# THE FLYING DUTCHMAN

ANATOLY KUDRYAVITSKY

# THE FLYING DUTCHMAN

*Translated from the Russian by Carol Ermakova*

GLAGOSLAV PUBLICATIONS

# THE FLYING DUTCHMAN

by Anatoly Kudryavitsky

Translated from the Russian by Carol Ermakova

Cover and interior layout by Max Mendor

Original photo at the cover by Maria Agustinho (shutterstock.com)



www.glagoslav.com

ISBN: 978-1-911414-87-2

A catalogue record for this book is available from the British Library.

# CONTENTS

# ACKNOWLEDGEMENTS

Grateful acknowledgement is made to the editors of the following, in which a number of these stories, or versions of them, originally appeared:

"The Red Canals of Mars, the Amber Spokes of Venus": *Far off Places*, "A Symphony's Farewell": *Asymptote*, "Brothers in Pens": *Prosopisia*. "Russian Nightmare" and "British Agent" were first published in *Dream. After Dream* by Anatoly Kudryavitsky, Honeycomb Press, 2013.

# THE FLYING DUTCHMAN

## A tone poem

Only the individual who is solitary is like a thing placed under profound laws, and when he goes out into the morning that is just beginning, or looks out into the evening that is full of happening, and if he feels what is going on there, then all status drops from him as from a dead man, though he stands in the midst of sheer life.

—Rainer Maria Rilke. *Letters to a Young Poet*

# PART 1

## Andante

### 1.

Houses swallow people. They toy with them for a while, then: gulp. And when the person quietens down and gazes out of the window, the window dims and the scenery becomes a poorly primed canvas. You can rip through that canvas, or you can get caught in its web.

N. managed to not get caught; he ripped through the canvas. But unless you are a spider, there are many webs which can snare you. N. would soon let himself be swallowed by another house – a large wooden one, standing alone on a riverbank.

He sailed unhurriedly along the byroad like a little boat, a suitcase in one hand, a bag of food he'd bought on the way in the other; the forest gradually took him in, absorbed him, then released him into a first clearing, then a second; a hazel, pines, then suddenly aspens and silver birch, then more pines. The scent of the river. She was the queen of this place. Birds on the wing would bow to her, paying homage; otherwise, to drink her waters was forbidden.

The house was her palace. It was dedicated to the river, it lived for her. Straddling the ridge pole, balanced like yokes, dragonflies sang for her. And someone called No One slung the yoke over his shoulders, carried dead water to the river and scooped the living waters from her. He lived off this water without food, and did not become Somebody because it was disgraceful, because it was unnecessary, because he had already been somebody.

An empty bucket stood on the veranda. Or maybe he was just imagining it standing there? Or maybe he was just imagining himself standing there on the veranda? For we are all artists imagining our own image. And now this is the still-life: a veranda, threaded on a tree. A "poplaspen" as N. christened it at once, unable to remember

Origin of the Plot.' Actually, the familiar story hammers itself out, and the Flying Dutchman sails along the typed waves of the Rheine – well, the typewriter is called 'Rheinmetall'!

Somebody is stomping around in the attic, sounds almost like a fight! Who else is up there? He goes to look, his feet playing the keys of the creaking staircase. The attic is empty, its windows cobwebbed over. Wait – not completely empty. There's a chest in the corner. Ancient, dusty and heavy, it doesn't let itself be opened, keeps itself to itself. There's an axe downstairs, on the veranda…

And the lock is broken. A smell of tobacco. Thick, almost putrid. Who's coughing? Nobody? My, how they're coughing!

*Fifteen men on a dead man's chest.*
*Yo ho ho and a bottle of rum.*

Well, there was *yo ho ho* all right but no bottle of rum to be seen. A maritime spyglass, a flannel cloth with two flint stones, an extremely long, ancient pistol with a dull, encrusted mother-of-pearl handle and – a large, lacquered casket. It was opened without the aid of the axe. Inside he found an old-fashioned maritime cap and a heavy bronze key.

"But where are the piasters? How can there be a chest like this without any gold?"

The tragedy was that N. thought about money, but money never wasted a thought on him. Ever. Money lives its own life, has its own likes and dislikes, its favourites. But why did he need money here, anyway? He had enough for food, and there was nothing else to buy, anyway. Wonder about that key, though. There don't seem to be any fitting keyholes in the house. But if there's a key for a door, there should be a door for the key!

He closed the chest and went down into the garden. The paths were long since overgrown, the vegetable patch, too. But the apple trees were laden with fruit. What's up there? The sun was wheeling overhead like a pancake in an oiled frying pan. He discovered a bench darkened by rain under one of the apple trees. N. sat down, pondering: what was a chest like that doing in the middle of nowhere, among the Valday Hills? What am I doing here in the middle of nowhere among the Valday Hills? Time hummed softly, seeping off somewhere between the trees into the 'twixt-trees.'

The house stood utterly unruffled, its pale, silent windows reflecting the grey-blue matt of the afternoon sky. A woman appeared at one of them. She was looking at him. N. shuddered – he had not been in that room yet.

He hurried back into the house, rushed up to the door, knocked, and went in. Empty. A double-bed with nickel-plated iron knobs at each corner, no mattress. A mahogany wardrobe. He opened the wardrobe door, as if expecting to see someone inside. No, the wardrobe was uninhabited but for the thick, sickly-sweet smell of lavender. N. recoiled, then peered inside again. Shawls were lying on one of the shelves, an ancient coat hung in the other side, nothing special, just a grubby orange throw-over raincoat.

Nobody.

He opened the transom, tucked a corner of the curtain into it to mark the window, and went back out into the garden. That wasn't the window where he had seen the woman! He went into the next room. It was completely empty. He hung the curtain out of that window, too. It turned out to be on the other side of the window with the woman. There were no other rooms between the two. It was a window into nowhere, he realised. Or from nowhere.

4.

Some things drop into memory's windows, some get lost, some can be seen in a flash, but others are kept in darkness… That woman – had he seen her before? Had she been present in his past life or in this present non-life? Who knows… He tried to imagine her with a child. There are women whom you simply can't imagine with a child, and she seemed to be one. Was she the spawn of this house, of its grey dust, its dowdy kitchen utensils, the river's dampness? You could not think of her as a mother, nor, for that matter, as a lover or a wife. No, she was simply the woman of this house, even if she didn't exist. Each place has its soul, a female soul.

"But what is the soul?" N. pondered, and that musing gave rise to an unpleasant ache in the pit of his stomach. And before his closed eyes, the contours of a fiery plane glowed green. "If there is a soul, then that means there must be a past. But if, as in my case, there is no past, then does that mean there is no soul? Or is it hiding, waiting for this present to become the past, for it to accumulate?"

Then it all seemed funny. Well, a house of ghosts – what better place to ponder the soul?! He had to end up here, of all places! And a rhyme came to his mind: 'all' – 'bawl'… Yes, the bawl, those jaws, this was what he fled from. But there's another rhyme: 'all' – 'fall'… At that, the green fire-plane in his eyes became unbearably bright and pain seared his heart. He lay down on the sofa with its worn office leather and tried to put an end to the philosophical games of his consciousness, or his subconscious, and to think of nothing at all. The pain passed, and sleep took its place.

5.

He woke up. It was cold… The sheet was wet, and the blanket, too. Lowering his feet to the floor – water up to his ankles. A flood!

He somehow pushed his feet into his boots and, throwing a windcheater over his shoulders, he rushed out into the yard. Oddly enough, it was dry there. A green lamp glowed in the garden, lighting everything around with an eerie, ghostly glow.

"How come? Has the river come gushing into the house, does it want to embrace me, carry me to the bottom?"

Water filled his eyes, waves beat against his brow.

"The house is chasing me!"

Frightened, he strode away, but the dense undergrowth caught him in grass traps, snagged him in snares. All of a sudden, a red dress flashed between the trees, a face appeared for a split second… It can't be, he said to himself. She's no longer on this earth!

Then everything became clear: he had not seen what one is not allowed to see; indeed, had he seen anything at all? N. lay down on the grass and closed his eyes.

Then his eyes opened by themselves. He was back in bed again – how had he got home? He had no idea, and there was no-one to ask. The sunless morning was turning grey outside the window. He was dressed – had he forgotten to get undressed? Oh, he hadn't even taken off his boots… There was no water anywhere, and, oddly, everything seemed dry. He wanted to sleep, terribly, so he tossed his boots aside. A button fell out of one. A red one? No – golden.

6.

Along the lane, around the corner, along the lane again, down the slope, between the barrels, over the ditch, around the cart, over the little bridge, hop, skip and a jump over the puddles, then back on the lane again, but he has already forgotten where he is going… no, not forgotten. Two more blocks, a left turn, then to the right, and straight ahead… Seems he has brought himself somewhere, and he is glad: it's good to have reached the final destination of any journey, although not all final destinations turn out to be pleasant resting places.

Take this tavern here in Rotterdam, for instance, this sailors' purgatory, with its fumes, tobacco smoke, dark corners, and low, terse hullabaloo where everyone talks at once. A figure in a rust-coloured camisole and a grubby neckerchief takes itself from table to table with obvious effort, stopping for a long talk here, barely mumbling one word there. Will they chase him away at once? No, the figure slides over to the next table, and once again: "blah blah blah…"

"Who is it?" the infantry officer asked a fellow at his table.

"Dirk Slothem," replied the old sailor, leaning over the table like a truncated mast. "Sailed with him once I did, he was the bosun on that ship. Now he's gathering a crew for the Crystal Key, an old piece of junk from Antwerp, a schooner or a bark, who knows. Wants to sail to the East Indies, on that old wreck!"

"Reckon it won't make it, then?"

"I wouldn't even risk riding it at anchor, roadstead!"

"So why's he rounding up a crew, then?"

"Who knows? Made it worth his while, I guess. A daredevil looking for his own kind. They'll all perish!"

The tobacco smoke coiled into a Pacific Ocean cloud turning the sea foam grey. The figures in the corners of the tavern braided themselves into tornado-columns and then unwound themselves again. One of the figures appeared dimly at the other end of the table. It seemed more real than ghostly, and the sailor realised there was someone else at the table, too: a young maritime officer.

"I've signed up," said the officer, whose name was Kees van der Weide. "They offered to make me First Mate. They really do pay well, whoever they are, and anyhow, I know that craft. She doesn't look too good, of course, but she can creak on another 50 years and more."

"You're a brave man," said the old sailor shaking his tousled grey head and topping up his rum from the jug. "With a risk like that you might as well buy a ticket to heaven."

"Ah, so you know the story, too!" said van der Weide with a wink.

"What story?" the infantry officer asked, squinting like a pharmacist as he measured the next dose of port into his glass.

"I'll tell you. An interesting tale, by the way," van der Weide began. "It happened many moons ago, back in the days when a large monastery stood not far from here. Well, one day the young novice Brother Ambrosius comes running up to Abbot Boniface and he presses his frightened face right up to the abbot's shrivelled ear and whispers: "Father, a young runaway monk is selling tickets to heaven in the next village." "Really?" says the surprised abbot, almost choking on his Moselle. "For how much?" "For a sum equivalent to the church tax," replies Brother Ambrosius, nervously running his fingers through what's left of his brown hair. "And the people find money both for him and for us?" asks the abbot. "Yes, Father." Now it's the abbot's turn to scratch his tonsure. "But we're missing out on that money!" he sniffs. "Can't we add at least a little to our profits? I want to talk with this monk!" The novice Brother Ambrosius's Adam's apple starts to bob up and down his salient chick-like throat. "But he's a blasphemer, Father!" Gnawing on his chicken bone, the abbot says piously: "The church teaches one should use the mistakes of her wayward sons to further her good." And so the monk was caught in some peasant's house and brought before the abbot. They found scraps of tatty paper on him, with the words: "We, the most merciful Archbishop of Utrecht, do hereby confirm that the below (there was a gap in the text here) has atoned all earthly sins and is worthy of our mercy. As such, we see no reason why he should not be admitted into the Kingdom of Heaven unhindered." The papers were signed 'Humble Servant of God Frederick, Archbishop of Utrecht.'

"My brother, you are not giving God's unto God," said the abbot when—at his own request—he was left alone with the sinner. Having obtained his interlocutor's full agreement, he continued: "My brother, if the name of Christ's representative is taken in vain, then that representative should be recompensed." The sinner's full agreement was obtained on this point, too. Father Boniface faked the archbishop's signature himself, since he was better at it. The peasants continued paying their taxes, buying their tickets to heaven, being brought to ruin, and dying out.

The Reformation came. The surviving peasants stormed the monastery, pitchforks in hand, and drowned Father Boniface in a vat of Moselle. As for Brother Ambrosius, they very humanely cracked his skull. The rebellion was led by that same rogue monk who decided it was better to be the lightning than the lightning conductor.

"And so, did the peasants get to heaven with their tickets?" asked the infantry officer, who had lost count of his drinks.

"That I cannot tell you," said van der Weide with a smile. "You see, I've never been there and, taking my future plans into account, I doubt I ever shall."

## 7.

The garden was calling him again. Leaves partly covered the sun. The minutes of the present oozed from the echoing emptiness of past years. You cannot look at the sun, but you can look at the point where the sun's rays land…

N. sat on the bench and closed his eyes. Silence. No, not silence, a cricket is chirping, the leaves are rustling; this is not silence. Silence is when there are no books, and it is good to think in such silence. Akhmatova said: you can live without books, and that is how he lives now. But in the city, in his flat, dozens of bookshelves were piled up with volumes and volumes, all read and re-read. But he couldn't read them any more: they belonged to his past life. Now there's nothing to do but watch the garden, ponderously green, frowning in the breeze.

The gate was green, too. Look, it's opening now, and in comes a beetle, a timber-worm. No, not a beetle, but something beetly, hugging a heavy iron sausage in its front paws.

"Gas."

But no-one had ordered anything, not even Noone. Then it dawned on him: maybe the runaway landlord had ordered it?

"This way," N. showed the gasman the kitchen door.

The canister was installed, but the gas man didn't straighten up, he stayed crablike. What else does he want, that dark-haired beetle?

   

"Do you have any water?"

"Ah, he wants a drink. Where's the kettle?" But the kettle was hiding, so N. showed the gasman the bucket. He lifted the lid – and gave a start.

"What have you got in there?!"

There turned out to be nothing but a bunch of pondweed in the bucket.

"I thought it was someone's hair!" the gasman calmed himself down after groping around in the bucket. "But it's seaweed not pondweed! Are you growing it?"

"Yes, instead of sea kale," N. remarked dryly.

And the gasman left, forgetting his drink.

8.

"Got seaweed there, you say?" asked Merinos, the head of the local police. He was bathing in the refreshing breeze of the old "Victory" fan with its rubber paddles like donkey's ears.

"Yes, sir, seaweed. Not pondweed," declared the phony gasman, the patch of sweat on his dark blue police shirt spreading.

"A scientist, then," Merinos stated, helping the fan along by gently waving his small, pink lady-like hanky. "I don't like their kind…"

"Who?" sergeant Vasily Safonov enquired hesitantly, donning his usual police uniform with relief.

"Those chaps, smarty pants. Students, doctors, professors of this, that or the other… Enemies, that's what they are."

"But maybe he's a Soviet intellectual?" Vasily was warming up to this intimate conversation with the boss.

"Dream on! Soviet intellectuals, for your information, are careerists, and as for real intellectuals… Oh, they're clever folks. But they're not Soviet. Can't even drink properly, don't like fighting, and can't utter so much as a single strong word! And that's why I don't like them. No simpleness in them."

Hanging opposite one another, the portraits of the two Ilyiches—one bald, one eye-browed—exchanged approving glances.

Vasily didn't bother to enquire why his boss didn't like doctors. He himself was none too fond of medical staff – he once got such a boil from an injection 'on the back of his face,' as he liked to put it, that he avoided sitting on it at all costs, like you would avoid sitting on a wasp.

"Well, you keep an eye on him," concluded his boss. "True enough, you can't do much damage with seaweed – he can take some algae off us, as a matter of fact, the river's choking up with it… But still, keep your ears pricked."

The drop slowly creeping down the ginger Merinos' freckled forehead finally reached the tip of his nose, and he swore, steadily and unhurriedly, as if to say that if swearing were a game, well, he'd play it on his own terms.

9.

To make a face… Well, what can you make a face from? From an apple, a pear, grass, fat, glue, dye, horse hair, Lego, breeze blocks, marble, bronze… But the most beautiful human faces, male or female, are not made of apples, fat, or dye or the like.

One such face was the carved female face which adorned the nose of the barque the Crystal Key. The vessel was indeed a barque, not a schooner or a barquentine, with a square rigged foremast and main mast, and fore-and-aft rigged mizzen mast. The heavyset bosun Dirk Slothem would punish the sailors not only for referring disrespectfully to their old ship, but even if he caught one of them insulting the wooden figurehead, calling it ugly or, even worse, Medusa. You mustn't give the ship's protectress obscene nicknames! They would never dare on a Spanish vessel, for fear of their maritime backsides; they don't spare the rod there! And it just so happened that the Crystal Key was indeed passing by the Spanish coast not far from the Cape of Finisterre.

The captain had not yet shown himself to anyone; orders were given by his first mate, van der Weide. More than once the tipsy sailors clapped the bosun on the back, hoping to make him confess that there was no captain but van der Weide on that ship. But Dirk Slothem was a sailor with decades of experience who had even sailed on Portuguese and English vessels, and such familiarity didn't raise a smile; he twirled and twirled his long red whiskers and, in his measured Frisian way, would let them talk their fill, then reply: we have a captain on this ship, and his name is Captain Falkenberg. He's simply indisposed and is lying in his cabin.

   

But one of the sailors who'd had too much rum, not convinced
by the bosun's explanations, was about to lay into him, fists flailing.
Slothem only hit him once, a short, lightning blow from his hand
the size of a bull's thigh. Coming back to his senses that evening, the
sailor joked that Medusa herself must have struck him with her full
force.

10.

Seventhly, you get peckish. No matter how much food there is
in the house. After some time—say, on the seventh day—you
discover that an odd hotchpotch is all that remains. A tin of green
Hungarian peas, say, and 'Theatre' toffees. Well, you simply can't
stomach that any more... And so you venture out of the house,
and make a great geographical discovery; without the aid of a
telescope, you find a new planet, fall under a bus or buy yourself
something to eat.

Foodstuffs – they are the fruit of someone's labours. Either man
labours over nature, or nature labours over herself. Man has not
yet mastered the art of producing something edible from himself.
Maybe he will learn. Definitely, he will learn.

N., meanwhile, walked along the woodland path, putting some
distance between himself, the house and the river, drawing closer
to human habitation, and—most importantly—to the village shop.
That shop sold grey white bread, rusty herring, tinned sprats in
tomato sauce, coarse ground salt, bay leaves in packets with a
picture of bay leaves, and an "Accord" record player with LPs of the
Choir named after Verevka and the vocal-instrumental ensemble
called "The Gems." There was a sales assistant there, too, curious
and rather unkempt. She began by asking:

"Who are you?"

"I live here," N. replied, to avoid admitting he was Noone,
although that was the answer the question begged.

"Ah, so it's you who's renting the old house by the river... And
what are you doing there?"

"I'm on holiday," N. said. "I'm thinking."

He said that, of course, without thinking. Never tell simple folks
of your ability to reason: it arouses nothing but vague surprise. Then

anyone you meet or come across will already be forewarned: you are a dangerous crackpot.

"Hmm, what is there to think about here?" said the sales assistant with a shrug.

"Well, one can think about anything, not only about the place where one is at the moment… Tell me, is there a post office here?" he asked, and then thought at once: "What do I need one for? Sending letters is dangerous."

"Yes, there is. On the next street," answered the shop assistant. "My sister works there."

"Alone?"

"Most of the year, yes, but a student's helping her now. His surname's Trampin. He's a bit of a simpleton."

"What do you mean?" N. asked, surprised.

"He's always getting muddled, putting the letters in the wrong place, and my sister has to sort them all out again. They nearly threw him out of uni last winter, apparently. That's the kind of young folk we raise out here…"

N. struggled to pack his goods into his string bag, tying the handle with twine just to be on the safe side. He could have bought the record player, too, of course, but the record selection on offer was obviously below par. If only they had Bach's cantatas or, just for fun, Wagner's 'The Flying Dutchman'! Actually, he knew that opera by heart, and he'd brought the score with him, just in case.

The string bag stretched his arm, the twine handles cut into his palm, and he stopped to wrap them in a handkerchief. And while he was carrying out that operation, sergeant Vasya was standing at the police station window watching him.

"Come and look at our intellectual, Comrade Captain!"

Captain Merinos was engrossed in pulling a splinter from his fat, freckled forefinger. He swore, dug into his long-suffering finger with a needle, swore some more, pulled out the needle, thrust it into the lapel of his police jacket and finally stomped across the painted floor towards the window.

"Him?" he said in surprise. "Bit old, isn't he? Grey. Doesn't look dangerous. Down at heel…"

Rested, N. continued on his way. Just then, the panting shop assistant ran into the police station.

     

"So, did you ask him what he's doing?" Merinos enquired as to how his instructions had been carried out, trying again to coax the splinter out with the tip of the needle.

"I did."

"And what is he doing?"

"He's thinking."

And Merinos caught the splinter at last, pulling it out with a shriek of pain.

"Ffffck," he said to the splinter, and then, after a pause, went on with the other conversation. "No, seems he's dangerous after all."

Meanwhile, N. had reached the boundary of his land. The border was marked by barbed wire wound three times between rough wooden posts pounded into the ground. N. could have sworn that just a few hours earlier, when he had left, the fence had been noticeably further from the house. He walked the length of the fence, but there was no sign that the posts had been moved. Was he imagining things? Or had the ring of barbed wire tightened by itself?

### 11.

Night. A white cloud on a dark background. A speaking cloud.

"Can I ask you something?"

"Ask me," sighs the cloud.

"Why can I find no peace on this earth?"

"Hmm, good question… Do you really want to know?"

"Yes."

"Because you are unlucky: you landed in the wrong country, the wrong century and, worst of all, you are not who you seem to be…"

"Maybe…"

"To put it very briefly, you cannot find peace because there is no place for you."

"Why is there no place for me?"

"Because you want to be something other than was intended."

"Something other?"

"Yes. You want to be better, cleverer. And that does not go unpunished."

Black steam came out of the white cloud's mouth, or at any rate, from where the mouth should be, from where the cloud spoke. Or was it laughing?

In his next dream he saw a man with a mirror for a face. N.'s own face was reflected in it, except that his eyes were closed and his cheeks were pallid.

"You don't know how to die," said the man with the mirror-face. "I will teach you. You have to have the knack, you see. You have to learn death, gain experience…"

The visitor began to teach him how to die, showing him an endless kaleidoscope with images of all sorts of death. That night N. died over and over – he drowned in the ocean, fell off the roof, choked on smoke and toxic fumes, perished at the hands of murderers and hangmen, committed suicide and quietly faded away in a geriatric ward. He understood that death could be boring, like any other ordinary activity, and he also understood that there can be no prior experience: each time you die anew. And in the morning, if you are lucky, you wake anew…

He did indeed wake up: someone was tickling his cheeks. The round face of the dressing table mirror searchingly trained the sun's rays right into his eyes.

## 12.

The waves run barefoot, playing football, chasing the ball of the sun, shattering it into a thousand shards, only to gather them up again and play again.

And so the Canary Isles are passed. The storm was lying in wait for them in warm waters. The wind shook the Crystal Key like a cat worrying a half-dead mouse. The sails were clewed down, but still the ship creaked and shuddered. The next wave rocked the deck and broke off a wooden plank, part of the outer hull. Panic broke out among the sailors; realising any one of them could be swept overboard at any moment, they ran for shelter anywhere they could. The bosun walked the deck, clutching spider-like onto every dangling rope or line, dealing blows left and right as usual in the hope of returning the sailors to their posts. But it was all in vain.

Just then a strange figure appeared on the bridge. He was dressed in a black Spanish camisole with silvery embroidery and a broad-brimmed hat. For a moment, the figure took in what was happening around him, then, audibly but without yelling, he gave an order:

"To your posts, all of you! Bosun, send two sailors to secure the lifeboats!"

The order came in the pause between two mighty waves, or it would not have been heard.

"The Captain! It's the Captain!" a whisper rustled through the sailors.

The order was carried out post haste. The Captain took off his hat and everyone could see his swarthy, even yellowy face and long grey hair. Those standing closer to him glimpsed rather harsh facial features and cheeks well ploughed with wrinkles.

"I, Michael Falkenberg, cured by the grace of providence from my ailment, am now taking command of this ship according to all earthly and heavenly laws."

He uttered this calmly but powerfully, and the sailors acknowledged this man's authority without a second thought. No need for him to shout or back up his authority with blows as Dirk Slothem did; his word and his glance sufficed.

"Aha, Michael," thought the bosun, who was himself seeing the captain for the first time. "Smacks of the Spanish 'Miguel.' Maybe he's that Spanish renegade, the former captain of the English frigate who later sailed on our warships? He went by the fictitious name of van der Dekken – 'man from the deck.' And I bet Falkenberg isn't his real name, either. No doubt our captain's a nobleman, and who knows what his real name is…"

Dirk looked at the captain again, but he couldn't see his eyes, they were too deep-set. And for the first time in his life, the bosun felt uneasy.

"The captain's obviously a foolhardy man," he thought. "I wonder if I'll make it back to my wife and children after this voyage?"

But Dirk Slothem was a man who knew how to handle himself, so his face did not betray his doubts. And anyway, his attention was diverted to another strange event: a second man in black now appeared on the bridge. Unlike the captain, this one was dressed simply, but there was something sinister about his impassive, parchment-white face with its hooked nose. Looking closer, Dirk realised that the worst thing about this man was his smile.

"And that's the physician. A cautious guy, never more than a yard away from the captain," came a voice behind the bosun.

Dirk looked around. The Malay cook was standing in the galley doorway. An ageless man, he now smiled his sugary smile. Just like the physician's.

13.

First, the Prophet Elijah turns to the heavenly hosts. His voice, the rattle of countless tin sheets. Then, it is time for the charge of the star-drawn cavalry. Stallions of fire and stallions of night's gloom stamp their hooves, thousand fold, on the celestial dome, scattering pale sparks and stirring up dust clouds. The powers of darkness are closing their ranks, heading for battle. And they are vanquished in an instant, on the run, celestial dust on their capes. And the battlefield is once more serenely, celestially blue.

Down below, we notice nothing more than thunder and lightning.

But in the morning, stepping on the smooth sand between the bushes on the riverbank on the way for milk, you would glance in the milky water-mirror, but the path leads us up, through the clearing, skirting the field. And there's the first roof, and hens are running underfoot. The village called Loss.

A jug of steaming milk, eggs, too, and even a bunch of dill, and a lop-eared lettuce. The old man is blind, it's the old woman who looks after the cow, her daughter lends a hand even though her baby is almost due. N. pays them—just pennies!—and gets a bouquet of white phlox into the bargain. Well, flowers do brighten things up.

The path shows the way back, skirting the field, through the clearing, to the raised bank, down, and home… He stopped short. My, doesn't the house look like a ship?! The attics were mezzanines—is that the right name?—kind of stuck on, built on, and the other side, it was like the stern of a caravel. But the deck side lines were straight, like those of a river steamer, not a seagoing vessel. And a tree was sticking up through the veranda. A mast? A misty mirage from a dream…

Where are we sailing to, my little one-mast ship? Well, no point in putting the classical question of the nineteenth century, formulated by Pushkin: "But whither do we sail?" Since we are already underway, albeit against our will. And the destination is unclear. Will we ever know?

## 14.

The Crystal Key had already reached tropical waters, saluted the sun with its orange pennon, and was now obediently following its scorching, shining pathway. But the sun kept slipping away from the ship, hiding behind a wave or a cloud, then behind the next. It winked, dazzled, blinded, and did all this with such enthusiasm that the sailors were forced to wrap rags around their heads. Drinking water was rationed.

Off duty, the sailors took refuge in their quarters and spun yarns.

"…he was married six times in a row, each time unhappily. And all his wives were called Dora Peters… No, no, he didn't keep marrying the same woman, they all just happened to have the same name. He was married to each of them for three months. And now whenever he sees a girl he fancies, he calls out to her: "Hey, Dora Peters!" If she looks up, he turns heel and runs."

The sailors guffawed.

"Hey, Jaap, you telling the truth?" asked someone curiously.

"What do you care if he's telling the truth or not, so long as it makes you laugh?" smirked another.

"What's in a name," declared one old sailor pensively.

Up on deck, Dirk Slothem was checking the rigging. Catching sight of the captain's young first mate as he happened past, the bosun asked him:

"What's he like, that physician?"

Van der Weide shrugged.

"Who knows… An Italian, born in Florence, but he speaks with a Spanish accent."

"I don't like him," Dirk said.

"Yeah, the philosophy of likeability," the young first mate said with a smile. He was an educated chap, had even studied at university once upon a time. "Let me tell you a story about a man who was very popular. They even sang songs about him."

It had to do with a certain Spanish colony known as Santa Anna. It was overseas, I won't tell you exactly where. The governor, Don Alvaro de Fuentes, liked his peace and quiet, but it was his lot to govern the colony, in other words, to busy himself with matters far from peaceful or quiet. More than anything else Don Alvaro loved to play the harpsichord while his officers were off chasing pirates. Actually, the governor hadn't given the order, but his officers were a very lively bunch. The pirate ships would scatter like wasps shooting from their nest when it's hit with a stick. Sometimes the stick struck one or two of the wasps, but they never managed to get the meanest and most stubborn one. He was called Chassan. He'd already sunk dozens of merchant ships, killing most of the crew; he never took prisoners.

The officers had been hunting him for eight years with no luck. Finally, Chassan came to them himself – he crept into town one night after some wench and bumped right into the sergeant the next morning, and the sergeant recognised him. When they took the pirate, he took that sergeant's life, unarmed as he was, just throttled him with his bare hands.

The prisoner was brought before the Governor, who was just sitting down to tea on the veranda in his mansion. This black-bearded creature stood before him – crafty, fearless, merciless, and the Governor's officers proposed an equally merciless hanging.

The Governor had dedicated that morning to Couperin's minuet. Don Alvaro's younger daughter had already mastered it, and he was about to demonstrate the subtleties of his interpretation to her, a daunting task which cast a concerned shadow over the governor's golden-haired brow.

'Execute him?' uttered Don Alvaro, surprised, as beads of sweat appeared on his brow. 'You want to do away with all your troubles— yours and his—so easily? No, let him feel the full weight of inevitable retribution, the barest necessity of a harmonious life.'

'But Don Alvaro, he's a murderer!' cried a scar-faced young lieutenant, de Castro, stepping forward. 'He's killed ninety-six people!'

'Well, that's not a hundred, my dear fellow,' smiled the Governor. 'The death sentence is such a dull solution. Throw him in a cell.'

Chassan glowered at him, his eyes like those of a rapacious beast given the chance to live, and a smile flitted across his lecherous lips.

And so the pirate was taken away. The officers didn't let up, but the Governor wrinkled his brow, pained. "It is unbecoming to insist."

Days passed. Chassan was sitting in the cell listening to the sound of the harpsichord through the air vents. After a week he was so bedevilled by these sounds that he broke through the wall with the bedstead, crawled through the chimney to the Governor's quarters and suffocated two of his daughters along with his wife. As for the Governor himself, Chassan snapped in him half and stuffed him in the harpsichord.

Fleeing the mansion, the pirate smashed the four guards over the head with a heavy candlestick and then, as if by way of compensation for his trouble, grabbed a pouch of coins. But on discovering they were not gold, the brigand flung them to the beggars.

The townsfolk woke next day to the gurgling sound of the French horn belching forth from the pirates' brig like an eruption from a sick bowel. Lieutenant de Castro unleashed a belated volley after them from the howitzer.

And so the pirate got his tally up to over one hundred, still not a nice round number. They said that if the next governor had been elected rather than nominated, it would most certainly have been Chassan.

"So now tell me what you think of likeable and unlikeable individuals, and of popular ones," said the captain's first mate, as he finished his tale.

But the bosun found himself at a loss for words.

15.

Sailing: the movement of a body through resistant matter. A matter which rocks itself, self-satisfied. "Who would take it into their head to move through me?" it thinks. "Even if they did, wherever I am, movement is only possible with my permission, with my participation. If I do bar them entry, they will not sail."

Nevertheless, each and every exception to this rule will one day plop unexpectedly into the water from above causing an indignant spatter. "Ah, you didn't expect that, did you?" croons the matter in its watery voice. "And actually, is it really necessary?" But as for Wind, well, it can't wait to make mischief. It's already shoving the sailing body towards some spot on the hypothetical shore. And this is called 'sailing.' Or maybe: fate.

It was evening when the watchman noticed the little boat, adrift, sail-less and lifeless. They went closer, caught the boat with the pole hook. Someone was lying in the bottom, face down. After having made sure he was breathing, they brought him aboard. He was getting on in years, and his clothes suggested he was of high birth. But now his velvet camisole was in rags, and the wound in the back of his head was caked with dried blood. He'd fallen victim to pirates, most likely, who'd somehow sailed into these southern waters even though the southernmost Canary Islands were not one of their usual haunts.

The physician came up, shooed the sailors away, and bent over the inert man.

"He won't make it," he said at last.

Dirk arrived just in time to catch an ironical smirk as it flitted across the physician's face, as though he were rejoicing in this stranger's misfortune.

The captain arrived, too, just as the physician was untying the man's belt. Coins fell out. The captain bent down, picked up a couple of coins, and examined them.

"Doubloons," he said. "A Spaniard. Chuck him in the sea."

"But maybe he'll make it?" the bosun suggested tentatively.

"A Spaniard," repeated the captain. "An enemy. Carry out my order."

"He's afraid that Spaniard will recognise him," thought the bosun.

Darkness was almost upon them. The physician took the Spaniard by the shoulders, Dirk grabbed his legs. The body swung, and was overboard. A faint moan – and the Spaniard sank to the depths.

"We've done a bad thing," said the bosun, shaking his head. "He might have pulled through."

"We'll die soon enough ourselves," said the captain quietly. "From thirst. His life is worth two of our people's."

"What shall we do with the money?" Dirk asked, practical as ever.

"It's yours, my honest Friesian," teased the captain.

The bosun reddened, and squinted at the physician.

"Well, that man's incorruptible," smiled the captain. "Like me."

Dirk picked up the doubloons and thrust them into a trouser pocket. A certain number of young children has a way of ridding a man of certain scruples.


16.

The wind blew in the evenings. It swayed the trees and the stars. "I shake up everything in the whole wide world," it boasted, for the wind is always full of promises. Yet a quiet, windless morning soon dawns. A silent morning. And everything remains the same as it ever was.

At night, a man in sailor's garb stole through the cotton wool of sleepy clouds and asked: "What have you done with our ship?" And then he asked: "Do you think we enjoy sitting broke, on a sandbank?" N. thought he was on about the coins, but turns out he meant the house. For some reason, the figure in the sailor's garb insisted on calling the house a ship.

There was no need to reply. But then came a third question: "How much time do you have left?" "No-one can know this," thought N. plainly, so the figure obligingly clarified: "Until you set sail." There was no need to reply to this, either. "You know nothing about the future," stated the figure before it disappeared. "That's bad. It's better to know."

After a dream like that, there is nothing for it but to wake up. N. got up and went onto the veranda. The other one, the one he'd not been to yet. Somehow he always went to sit out on the one skewered by the tree, 'the veranda with a mast' as he called it. The other veranda looked out over the water. N. positioned his chair, and sat down. The far bank was low and overgrown with bushes. Golden lights twinkled somewhere in the distance; there must be a village somewhere over there. The river exuded a smell of damp, silt and secrets. Why did the river loop around so close to this house? Or: why did the house stand so close to the water? Or: why was he, N., in this house?

The sky began to brighten ever so slightly. An owlet moth flew by. "How long before you set sail?" Well, do I want to set sail? Where to? It's so quiet here… And those little stairs from the veranda, where do they go? The little wooden stairs led right into the water.

And at this point N. did something he had never done before: he took off all his clothes and went right into the water. It was black and warm. N. decided to swim across the river, which, fortunately, was not too wide just there. He clambered out from under the veranda and swam in a straight line; there was nothing to give him his bearings.

"When you swim, you have some sort of goal," splashed his thoughts to the rhythm of his arms. "Even if it's just to swim a length. It's a nice feeling, to have a goal."

After a while, his feet touched the bottom. The far bank. A dark reed palisade was before him, determinedly imitating one of the local fences which were just the same colour. N. did not get out of the warm water; he rested, surveying the hulk of his house. From here, it looked like a black splodge on the purple sky.

He decided to get out onto the bank after all. The reeds gave way and led him into the embrace of the low bushes which tenderly caressed his legs. The bushes were taller further on. Beyond them something shimmered golden. He heard a voice, and a soft rustle. Some holiday-makers around a campfire? Well, if there was anyone he didn't want to run into, it was holiday-makers! That word, 'holiday-maker,' roused some mechanism lying dormant in his memory, which in turn triggered the strains of Communist youth anthems or even prison songs accompanied by the sloshing of vodka in knapsacks…

He was on the point of heading back into the water when a groan came from the rushes. "What the devil is going on there?" he asked himself, and, making up his mind to go closer, he spotted a little gap between the willows.

He found himself looking at a clearing overgrown with low grass. A campfire was burning out resignedly. A camelhair blanket lay between the campfire and the bushes fringing the far side of the clearing, and on it two naked bodies slowly wove themselves into a kiss, then unwound themselves again.

"Mhm, so an uninvited guest has come to the feast of flesh," thought N., suddenly noticing that both the bodies were female. "Now that *is* interesting," he smirked to himself. "They say there is no 'fraternising' between the sexes, or rather, within the sexes."

The silhouettes moved with more vigour, gathering momentum and N., who had thus far only been privy to the movement of hands, breasts and buttocks, now had a face in his line of sight. A young, broad face, a pleasant face with a dark mole on one cheek almost covered by tousled blond hair. There was something rapacious about that face, yet it was also somehow defenceless. And now it hid itself behind elbows, and another face surfaced. This one was almost childish, a round, white face covered in freckles framed with long, ginger hair. "That one's just sixteen," N. realised. "Maybe it's her first time. The other one's older, more experienced, probably around thirty."

The older girl's head hid itself between the redhead's legs, pale in the light of the campfire. The redhead moved, moaned, bit her lips. N.'s heart froze, maybe picking up some signal or some vague command from his male organ, as it rose up against something – surely not against its own inactivity? N. withdrew in a panic. His legs moved automatically. Reaching the water, he gave himself up to it, stretching himself comfortably on its cold bosom.

"Ah, afraid of the call of the flesh!" he scolded himself as he swam back. And then it dawned on him: those two bodies were not for him anyway. Was there any body for him, especially after... After that never-to-be-mentioned event, never to be remembered because it was not allowed, because he had forbidden himself to remember, strictly.

"Actually, there's no such thing as a body for a body, since the soul interferes, makes its demands, makes us long for the ideal, and all that searching results in utter alienation from the corporeal world."

The water replied to his musing with a soft, black splash. Water always agrees with everything, water always accepts both body and mind, and sometimes even the soul which searches for the ideal. And sometimes it even forces the incomer to check their body in for eternal rest.

He swam back. Swam and swam, and finally arrived. The veranda is close now – where are the little wooden steps? But he swam past them in the darkness, and found himself under the veranda. His hand brushed against something metal. It was a chain.

N. smiled: "Wouldn't it be funny if the house turned out to be at anchor? A man without an anchor living in a house with an anchor!"

## 17.

The Mirror of Venus is not merely a mirror, it is a mirror with a cross. A mirror to reflect the body, a cross to legitimise the reflection. Furs remain in the imagination of the writer, but the body shines out of emptiness. Some see the spreading clouds of vainglory, but the mirror merely reflects whatever steps into the sunlight. Some see whirling demons, some see angels, some think of Titian, Tintoretto, Velasquez, Veronese, some think of love. Some curse themselves for their visions... All this is naught but the triumph of the subjective over the objective, the victory of the view over vision. A temporary victory, of course, but lasting long enough for those who wish to enjoy it to do so.

Beauty is the 'heads' of the coin while fertility is the underside, 'tails.' Much celebrated by progenitors of both sexes as an antithesis to the 'fraternising' type of interpenetration. "Fertility, of course, is good," thought N. "I'm all for it, let's increase our potency artistically, too, of course, nationwide, but then what should we do with the phallus standing as high as human development? It slinks over you like the snake slunk over Laocoon. A blue tablet, a yellow tablet – and the fleshy snake is already clapping you on the shoulder, poking into your ears, the three graces are replaced with three phalluses with angel's wings, while palm trees bashfully cover their coconuts, and finally the phallic temple is built. And most importantly, what female receptacle is able to accommodate this cathedral-sized phallus?"

## 18.

Unbearable heat. Rotting water. Nothing but red fog. The air around has solidified into a tepid jelly, holding the ship, stopping its sail so it barely slides over the yellowy-green carpet of seaweed. Drinking water is in short supply; two sailors are already dead, buried in the seafaring tradition: thrown overboard.

"Let's put ashore! Why aren't we putting ashore?!" grumbled the disgruntled sailors.

But they couldn't put ashore: the shore they could see in the distance was equatorial Africa. No-one but cannibals will greet you there, while the jungle belongs to monkeys who open their séance by throwing coconuts as soon as you come anywhere near. There are a few settlements somewhere on the shore, but they're Portuguese, so in other words, a Dutch ship had better steer clear. Portugal and the Netherlands' northern provinces are rivals in these southern seas. Or enemies, strictly speaking. The captain announced:

"We'll put ashore at the mouth of the Orange River. Till then, we hold out."

Southern Africa is the last refuge for Dutch runaways. For those who have had more than enough of life under the Spanish crown—or under the Spanish boot, to be more precise, or maybe inside that boot—and have made up their mind to withdraw from the reality of Europe and reinvent themselves in a new place. Settlements in southern Africa offer assistance. It's a friendly shore there, if indeed any shore can be 'friendly' towards a ship. In the sea, a ship is forever lonely; it is both the hunter and the hunted, and everyone is hunting everyone else. There is no cover, nor will there ever be.

How can you sail on, how hard it is to move your legs over the deck of this ship, how hard it is to hold onto your own life, which is already yearning for some other expanse…

"Hey, Malay, what did those two die of? Maybe you gave them a helping hand into the other world?" It was the lean sailor who put this jaunty question to the cook; he could bear the heat better than the rest.

Standing nearby, Dirk noticed that the cook didn't smile; it was dark fire that burned in his eyes.

The next day they 'buried' the lean joker.

The last barrel of drinking water was standing in the captain's cabin. Two loaded pistols lay on top of it, and no-one doubted that the captain wouldn't hesitate to use them.

19.

The heat infiltrated his dreams. N. saw himself in Red Square filled with sunshine. A statue of a naked leader stood in the centre of the square, his nakedness no doubt a symbol that he had nothing to hide from his people. The sun reflected off the frail, freshly cast extremities and the round belly: the bronze leader was certainly no Apollo, neither were the townsfolk whom the statue's unembellished countenance should have pleased. The pigeons were searching for something among the cobbles, occasionally flying up to land on the leader, choosing a most unexpected perch.

Naked buskers arrived. The pigeons made way for them. The buskers pulled more musicians from their instrument cases. These musicians were smaller, but also naked, and the buskers began playing on them.

"Ah, well, we know why they don't have brass instruments, of course," said one naked beggar. "We know where all the bronze has gone – except the bronze for this statue, that is. But where are the strings? Surely they've not been sold off, too?"

A police sub-unit went by, all naked except for their police caps. The policemen fell to in rhythmic exercises. Naked spectators gathered.

Just then, a door opened in the statue of the leader. A naked person jumped out onto the ground and went off home.

One of the policemen said with a smile:

"So, anyone else fancy pretending it's the old days? Being in power and wearing clothes for a while?"

There were no volunteers.

"That can't be," N. said to his dream. "Surely they haven't broken the habit…?!"

## 20.

When a person so wishes, the boat sails. When the wind so wishes, the boat sails where the person wishes.

The Ost Wind—in other words, an east wind—carried the boat from the coast of Africa.

"Excellent!" the captain exclaimed when told. "That means we won't flounder on the reefs. Don't furl the sails tonight!"

"But that's not done! It's dangerous…" Dirk was taken aback.

"I'm not afraid of danger and I always do what's not done," smiled the captain shaking his curly grey locks. "Isn't that right, Niccolo?"

The hook-nosed physician was standing too far away to hear, but he nodded nonetheless and smiled his ambiguous smile.

The bosun grew uneasy.

"Oh, Niccolo has a great sense of hearing, by the way, as do all Florentines," said the captain. "He can even hear what we think, let alone what we say. Isn't that so, Niccolo?"

Standing in the same spot, the Florentine gave a bow.

## 21.

This house tempts with illusion. N. went into one of the rooms – he was looking for an axe to fix a wonky step on the veranda. He went in – and stood stock still. He was surrounded by mirrors, by myriad emanations of himself. A small boy wearing a child's hat embroidered with little cats. Or a student with a notebook under his arm. And here, the Someone he had been before he became Noone. And here, as he is today. Or here, a strange stranger with a predatory grimace, an axe in his hand, a readiness to kill written on his face… Kill… For some reason, that word arouses an odd pain in him… Pezzo Capriccioso Something had happened earlier, he was familiar with this nagging pain, this odd state. Anyway, it was most likely to do-with someone else, not with him. With Someone. But he, well, he is Noone. But he didn't like that reflection with the axe. And the reflection didn't like him, either. It threatened him, taking a few steps forward.

Where is the door? How could he escape? He was surrounded by mirrors. Should he enter one? He tried to go into his current self but it spurned him. And then N. realised he had to search for an empty mirror. He found one right away, entered, and came out in a corridor. He stood there for quite a while, wiping the sweat from his brow.

"So many 'me's' everywhere!" he thought, the mirror images were whirling in his head.

He gave up looking for an axe and propped the step up with a brick.

Another odd thing about that house was the lack of echoes. Like out at sea. He could shout as loud as he liked in the empty rooms, knock over chairs, beat the peculiar drum he'd found in some cupboard or other, but all in vain: the echoes kept mum. Echoes keep mum in the city, too, N. remembered. The newspaper echo, the conversational echo, the television echo. That's how it was, life without an echo.

But sounds arose by themselves in the city. They do here, too, by the way. Life in the city was mute, latent, unnoticed; it bubbled and gurgled quietly. Inside, all was silent; outside, all was garrulous. And everyone had their own opinion, held down there somewhere, in their own special surroundings, near the gall bladder. The fools in particular. Fools always have their own opinion. They are ready to strangle anyone who disagrees with them. Because he, the fool, cannot be wrong. Otherwise, chaos ensues.

In one of the rooms, an unseen radio began talking with a sexless, touristy voice. N. was on the point of going in, but then he realised he could hear the voice all the same.

"And now here is our broadcast for our fellow countrymen abroad," said the radio blithely. "If you live on an island, you can use the fish post to communicate with the outside world. It is easy to recognise the post fish – they are blue with white stripes, like letter boxes. The fastest is the plane fish. There is also recorded fish and 'signed-for' fish. Parcels are delivered by sperm whale. Pack them carefully, keep the weight limits in mind.

Fish post is reliable and free. The fish are motivated solely by their enthusiasm to work. Today we celebrate the third millennium of fish post. We praise these modest and tireless workers of the deep!"

The radio rasped, went silent, and N. heard his own voice, reaching his ears as if from outside.

"The question is, of course, what to send, and against which current."

22.

A knock at the door. A knock at the door? Impossible! Maybe it's one of those mysterious noises that sometimes roam the house?

But the knock was repeated. A genuine, insistent knocknocknock. Only a visitor knocks like that…

N. opened the door. A man of around fifty was standing on the doorstep. He had a greying hedgehog of hair, was clean-shaven, self-assured, smiling, wearing an English sports jacket and carrying a reddish leather briefcase.

"I couldn't help but come and visit my neighbour," the visitor began. His manner of speech was very correct, intelligent. "Allow me to introduce myself. I'm Porozhdestvensky. Yes, that's right, I have a strange surname. But my friends call me Kesha."

N. burst out laughing – such a childish name really didn't suit this grown-up gentleman. Although if you take a closer look, N. realised, there is something childish about this visitor. Disarming innocence, maybe? And he decided that a name like Poro would fit this man well.

"No, Kesha isn't from the English 'cash,' if that is why you are laughing," the visitor explained.

N. apologised and introduced himself:

"Noone."

"Ah, so you are of Irish descent, maybe even from the nobility," Poro drawled. "I am far removed from you. I am undoubtedly the spawn of an Orthodox priest."

"I am no Irishman!" Taken aback, N. almost blurted out: 'I'm no one.'

"What do you mean? It is a Gaelic name, *O Nuadhain*, pronounced O'Noone. The Noones, or Noonans, were nobles from the West of

     

Ireland, near Sligo. It's just that one of your ancestors was born there…
No, no, don't be surprised. By the way, there is a very famous doctor in
your family, Jacqueline Noonan. Don't know if you've heard of Noonan
syndrome… I'm also a medic…"

"Won't you come in?" N. asked. "I'm afraid I don't have much to offer
you. I wasn't expecting visitors."

"Nonsense, nonsense, it is I who should be apologising."

And a bottle of 'Napoleon' cognac appeared on the table like a tower,
and a large flat waffle cake emerged from inside the red pigskin briefcase.

"It's just a neighbourly visit," the guest said once again. "I'm living
in a dacha near here, it belongs to my uncle. Drop by some time, I have
plenty of books, and records."

After a few drinks, the conversation turned to books and music.

"Don't you find it boring here?" Poro asked.

"I'm never bored," N. replied. "I know how to entertain myself."

"And what do you do?"

"I think," N. replied, and at once remembered he was saying this for
the second time in two days.

"Do you make a note of your thoughts?" came the next question.

"Well, I wouldn't tell you even if I did," thought N. to himself, and
answered jokingly:

"Do I look like someone who makes notes? Writes things down?"

"You do, you do," his guest attested. "Although you are obviously an
ascetic, your brow is wrinkled. Intellectuals don't live that way, neither
here, nor there,"

"Aha, that means he's been 'there'!" The thought flashed through N.'s
mind. "That means, *they let him through*. Just as well I didn't tell him
about my writings!"

"You don't have any books here at all. How do you manage?" asked
Poro, getting up from the table at last.

"Oh, I get by somehow."

"No, no, that won't do at all. We'll think of something," said his visitor
as he left.

That night N. tossed and turned, unable to fall asleep. He was
trying to remember where he could have heard that strange surname,
Porozhdestvensky…

And he did remember. Not that night, admittedly, but the night
after. Sometime back in the days when he still read the papers, he had

read an article in *Pravda* about a young doctor-cum-gerontologist, with a PhD, by the name of Porozhdestvensky, who had taken part in a conference in England. He was allegedly kidnapped by English intelligence who wanted to force him to stay in the West. The article spoke of forced injections, of a Soviet man's heroism as he resisted all torture and returned to his motherland unbroken.

"Is he really such a prominent scholar?" N. had asked a doctor he knew.

"Of course not, he's a typical cissy, a loafer and a playboy. His father, on the other hand, now there's a really good surgeon, an academician. The son is quite another matter."

"So that's the man who paid me a visit," N. said to himself as he fell asleep.

23.

Sooner or later, later or sooner, a shitty day dawns. Everywhere at once. And then the human shit and dog shit lavishly garnishing the meadows, park paths and pavements starts to stink particularly artistically. And the shitty people get drunk on this smell, they emerge from ice holes and shitty laws are passed, shitty ideology is spread, and sometimes some shit even surfaces in decent folk. And the country is then called Augean Stables and everybody is waiting for Hercules, the great foreign saviour. Hercules comes and causes a semi-universal flood on a certain part of the earth. But even then, after the flood, when everything is washed away, smashed, swept away by the water, people with the light of shit sitting deep in their eyes exchange glances: "Well, wasn't that fun?"

The future Cape colonists fled this shitty stench, leaving Flanders and Holland. It was not only Spaniards who stank like this; their own religious fanatics and meddlesome grassers did, too.

In Africa, of course, shit is natural and doesn't stink so badly. Even if a rhino shits, the smell is nothing like the stench billowing from the deeds of certain European folk. Or to be more precise, certain shitty folk. We shall not take that pretty name Europe in vain. Shitty people are not Europeans, Americans, Spanish or Dutch – they are simply shitty people.

24.

The bay ope's wide its jaws and swallows the ship. Its face distorts in an ecstasy of chewing. It frowns, then smiles, then frowns again, then, having apparently chewed the ship up, once finished with it, the bay falls silent and still once more, with an innocent expression on its face. But it is lying in wait for its next prey.

After crossing almost the whole of southern Africa, the great Orange River meets the Atlantic at a smallish cove, and it is here that the Crystal Key dropped anchor.

Now it is the swallowed vessel's turn to flex its digestive muscles. Like a swallowed fish which continues to push any small fry swimming towards it into its belly, the vessel in the bay eats and drinks. All evening and all morning, small lifeboats filled the leviathan innards of the vessel with vittles and barrels of water. Van der Weide oversaw the operation. And even a distant bystander could see: the ship had a long sail ahead.

The crew loaded their bellies with food, too, slaking the unslakeable. Out of the entire crew, only three faces did not betray their ordeal: the captain, the hook-nosed physician, and the Malay cook. The sailors avoided the latter two, afraid.

The hook-nosed physician… Such a familiar face, who does he remind me of? The bosun thought long and hard, but to no avail. And then in the evening, leaving the shack of a colonist who turned out to be an old acquaintance of his father, Dirk noticed a coin in the dust and picked it up. A hook-nosed profile gleamed on his palm in the torchlight… who would have thought it? The late King of Spain, Philip the Second.

25.

"I'll think of something! I'll think of something…!"

And he did think of something, yes, and he called, persuading N. to go with him. Or rather, travel with him – first by local electric train, then by tram.

"Bookworms gather at the third tram stop after the station. You can buy a book…"

Yes, that's what Poro said: a book. Curious, did he mean one book in particular?

They miscounted the tram stops and got off not at the third but at the second. There was forest here, ancient, reddish pines. They walked on, following the sleepers. No-one to be seen except some startled squirrels. A woman with an empty zinc bucket appeared from the bushes.

"There's no point in going any further," N. said. "Did you see the bucket? It's a bad omen."

"Yes, I did. We can go back if you like, but we've almost reached the next tram stop."

And he was right – there was a tram stop in the clearing. The sign was nailed right into a pine tree.

"I wonder how the pine tree gets along with a sign nailed into it," N. thought to himself, and then answered himself: "Well, I suppose people have signs, too – their faces..."

Surprisingly, there was quite a crowd at the tram stop. They all had bags, and somewhere there, in the depths of each bag, hidden under some cloth or loaf of bread or a bath-house broom, were books.

"I'll look for one about myself," N. said.

And he found one.

"Let me see," said Poro.

On the cover it said: "Samuel Taylor Coleridge: *The Rime of the Ancient Mariner.*"

"Is it about you?" Poro asked.

N. nodded.

They walked back in silence. The tram did not come – it had just been cancelled.

26.

By way of each wave, by way of the corridors between the waves, through hard wind and hot rain, down the map, beyond the equator, drawing closer to the pole... The next stop was Capstad, a small new settlement with a harbour which had already made a name for itself among those who sailed these waters. Today's exuberant conglomerate of voices, noises and smells known as Capetown was in its infancy, but even back then any and all ships heading East to the Indian Ocean for spices would stop there. Here, letters to and from home could be left, or collected from passing ships.

Sometimes ships stayed a while in Capstad harbour, waiting out bad weather; no-one would ever risk rounding the Cape of Good Hope in a storm – not after several ships had gone down here. And so the Crystal Key had already been standing at anchor here for a week. Admittedly, the wind had dropped a while ago, but for some reason known only to himself, the captain was in no hurry to set sail. Again and again the sailors shot wistful glances at Table Bay, where their ship lay at anchor, rocked by lethargic sleep, then turned their eyes towards the low Table Mountain; after all, there was nothing else to look at.

"Ah, the weather's turned bad again. We can't set sail now with this squally wind," the bosun grumbled to himself. "We should go deeper into the bay and shelter from the storm. Aha, the captain's giving the order to raise the anchor now…"

But this was followed by a second order: to raise the sails. Dirk couldn't believe his ears – not now, surely?! There's a storm brewing!

A rumble of grumble rose from the lower decks where most of the sailors had congregated: why take unnecessary risks? The captain turned to the bosun again and ordered him to call everyone up on deck.

"Whoever's afraid of the waves is a coward," the captain pronounced audibly, strands of his grey hair prancing around his yellowy brow as if trying to detach themselves from it. "We're about to leave the bay. Whoever wants to can climb into the lifeboat and take off wherever he pleases."

Three sailors at once lowered the little boat and it tossed off into the high waves.

"I'll wager a gulden it'll go down," one of the sailors yelled.

The bets were laid in haste, and the sailors watched with interest as the waves beat against the little vessel where their comrades were working the oars with difficulty.

The gulden was lost. The little boat made it.

For a brief moment, Dirk toyed with the idea of getting into that little boat and leaving this madman to his fate, but the first mate could not imagine abandoning his ship, nor even less, leaving his crew in the hands of fate.

"To your posts!" he ordered in his usual confident tone, although there was not a drop of certainty in his soul.

The Crystal Key left Table Bay and now it was the larger vessel's turn to take a beating from the wind and ocean breakers.

27.

*A sadder and a wiser man,*
*He rose the morrow morn.*

N. awoke that morning and asked himself:

"So am I wiser?"

"Yes, but it's too late," came the automatic reply. "You learnt not to trust people. And that is sad. 'For with much wisdom is much sorrow; as knowledge increases, grief increases.' And all is lost. And you cannot bring her back… no need to remember who. 'He went like one that hath been stunned.' Yes, that is how it is. But not 'of sense forlorn,' not deaf to good and evil. No, I am trying to shield myself from that evil here, but evil, well, here it is, knocking at my door…"

Someone was indeed knocking at the door. Ah, no, they're knocking at the window. Who's there? The apple tree. The wind is bending it, trying to break it. Seeking shelter, it knocks. Where is this wind coming from? It's an out and out gale. 'And now the storm-blast came, and he was tyrannous and strong.'

It's coming from the kingdom of winter blizzards. From whence he, too, had come. Does it herald something, this wind? Will the most biting winter blizzards follow on its heels? Or perhaps even the whole 'kingdom'? That was the last thing he needed here… The raindrops were also begging to come into the house during the downpour, but so far the roof had not let them in and they drummed on it, enraged, crying on the window panes…

The gusty wind quietened down towards evening. The crown of the tree which stuck through the veranda had snapped off, it looked even more like a mast now. Somewhere in the bowels of the house, someone was playing Tchaikovsky's *Pezzo Capriccioso* on the cello. The house played an accompaniment: a pitiful screech. N. shook off his habitual evening stupor, straightened up and set off to find the source of the sound. The cello was being played in that same non-existent room with the view to nowhere.

## 28.

Wagner disliked injustice, the city of Leipzig (although he was born there), Jews and the composer Mendelsohn in particular. When he was writing *The Flying Dutchman*, it had not yet dawned on him that everything he disliked was connected and formed something akin to a spider web: all injustice stems from the Jews, especially from the composer Mendelsohn living in Leipzig. He arrived at this fundamental understanding later in life. Meanwhile, Wagner was creating revolutionary circumstances in the country and in opera, conducting orchestras but also, in cahoots with some rabble-rousers, composing pompous symphonies with vocals, which were then performed in opera houses, much to the amazement of the great German composer Brahms, since such a thing was quite beyond his imagination. Walking into the theatre during a piece by Wagner, Lev Tolstoy, frightened by the green cardboard dragon with little green lamps for eyes roaming freely about the stage, promptly fled the theatre willy-nilly, and found himself writing about Beethoven's Kreutzer Sonata as though it were the first shy shoot of musical erotica. Becoming acquainted with Tolstoy's impressions of Wagner, Romain Rollan concluded that Tolstoy had a right to his own opinion, since he was not even fond of Shakespeare, and that, on the contrary, Tolstoy's opinion was in fact proof that Wagner was the best opera composer of all time. In a footnote, however, Romain Rollan stipulated that Wagner would be better off calling his operas symphonies and recommended listening to them with closed eyes. Odd, and—we should note—very coherent thoughts roam the heads of the great.

## 29.

The table was set. Glancing at Table Mountain as they prepared to take a bite out of the reckless vessel, the waves grew green with gleeful expectation, wheezing with tufty, cotton wool foam. The clouds scratched at the tops of the mast. The sails were furled, the vessel listed, leaning into the water, looking for salvation there. Those on deck clung to the stays – everyone dreads being washed overboard. Many were in the flooded hold, baling out water. Like a giant firecracker, the wind exploded over the ship again and again.

This is the scene which met Kees van der Weide's eyes when he made it to the captain's bridge as the ship listed towards starboard. The captain, as it turned out, was in his cabin, having retreated there as soon as they left the bay, as though unwilling to help the ship in its battle against the elements. He was sitting in his berth; he had tied himself to the post with his belt. There was a bottle of rum in his hand, and he'd clearly just taken a swig.

"Who's there?" he asked when the door flew open and spray burst in. "Aha," he drawled, recognising van der Weide. "Weather's bad today…"

"It's still not too late to turn back, Captain. But why on earth did we leave the bay?"

"We had to, Kees. Donnerwetter, I made a bet I would round the cape in a storm…"

"What, it's all for some empty bet!"

"This bet's no empty bet, though I was very drunk when I agreed the odds. If only you knew what's at stake for me!"

"But we still can't round the cape, Captain. It's an easterly, head on."

"Raise the topgallant sails."

Van der Weide stared at the captain, wide-eyed. Such an order was tantamount to giving the command: "Go to the bottom!"

"Just kidding," said the captain, retreating under the wild look in his first mate's eyes. "But we have to round the cape, Kees. Think of something."

But no matter what he tried, the heavy ship refused to heed the rudder, slipping back West time and again.

Now the young officer sent the bosun to report to the captain's cabin. This time, the hook-nosed physician and—the bosun could scarcely believe his eyes—the Malay cook were there besides Falkenberg himself. The two of them gave Dirk a very odd look as he entered the cabin.

"Well, let's have it, then, Dirk Slothem," ordered the captain, grasping the neck of the bottle so hard his hand shook. "Have we managed to round the cape?"

"No. The wind is stronger than we are," answered the bosun with a heavy sigh.

"How many times have we tried?"

"Three, Sir. But all in vain."

    

"Three tries." The physician and the cook spoke in unison, and their eyes shone green in the gloom, piercing as a lynx's. "You've lost the bet, Captain. Now the boat is ours!"

They got to their feet, raised their arms, and seemed to grow. Indeed, the whole cabin seemed roomier, its walls reflecting an eerie green light. The faces of the cook and the physician were clearly visible now. They were rosy-cheeked, like women. Their eyebrows painted, their lips flushed red. Red rays shone from the rubies on their rings, dancing on the ceiling, the walls, the table. One ray landed on Dirk's face and the bosun sensed something uncanny happening to him. His legs went cold, goose bumps crept up his spine.

The captain, who had, in all evidence, deliberately drunk himself into a state of utterly inhuman calm, now eyed that game of shadows dispassionately.

"But which one of us will get the captain, then?" asked the figure of the former cook in a metallic voice, drawing out a long, crooked forefinger. "It was me who had the bet with him."

"He will become mine. You'll see now." The white eyes of the other figure bulged. "Reminds me of King Philip the Second," thought Dirk. "In a dress."

They set to playing dice, and the vessel groaned, creaking at the seams with each throw.

"Yes, Death, he's mine," said the image of Philip the Second.

The other figure flicked the bone-dice across the table so hard that one leg broke and everything was thrown onto the floor. And Dirk suddenly realised: the storm had passed, they were no longer pitching.

The ruby rays of the ring were trained right on him, and Dirk saw terrifying faces, the likes of which he had never seen before.

"Then maybe *that* one's mine?" Death asked with a snaky smile.

"No, another fate awaits him, and all the others on this ship. Now this boat is mine. Forever."

And Death disappeared, snuffed out like a lamp. The second figure turned his princely, icy gaze on Dirk.

"You remember that Spanish merchant? Go up on deck, he's lying there. Throw him overboard."

And the figure vanished like the first one.

The captain was sitting in silence, staring into emptiness. Dirk shook him by the shoulder.

"Who was that?" he asked.

The captain turned an uncanny countenance to him; his face was covered in yellow wrinkles; he looked over a hundred.

"Who was just speaking with us?" The bosun repeated his question.

"It was Death-in-life," the captain replied through clenched teeth. "We're in its power now. From now on, we're doomed *to go against the wind* for all eternity."

30.

When the evening sky pulls together the lapels of its dressing gown and the pain the day brought with it slips behind the horizon like a crimson ball, the eyes of the constellations look out at nocturnal life through the dark shroud of non-existence. "Death claims his own, but he cannot claim everything from everyone," sang the moon milkily, her light masking the night's endlessness. Dreamless sleep seeps through the gloom; our past soundlessly sinks into it. Our present depends on whether we wake; as for our future, who can say with certainty whether we have one or not? Some of our affairs have a future, though; even some of our words, too…

Such muddled thoughts were roaming through the half-awake N.'s head until the sound of his notebook falling off the bed finally roused him.

"Why aren't there any records in the chest?" N. pondered over breakfast, his memory replaying his recent visit to the attic like a worn record. But then he remembered: old skippers didn't like to keep records, sometimes they just kept the accounts. You had to figure it all out for yourself. Wagner, for instance, had "deathless torture," "wandering," "shore leave only once every seven years"… That's torture, not a curse. What might a curse entail?

"Endless haplessness," thought N., remembering his own story. "Smouldering but never blazing, flickering but never flaring." And the wind flung open the windows, howling its agreement into the room.

"Yeah, and the inability to burn up, and the lack of oxygen to do so," N. said to himself as he closed the window. Living like Einstein among the Eskimos, always going against the wind, getting blown right back to where you came from. And no woman's love can help you there, no matter how often Senta throws herself from the cliff, in the third act or even in every scene. Yet there is a curse in this opera, and here it is: "Around the ship the sea is restless and waves produce foam, while everywhere else the sea surface is still and smooth."

## 31.

"Run for it," Dirk decided. "The storm's passed, I can lower the lifeboat. Not a second longer on this cursed ship!"

His numb, wooden legs somehow carried him up on deck. The sun was dazzlingly bright. The deck was bare, the gale had wiped it clean – the lifeboat, the bulwark… and all the people? There was no-one to be seen, only the tattered sails barely fluttering on the guys. And – a body lay near the mast. The body of that Spaniard. A dead body.

Dirk walked over, picked the corpse up by its legs, dragged it to the side and heaved it overboard.

"See you tomorrow!" said the dead Spaniard as he fell, then disappeared into the transparent blue water.

Dirk felt his hair stand on end. He looked about. The ship lay still in open waters.

"I'm on my own," he said to himself. "No, wait, there's the captain, too."

Then came the next thought: Maybe the others are somewhere on the ship? And he headed for the crews' quarters. But even before he arrived, he heard the sound of merry voices and heaved a sigh of relief: they'd survived! And he opened the door. The quarters were empty, but beer glasses clinked and conversation hummed. Van der Weide was telling some tale, then they all fell to discussing it.

"Hey!" the bosun roared. "Can anyone hear me?"

But the conversation continued, and no-one bothered to reply.

Dirk shot out of the mess-hall. Must have a sweaty brow, he thought, and was about to wipe it with his neckerchief when he realised he wasn't wearing one. Neither was he wearing a shirt, breaches or boots. Nor did he have a neck. Nor a body. Only a voice. And invisible limbs. And hands with which to throw the dead Spaniard overboard. And legs, to carry him to the corpse.

"Essentially, the opera begins where the legend ends. In the legend, what has gone before is paramount whereas in the opera, it's the consequences, Senta's self-sacrifice, and the Flying Dutchman himself that are central. Lofty love and other such romantic notions. The only interesting point in the plot of that opera is the attempt to portray the Flying Dutchman's end, in other words his salvation. Salvation from what? From forever roaming the seas, from loneliness. But surely total annihilation cannot be the only salvation from loneliness? What should he do, the Flying Dutchman of the real world, not the operatic one? The one whose 'grief is deeper than the seas he sails?' Does he settle accounts with non-life or continue living it, examining the depths of this inhospitable world, using himself as a probe? For us, mere observers, the main point of the Flying Dutchman's story is, as we have already said, what comes before, whereas for the Dutchman himself it is his subsequent sailing, the chance to see other countries, other towns, to roam the centuries and the seas, to be alone and free… 'His ship is without an anchor, his heart without a hope.'

N. sat on the veranda of his strange house and, absorbing all the moisture of the coming light rain, he wrote and wrote.

"*The Flying Dutchman* is believed to be the only opera on this subject. But, actually, it isn't. There is another opera, which may in fact better reflect the essence of the legend than Wagner's does. It is Vincent d'Indy's 'musical drama' *L'Etranger*, or *The Foreigner*. The Foreigner lives on the seashore among the French sailors but differs starkly from them: he is sad and noble, prepared to share his catch with the needy, whereas they, on the other hand, are coarse, bad-tempered, and suspicious. They reject him, seeing him as something alien. This life amidst the unworthy, that is the real curse, far more terrible than the curse laid upon the Flying Dutchman. There is only one who loves the Foreigner, a girl. Well, how can you have a good opera without a girl?! It simply wouldn't do, you see. And so the Foreigner reveals his true self: "My name? I don't have one… I am he who dreams. I am he who loves. Loving the poor and inconsolable, dreaming of happiness for all people, my brothers, I have traversed many worlds. Long have I sailed, over many seas…" Stop. Here we shall first see wonders with precious stones, then our lovers shall be plunged into the watery abyss; in other words, the full arsenal of romantic tricks. What interests us, however, is that the hero is not merely roaming aimlessly – he is seeking. "Under the sultry sun of the East, amid the white oceans of the poles" he seeks out two things: beauty and love. And he finds them – and then he perishes. Not because he is not forged for happiness, but because this particular world populated by these particular people is not forged for happiness.

Vincent d'Indy's work is at its musical best in the most improbable scene, in which an enchanted emerald is hurled into the sea, spreading a "supernatural green light" over the waters as far as the eye can see and causing the waters to "rise stormily." The most unlikely things sometimes stir an artist's imagination…

Neither opera is often performed, though *The Flying Dutchman* is played more frequently, of course. The premier of *The Foreigner* took place in Brussels on January the seventh, 1903, precisely sixty years after the first performance of Wagner's *The Flying Dutchman*, in Dresden on January the second, 1843. After another sixty years, the author penning these lines completed his studies in the history of music at the Moscow Conservatoire…

Such were the rather disjointed notes N. jotted down, *staccato*-style, in his notebook on that rain-pierced day on his one-mast veranda.

<h2 style="text-align:center">33.</h2>

That night, the sail of his sleep was swelled by the winds of time. And it tossed a handful of phoney snowflakes in his direction, and a short man with rather bulging eyes, long hair and a fleshy nose. This person was dressed in a blue jacket and raspberry-coloured trousers hastily tucked into his boots. A black beret crowned his head. He looked like a craftsman or a merchant. He was walking somewhere, dragging a small sled of books behind him with obvious effort. Sometimes snow lay under the slats of the sled, sometimes it glided over tarmac, emitting spine-chilling, grinding sounds as it did so. N. found himself in the path of this man in the beret, so both were forced to stop. N. looked into his face.

"Allow me to introduce myself. Wilhelm Richard Geyer," the man said reluctantly, raising his hand to his beret.

N.'s face must have betrayed his doubt; the figure scowled, wrinkles appeared on his fleshy nose, and he declared through his gritted teeth:

"Very well, I am Wagner, although in my youth I used the surname Geyer. My *Flying Dutchman* was prophetic, it would seem, in that even after my death everyone ogles at me, not granting me any peace!"

"Forgive me, I did not mean to bother you," N. muttered politely. "Though I must admit, I am fascinated by precisely that opera."

"It has fascinated many, since the day it was written," said the man in the beret with pride. "Even those who hate me. Just imagine, many artists are hated. How they hated Mozart! And Gauguin! Yes, and even your Pushkin and Shostakovich... Actually, that is as it should be: you will hate us, but will listen to our music, read our books, and hang reproductions of our paintings above your bed! Ah, you would like to know why?" he went on, although N. had not prompted him. "Because each of us won his battle and now we are on the other side of time. I hated Bismarck, with his stubbornness and warmongering, but I began to love him when he became the German nation's only hope."

"Some people express their doubts about your views," N. said cautiously.

"Yes, I could not stand Jews," Wagner replied simply, adjusting the collar of his jacket. "But surely you don't think I preferred Germans? We bourgeoisified and mixed with the Latin peoples, that's the root of this tendency towards laziness and debauchery... Some people!" he suddenly said forcefully. "If you could only see the people who hate me, you would begin to love me more!"

"Your music was popularised by certain rather unpleasant individuals in this century."

"I know, I know, the Nazis loved me. And what of it? Fascism is just a matter of terminology. Or belief, if you prefer. They believed in killing, but they did not understand that the cultural assimilation of the Jews would have led to the same result without the need for any casualties. Do you know that they banned my *Parsifal* in 1939, claiming it was a pacifist piece? So I am no Fascist, but a German nationalist. And if the Nazis loved my music, well, so much the better. My works stirred the love of greatness in the hearts of even those petty shopkeepers."

"A love of greatness, as those petty shopkeepers understand it," said N., unable to contain himself.

"Greatness is greatness," said Wagner severely. "And great things can only be brought about through great effort. See how many books I had to wade through before I could write *The Dutchman!* And as for *Die Nibelungen*, well, it would take more than a sled to carry them, much more! Now I am gradually taking all these books to the wastepaper recycling point. I am destroying what they call the interim link, so to speak. It is always vital to destroy this link in a timely fashion, in art. Rough drafts and diary entries, for instance… I didn't manage to burn them all, you see, and I regret that now…"

With an almost involuntary motion, N. picked up the book lying uppermost on the sled. It was a heavy volume with a green leather sleeve; there was no title to be seen. It turned out to be Captain Marryat's *The Phantom Ship*.

34.

"There's a well there. They threw a nun into it, once upon a time," Poro told him. "There's shade without trees and a church without a roof, too."

Any of these facts were reason enough for N. to feel drawn to this mysterious 'there.'

"I'll go with you," said Poro. "We can take a bike or a canoe. It's much faster and easier by canoe, of course."

N., however, had never paddled a canoe, and that reminded him of a song he had once heard to the strum of an out-of-tune guitar while sitting by a campfire:

Don't sit in the same canoe
If you're not a couple but just two.

"Well, this chap and I certainly don't make a couple," N. stated. "But it doesn't matter, because nothing matters any more."

"Well, I wouldn't mind cycling there," he said lamely.

Poro wheeled over two bikes. One was English, a Dunlop, the other was a rusty local steed. Perched on the Dunlop, Poro looked like Lord Astor cycling around his overseas domain.

Turning the pedals side by side, it took them over an hour to get there.

Silence lived in the church without a roof. It took the form of chance mute words drawn on the walls in charcoal and chalk. It lived there just by itself, too, as a clot of peace and quiet.

"I should come here and draw," Poro said. "Although summer's all but over…"

They didn't find the well. The shade was there, but not without its object; it was cast by trees. N. and Poro went out onto the riverbank and laid the bikes on the sand. Poro spread himself out to sunbathe.

"I'll go and take another look at the church," N. said.

The silence swallowed him at once as if it had been poured down from somewhere on high. He didn't feel like going anywhere; maybe he'd already arrived at the final destination…

Then he caught sight of a small door in the side chapel. It was hanging by a single hinge. N. walked through it. As he crossed the threshold, the sun dazzled him; he was blinded. N. screwed his eyes up against the glare, gingerly took a few steps and was in shade. The shade was particularly clammy. Raspberry canes were growing in it; he picked a few berries, gathering them in his left hand to eat all at once, relishing the sweet tartness which burst into his mouth. Then he lay down on the grass, turned his canvas jacket inside out and tucked it under his head. The sky over his head pealed back layers of feathery cirrus clouds, revealing not the sun but the warm light of a daydream.

He was picking raspberries in his dream, too. He's just reaching for one now, a particularly plump one. He leans closer, and suddenly finds himself in a hole. He hits his head against something wooden as he tumbles, and everything goes dark… N. is sitting on something soft. It's dark, his legs are aching terribly. He wants to get up, but can't. As his eyes gradually grow accustomed to the gloom, N. realises he has fallen into the well they had been looking for.

Somewhere high above, the sky was blue, but down here it was dark and dry; there was no water in the well. N. was lying on a cushion of moss.

"That was lucky," he thought to himself. "I could have hurt myself. Yes, this is the well, and up there is the shade with no trees, right after I walked out of the church. Why did I have to reach for that raspberry…? And now what? Poro can't haul me out of here, he'll need a rope. I wonder if he'll call for help or just leave me here."

   

And then N. began to shout. His voice sounded eerie in there, his words seemed to shatter into individual syllables and roll around his head. Nobody appeared. N. shouted for a long time, pausing occasionally, until he was completely hoarse.

Dusk fell.

"Poro has probably left," N. decided. "He must have thought I'd got lost in the woods. Hid my bike in the bushes, most likely. I'll have to wait until morning."

The pain in his leg was unbearable. Stars began to glimmer in the darkness, peering down at him. It was then that N. realised he was not alone down there.

"Well, who will they come for first?" A soft voice sounded right in his ear.

N. started. He groped about in the darkness but his hand met with nothing. Laughter. Very close.

He felt uneasy. The voice was female, but not very distinct.

"I usually while away the nights alone," came the voice. "But not always. I'm loved and in love!"

Somewhat jealous, N. asked with a sigh:

"When will they come for you?"

"When the sun's rays shine down into the well. But it's always dark in here. The shade covers it, even in winter."

"The shade without trees," N. said solemnly.

"What did you say?"

"There is shade, but no trees."

"Yes, shade. There are many shadows in this world, and many in our souls, too…"

Everything sunk into silence; soon, no doubt, dream would follow – or rather, a dream within a dream, then he would wake up in that dream, for the next thing that N. became aware of was a square of sky above his head. And the sky was suddenly blue again. A sunbeam bounced into the well.

"Oh! They've come for me!" The voice was close even though there was no-one next to him.

A silhouette flashed overhead. A light breeze brushed N.'s cheeks.

"Farewell!" The voice floated down from above.

"And when will someone come for me?" N. wondered morbidly.

And someone came at once: a familiar face appeared at the opening of the well. It was his father. Peering over the rim of his glasses as he bent over the well, his father enquired:

"Why did you let yourself fall into a pit? I'm disappointed in you. I hope you can get out by yourself? You're already late for dinner."

And he disappeared. Left. Just like that.

Then another face peered into the well. A pale, made-up face. His mother.

"Ah, there you are! Up to your tricks again! Don't come home until you've come to your senses!"

And the face disappeared. It was replaced by emptiness, and then by another face, a very young one this time. Long hair dangled into the well… Vera, his childhood sweetheart. He had almost forgotten her face.

"I knew it! So now do you see you're a loser? I don't care anymore, rot if you like…"

And that face disappeared, too.

"I thought she was fond of me," N. pondered sadly. "I suppose I didn't read people well back then… My parents are strange, too. I don't remember them like that, they were always so kind to me… But people change their attitude, the state changes its attitude, too, one has to be ready for anything… I wonder what face the little breeze will bring next?"

But no face came. The little breeze gained strength, grew into a gale, shook his shoulders and urged him:

"Wake up, for goodness sake! Good grief, you sleep a lot!"

Poro was shaking him by the shoulders. Sitting up, N. realised his leg had gone numb. Poro was towering over him, massive as a well-fed English gentleman. Is there so much as a hint of concern in this man's eye? No, only shade without trees, a church without a roof, and light without warmth…

Warmth poured down from on high, and the raspberries' red berries smiled up at the sun gratefully.

35.

*"If you sleep, sleep with open eyes, if you sit down, sit on the ground, if you walk, walk where Death goeth not."* N. discovered this sign

    

while he was examining a lacquered box. It was in German. Germans had always been fond of oriental wisdom, and even Goethe, with his *West-Eastern Divan*, is no exception here. It's good advice, by the way, but where is off-limits for Death? Is there such a place?

There is. The Flying Dutchman's ship. Death is forbidden to set foot there. Those on the ship live in another world, where there is no Death. A different dimension…

N. opened the casket again, cradled the snug little pistol in his palm. "This fascination with weapons comes from my father, I expect," N. said to himself. His father was an infantry officer, he had died long ago; having survived the whole war, he died at the beginning of the 70's in a freak accident on Lake Ladoga: his sailing boat overturned in a storm. N.'s mother died a few years later.

"My father was no unsinkable Flying Dutchman…"

N. picked the telescope up and took it over to the attic window. As a boy, he had dreamed of owning binoculars or a telescope and would stare at them through second-hand-shop windows, but no-one bought one for him – they put it down to a spoilt boyish whim.

The attic window became a picture framing the wooded riverbank and the crowns of the pines lush with their green carpet. Ah, there's the distant village on the far bank, there's the unhurried grey water and the parchment strips of sand, and there—right in the distance —a dry channel where the river had once flowed, then there are the meadows of the river estuary, and there—beyond—the holiday resort. And what if he looked in the other direction?

More forest, another pine carpet, then there's the village shop where he had bought groceries, and the building nearby, the red brick one with the square windows. The window swung open, and in one of them…

N. started, dropping the telescope. There was a man in a grey shirt in that window, holding big field binoculars to his eyes, and that man was looking right at him.

You see, it was time for sergeant Safonov's patrol, and, thanks to his father's prized binoculars, he would complete his patrol without leaving the familiarity of the police station. At this very hour, the sergeant was busy keeping a watchful eye trained on the dubious house on the river bank.

36.

N. got undressed, stood in the washtub and poured a bucket of cold water over himself. He gasped, but the sensation of being watched remained on his skin. It didn't wash off; it was sticky, cloyingly sweet, like jam in a jam tart that has been lying around too long. N. picked up the loofah and began fiercely rubbing his skin.

After that incident, he only sat out on the other veranda, the one with its back to the man with the binoculars, and facing the water. And he drew all the curtains of the rooms facing the front. All rooms, that is, to which he had access; the others lived a life of their own, quietly, modestly, disturbing nothing. N. checked: the man who had been observing him could only see the attic. However, this didn't cheer him up particularly: the feeling of being watched did not pass. It was as though the city had muscled its way in here. Here it is, "the kingdom of winter blizzards." That is not what he had come here for; quite the opposite, he had come here to become invisible. But is it even possible to be both alive and invisible in a country of eavesdroppers?

"Maybe it's time to move on, to go somewhere else?" N. asked himself the question which dogs every fugitive.

But the house had already swallowed him whole; it was nice and quiet here, and anyway, where could he hide? So he closed himself away deeper inside the house's silence.

37.

With its single eye, green as the needles on a freshly felled Christmas tree, the well was watching from under its murky, cloudy veil. The water was cold and smelt rusty, as ever. Having turned the winch and fetched the bucket, N. greedily drank of the green needles and murky clouds, but they were not depleted, and the bucket remained full of them.

Next he took a look inside the well. The shaft was dark, moss peeped out here and there. Suddenly a face appeared between the needles and the clouds. Or rather, not so much a face as a kind of grimace, vulgar and sickly sweet, and a mouth appeared. Gaping, it declared with its lips alone:

"Come sleep in the water."

      

And the needles with their clouds wrinkled in expectation.

"Tempting," N. admitted. "But that smile is most unpleasant, and the face only knows the bad side of you—no, not quite—but it's certainly a case of 'nothing human can be alien to me.' What happens if we turn that around? 'Human nothing.' That's who is calling, not that nothing which is essentially non-existence, but the nothing which is inside you, grey and cloud-coloured!"

"I won't surrender!" N. bit his lip and hurled the brash zinc bucket into the smug grin.

<h2 style="text-align:center">38.</h2>

Death is an immigrant with a light overnight bag, a little red leather suitcase containing not a sickle but a clepsydra or an hourglass. Death is a stranger everywhere, yet you cannot banish it beyond the country's borders. Death is understood by all: it speaks the language of deeds belonging to the same linguistic group as earthquakes and thunderclaps. Death knows no doubt, and in this alone it differs from people, for in all other aspects it has fully humanised itself – or rather, it likes to think it has humanised itself. At the same time, its humanity is but an empty human shell, and the inner emptiness of death inexorably sucks in all and everyone. Listen – you, too, hear that seltzer sound in the night; it is the voice of Death.

Tired of the sounds of non-existence, N. pulled the covers over his head so he could hear only nothing. A dream came. And in that dream N. was walking along the streets of London he had read about: a Russian's dream, the dream of a man whose feet are tied down with border wire. Near Covent Garden, a rather dubious beggar sold him a ticket for the nearby theatre and even offered him some snuff.

The ticket said: "Hamlet. The Tragedy 'William Shakespeare.'" Wondering at the strange wording, N. made his way to his box, sat himself down on the red velvet-covered seat and began looking around the half dark stalls. There was quit a commotion, the audience were taking their seats, talking and laughing among themselves.

Finally, the lights went out and candles were lit. And N. noticed the audience were all in fancy dress – Roman togas, Venetian camisoles and even knight's armour. The ladies were dressed no less strangely, either.

The buzz of conversation stopped abruptly. A man in a long black cape appeared in the adjacent box. His stern, unsmiling face reminded N. of someone.

"The author! It's the author!" The whisper rustled through the stalls.

And N. no longer understood where he was or what was happening. "Well, I'm still just a spectator," he thought woefully. "Others usually take centre stage…"

The man in the black cape bowed to the audience and raised his hand commandingly. A hush descended.

A fanfare sounded, the curtains were raised – and a medieval English town was revealed. The first scene portrayed the birth of a baby into an affluent glover's family, the second showed his childhood. The action took place in Stratford-upon-Avon, and N. was finally convinced that the play was indeed about Shakespeare's life.

Now they'd reached the composition of sonnets, then plays – it was already 1600 on the stage, the year *Hamlet* was written.

The intrigued N. tried to imagine what would happen next, but no 'next' came; the Queen asked Shakespeare to recount his life story. The lights went out in an instant, then went back on, and the play started all over again.

"Of course," N. reasoned. "If the author of this play is Hamlet, how can he know what happened to Shakespeare after he had written the tragedy about him – he had become a character, existing only within the author's mind."

The play played itself out three times, and was about to begin again for a fourth time, when N. realised he had to do something to stop himself losing his mind.

He grabbed a chair and threw it onto the stage. The never-ending show stopped. A bright light went on and everyone in the stalls turned to stare at N.

Gosh, everyone was there! Prospero and Mercutio, Juliet and Ophelia, Falstaff and Macduff… Even the ass from *A Midsummer Night's Dream* was sitting there! N. recognised many but not all of them, even though he considered himself a bit of a Shakespeare connoisseur. Now, however, all those faces turned towards him expressing only indignation, as though asking: "How did he get here, and why is he spying on us? And what shall we do with him?"

Prospero came forward and asked:

"Are you a character or a real person? Don't lie to us!"

"I am a character," N. said with some hesitation. "My book is The Book of Life."

No sooner had he uttered those words than everything disappeared. N. found himself on the street in the rain. The familiar beggar was counting coins nearby.

"Well, sir, did you enjoy it?" he said with a smirk. "And now follow me. You have a role to play, a role no-one but you can play."

And leaving his tattered black cape in a doorway, the beggar stepped into the yawning dark of a passageway. N. followed him – and, leaving the land of dream, he came out on the other side, the almost tangible side of reality.

39.

"No living soul nor book to hand…" How well these words of Mahler would fit with the motif of any folk song! A travelling song…

N. had set off early that morning to wander wherever his fancy took him. He wandered the hills, sat on a tree stump, listened to the frogs and the scraggy cows, pondered herd mentality and close-knittedness. His trouser legs were soaked with dew, thorns clung to them, but he was oblivious to this and all else, and, when tiredness overpowered him, he would sleep in the shade on dry hillocks before setting off again. Sweet nostalgia was singing within him. It always lived inside him, like the sound of the sea inside a shell. "Everything might have been fine, everything could still be fine," the warbler repeated from some abandoned garden. An apple tree was growing there, half wild now. He bit into a tart apple. Apples, dill, lettuces, a few red currants… N. remembered the white currant bush which grew under his window in the city. Every year, on the fifth of August, he would gather his "harvest" and lay the birthday table… no need to remember whose birthday it was. No-one else picked the white currants; they probably mistook them for poison sumac berries, even though a lot of people walked beneath his window… He wasn't thirsty, he wanted to sleep. But actually N. couldn't be sure he was not already asleep and this walk was not a dream.

He came out on the high bank again. He was far from the house now. People were sun-bathing and playing cards on the sand below. Someone was paddling a canoe. Two slender midget ships were racing each other. A woman's laughter reached him, and the paddles worked rhythmically. The day was already asserting its rights, the midday sun was baking, and the crickets were chirping their bicycle song.

"So life goes on, despite everything. Newspapers are read, TV sets are switched on, people do sport and find something to breathe, the city does not cramp them… How come? Well, the city didn't cramp me, either… Or did it? Well, they probably feel cramped there, too, and that's why they are here, with their portable radios and their songs. They've brought the city here, forced it to sing, hum. Buzz. Tell me about silence! What was that in Mahler's first symphony? Nature and 'the respectable public' in the countryside… Animals bury the hunter, sounds bury silence…"

N. stopped short of the resort and turned back.

40.

No books? That can't be! And to prove it, the house turned the old chest inside out. Inside, it was concealing – no, not a book, but a tattered fat journal with no cover and some torn out pages. It turned out to be a copy of *Foreign Literature* magazine. Seems you can't get through the summer without at least some reading…

The evening sun was pouring over the garden bench, and, having made himself comfortable there, N. opened the journal in the middle and began to read the story there, translated from… Part of the page had been torn out. The short story described a mountain lake which, in some mysterious fashion, reflected the eye of God, and everything was laid bare before this eye…

"Hmm, applied theology in action." N. was tossing sleepless in his bed. "But the eye really is keeping track of us, unblinkingly, and we never even know whose eye it really is…"

And he pulled the covers over his head instinctively.

<h1 style="text-align:center">41.</h1>

An unfamiliar fisherman arrived the next evening. Striding straight up the little wooden stairs right onto the veranda, he held a large piece of carp pie out to N.

"I fish not far from here," he said with a shy smile, the wrinkles on his narrow, unshaven face smoothing away. "I see you always have the light on at midnight. It's obvious: the man's working, not looking after himself, I must take him something! My wife bakes these pies… Take it, please, as one ship's captain to another…"

N. broke a piece off right away. The fish was tender and surprisingly tasty. N. didn't even know how to thank the fisherman.

Having bade farewell, the fisherman retraced his steps down the little stairs, untied his rowing boat and sailed on; he worked nights and early mornings. N. felt a warm sensation spreading in his chest, and he gazed after the fisherman for a long while.

"As one ship's captain…" The words rang in his head. "Captain… as for the boat, well, I'm my own boat. And I steer this ship with an unusual lack of skill…"

<h1 style="text-align:center">42.</h1>

There was a soundless voice in the room at night, a voice from those days which never were: "Remember how I lay down on the tarmac?"

No, he doesn't remember, he mustn't remember. He doesn't remember the attic, either; he remembers a face, a woman's face, pretty and asymmetrical. A face where everything—eyes, eyebrows—is in flight. A beloved face. How could he forget? It would be like forgetting himself… but as for what had happened, well, he remembers nothing. And he must not remember!

But the figure lying on its back on the tarmac has no intention of forsaking his memory.

And an answer comes, the key to salvation: "It didn't happen to me." Yes, that is how to think of it: it happened to somebody else. It happened…

# PART 2

## Allegro. Adagio. Allegro

### 1.

For some reason, a chalk outline is always drawn around someone who falls from a window. All that's left are the contours, which look like a plane. A plane that will never take off.

When I ran up—the tram didn't come for ages—they'd already taken Beta away, so I never did see how she lay there on the tarmac. But judging from the chalk plane, she'd lain as if asleep. That's how she slept, on her side, with one arm stretched right out, her head nestling on it. Maybe it was easier for her to cut through the waters of sleep like that, in that seemingly purposeful position… Beta, Beta!... Why is everything so dark?

I gathered from the onlookers that she'd been taken to the morgue. But where is Gamayunov? Probably went with her. Beta plus Gamma… An equation which had never happened in real life. But a corpse goes well with any living soul. Well, at least the corpse won't protest.

The tram. Faces, faces, faces, shopping bags on the floor, on knees. Movement – but where were we going? Was this the direction Beta's outstretched arm was pointing towards? But I knew where I was headed: to her. Because she still needed me, even if she was no more…

### 2.

The morgue. Cracked tiled floor, tiled walls, too, and – the smell. I wait, standing up; I can't force myself to sit down. But now I can't even stand still, either. I pace around in circles. Suddenly – Gamayunov. Now it's Gamma plus Alpha. That equation had happened – maybe a friendly combination, maybe an indifferent one, but a combination nevertheless.

"Sorry, I couldn't stop her..." He's talking, so calmly... but what about? "She was sitting on the window ledge, she burst out laughing, leaned back..."

What, he's talking about HER?! Like that?! SHE WAS LAUGHING! Laughter cost her her life. But he, Gamma, well he knew how she laughed, too – she would throw herself back and scatter into beads of laughter. He knew it, and he made her laugh, she, Beta, sitting there on the window ledge! Not on purpose, he says, not on purpose. But what was it we used to say about 'not on purpose' when we were kids?...

They call us into the hall. A metal cupboard scrapes. A white sheet, and under it... Her arm's no longer outstretched. Yeah, no longer outstretched... Her arms are folded over her head. She would sleep like that, too, Beta would... Beta's asleep. Wake up, Beta! She looks alive. She is alive!!! No, the back of her head is split. She's in pain. Let me hug her... I don't remember anything else...

3.

No, I do remember – I remember how I carried those three roubles I'd found to the bin. The three rouble note is green and rustles temptingly. I have to make it to the bin. I would have run, but I'm too small. So I just move my legs quickly.

The chase is already closing in. Granny had heard that pleasant green rustle, too.

"Three roubles!" she shouts hoarsely. "That's money! Stop!"

I hurry to the bin. Granny's hurrying, too: there are people around, it's unseemly to run. But in the evening the park is quite empty. Nobody watches as I win my first victory. Granny is catching up, the distance narrows mercilessly, and – there is it, the bin! And like a basketball through the ring, I pop the green paper right into the target, into the gaping black hole.

"Eh, you rascal!" says Granny, hotly, rummaging in the bin for the three roubles.

I smile inwardly, as I often shall when I grow up. And so there I am, being led like a criminal along the avenues of the Kislovodsk park...

4.

No, not along the avenue, but along Pirogovsky Street, to the Metro. The pigeons are in a frenzy on the eaves of the grey, Stalinist, barrack-like houses. It is Gamma who is leading me. Gamma plus Alpha. But Beta... Oh, Beta!...

I stop. I'm trembling.

And we go on. A bell is tolling in Novodevichy cemetery... Or am I imagining things? Never ask for whom the bell tolls... It's clear: for you…

Home – Beta's things, underwear… Dear God!

Just three years, yet already so familiar. I'd got used to it, although she didn't live here, would just come over… And me, I lay down where the chalk plane had been and it carried us both away – then crashed into the tarmac.

5.

The police. "We have a witness that your texts..."

"What texts?" Look surprised. Of course I know what texts, but then they know, too… Well, so what?! The main thing is not to admit it. Like a spy from a kids' book. The valiant Soviet spy. Hmm, a spy… For Them, saying what you think is tantamount to being a traitor or a spy. If only they'd seen how we were spreading pamphlets through the letter boxes late at night while it was all going on in Czechoslovakia! If someone comes into the foyer, you run up to the next floor and wait… Trying not to breathe. Until the lift has gone. Then you go down a flight of stairs, and carry on. Like a spy. The main thing is not to admit anything. The police cell, bars on the windows. Lucky for me I wasn't wearing lace-up boots, or they'd have confiscated my laces. They tie up a dog outside my cell – a huge German shepherd, bigger than I am. They goad it, then say: "Don't you want to sit with it?" I keep mum. Heart pounding. They're trying to scare me. In the report, I fill in everything which has been deliberately left out. And then I sign it, only then. I remember some advice like that in an instruction note by the dissident Yesenin-Volpin, son of the poet Yesenin. The investigator was livid with me, that's why they threatened me with the dog. But they can't prove anything anyway!

   

"How long have you known Elizabeta Osiptseva?"

Ah, yes, this is now, not then. "Elizabeta..." I had never used that name; I'd even forgotten that she was Elizabeta.

Meanwhile the policeman rustles papers in his file.

"Ah-ha, it says here, three years..." he declares. "What was the nature of your relationship?"

I keep mum, look at the policeman. A handsome, rough face, red, with sideburns. The likes of him can never understand psychological subtleties. Back then, more than a decade ago, it had been a different one. Pale, with glasses, like a first-class swot. "Don't you sympathise with us?" How can you answer that? "Well, you know how it is," I said.

Red-Face decides to clarify his question:

"She was almost your wife, they say."

Almost! She was more than a wife, she was half of me, my better half, at that. But I reply:

"We were going to get married."

This suits the policeman. A ready formula. That must be the way to reply, in ready formulas, clichés. If only each new question wouldn't trigger these inner dialogues!...

He's asking about Gamayunov. Well, what can I say? A school mate, Garik Gamayunov, or Ga-Ga for short. It was only later, in the 6th form, that Beta came up with the idea of calling us Alpha and Beta, and so Garik became Gamma. He was a natural at copying; he would copy natural sciences from Beta, maths and physics from me. He was easy to get along with and his face, round as a pancake and smooth as a baby's, wore a ready smile.

"A school mate, then? A joker? And was there anything between him and your fiancée?"

I got so outraged that the policeman apologised.

"I mean, did they work together, for instance..."

Yes, they did have something in common, a hobby, rather than work. Beta taught in the Gnessin college and would sometimes play the violin in the House of Scholars amateur orchestra. And sometimes I played in that orchestra, too; I played the piano, an instrument occasionally used in orchestras. Garik scraped through music school—he played the bayan—and then astounded everyone by taking to the triangle like a duck to water. The triangle. An odd orchestral instrument, looks like a bent steel twig. They hang it up and hit it with a metal rod. Well, could you call that 'working together?' Beta is sitting there in the first violins by the concertmaster, and Gamma is somewhere at the back, there's a lot of people between them. They are both performing the same task, me as well: creating music.

"All three of us played in an amateur orchestra," I say.

"Aha, that's no place for a duet," remarks the policeman pensively. "Fine. If you remember anything, give me a ring."

And he hands me his calling card: "Inspector Volov." A palindrome surname. Perfectly streamlined both forwards and backwards.

6.

Back home, I pace out circles again. Something is bothering me, something is amiss. But I can't figure it out. Something Beta had said to me shortly before she died. Something she'd said... No, I can't remember.

In my room, the furniture stands around the perimeter. Once when we were playing Battleships I stationed all my ships right at the edges, just on a whim, and I beat everyone: there was more empty space left that way. The four-square ship in my room is the bed; the three-square ships are the wardrobe, the piano and the desk. The two-square ship is the bookcase, and the one-square ship is the chair. Who can I play Battleships with, room against room, to get these objects out of my life? There are plenty of objects in my life, but few people. And now... No, don't think about it, don't think about this 'now.' Don't think about Beta either, otherwise I'll go to pieces... But what was it she'd said?

7.

I don't want to go on living. But how can you do that, how can you 'not live'? I go over to the window. As if to spite me, my window is on the ground floor. But if it were *that* window! What else can you do to 'not live'? What tablets do I have lying around?

My archaeological dig in the medicine cupboard was interrupted by the phone's impudently persistent ring. Forgot to take it off the hook, again...

"Hello!"

　　　　　　　　　　　　　　　　　　　

It's Vassa, the elderly flautist from our orchestra. A lady with a face from a foreign laxative ad, Beta would joke. But Vassa evidently took this grimace which stretched her painted lips for a smile. I don't really like her, of course, but I'm giving her son piano lessons: Vassa herself doesn't play well, she can't teach him. But she's not calling about her son now.

She's sympathising, wants to know more. Horrid old gossip in her cat shawl. No, she won't get any details from me!

"But are you sure there isn't some catch?"

What does she mean?

"Well, that it's just an unfortunate accident. Are you sure? Maybe it wasn't an accident?"

I redirect her to her favourite conversant: Gamayunov. Like it or not, he was there when it happened. When *it* happened…

A wave of pain crashes over my heart, as if it were a tiny sailing ship. I lose track of the conversation.

"Never mind, don't worry," Vassa is saying.

Well, I like that! 'Don't worry!' I hang up, angry, and pace, pace about the room. "Not an accident"! What, Beta jumped out deliberately? Good God! No, impossible. Not her…

8.

Beta comes to me in my dreams. With a dog. Like back then. We all go for a walk in the forest, the spring forest of three years ago. And Beta sits on a hillock among the yellow lamps of coltsfoot. The dog's a big, amiable Airedale terrier, a bit on the daft side, and for some reason it reminds me of a friend from St. Petersburg: the poet Zhenya Rein. It jumps on Beta and, laughing, she throws herself onto her back. Her blouse rides up, baring a white strip of tummy. How I loved her then! But I didn't say anything, kept mum. Because it wouldn't do to say anything, because it wasn't voiced yet. Though it was implied.

And then Beta and I go home – but we can't get back. "Where's our block of flats, Beta?" But no, it's not there, our block isn't there, and we roam the streets till dusk, and then darkness falls, pitch black, so I can't even see Beta any more. "Beta!" I shout.

No, I'm whispering, not shouting, because I've already woken up. It's dark and cold. Utterly dark. I was always afraid of death when it got dark – something would loom up, and I would sense an *absence of me*. It was so terrifying that I would always switch on the light and try to distract myself. But now, in the darkness, I realised I wasn't afraid of death now, that indeed, I wanted to die and had the power to do something to myself any moment. Strange though it may seem, I felt relieved: it's so much easier when we don't fear non-existence!

And with that thought still in my mind, I sink into dreams again.

Now Beta is playing her violin for me. Brahms' 'Scherzo.' Fast and furious: da-da-da-daam. Almost like Beethoven's fifth symphony. da-da-da-daam. And the violin's voice is worried, telling me something.

I wake up and can only recall the tail end of that dream: Beta, lowering the violin, and: da-da-da-daam. That's right, she *had* told me something about the violin. But what?

Now I remember: she'd asked my advice about what to do with her second violin. Beta's mother died a year ago, as it happened, and she was a violinist, too. She'd burned up with cancer, and so Beta found herself with two violins. They were both Italian, not factory made but hand-crafted, so they were worth quite a bit. Beta was used to her own violin and didn't play on the other. She'd picked it up once, tuned it and started to play a Bach Prelude, but then suddenly stopped short and all but hurled the violin onto the sofa, sobbing. It reminded her of her mother. Beta loved her. She was the embodiment of her mother's dreams, a wonderful violinist, even though she didn't become a soloist. She and her mother had played Bach's concert in D-minor for me once. Beta played first violin, of course, and her mother was so proud of her pure, clear tone.

I had said to Beta back then: we don't need money now. If we get married and want to go on a honeymoon, well, then maybe we'll sell it. Beta had laughed, and we didn't speak of it again.

9.

I wake up. Morning. The phone is over-exerting itself. It's Auntie Manya, Beta's auntie. The funeral is the day after tomorrow. Did I know my passport is lying on the piano in Beta's flat?

No, I didn't know. I don't want to know. But Auntie Manya insists. She's an accountant, goes by the book: a person should always carry their documents, the sun should always rise in the East, you must pay for your tram fare. If she ever forgets to pay and gets caught, well, she would probably lose her marbles. Beta was different, thank God. Was… And suddenly nothing makes any sense anymore…

Auntie Manya doesn't let up: we should go to Beta's flat today so I can pick up my passport. At least they haven't sealed off the flat: Beta's grandmother is the registered tenant although she lives with Auntie Manya, not at the flat.

"After work," she'd said, though I had no idea what time Auntie Manya finished work. I got the impression she was always at work – she was one of those quiet, agile old ladies, small and dry but with a tenacious sharp eye, the type who is always busy doing something, either at work or at home. You don't see the likes of her with a book or in front of the TV. I reckon they are the ones who keep the world turning. Or at least, society revolves around them. Certainly not around hermits like me!

10.

My passport was indeed lying on the piano. Not surprising – anything of mine could show up at Beta's and vice versa, anything of Beta's could be at my place. A sort of mutual interpenetration, diffusion, as the scientists say. A thin layer of dust already covers everything – the table, the piano, the violin case… The violin. It was like Beta's living soul, and now it drooped. The case is not standing in the corner as usual but is lying on the coffee table. It's anxious. Alone. Where is its friend?

That's a point – where is the other violin? I go through the flat looking for it, but it's nowhere to be found. Auntie Manya doesn't know anything about it, either. Who could have taken it? Who was here last? Gamayunov. *That* day. Surely he hadn't swiped it?

I call him that evening.

"What are you talking about, my dear fellow? What's got into you? I can't even play the thing…"

I feel embarrassed.

"Maybe she lent it to someone?"

Gamayunov's suggestion is perfectly plausible: Beta was such a generous person, she could easily have lent her violin to someone, and not even to someone particularly close to her.

Maybe we'll never know what happened to the violin, I think to myself. Beta's grandmother is the heir, and she's too old to chase up part of her inheritance.

I tell Gamma the funeral is tomorrow.

"I'll be there for sure," he says, and then—matter-of-factly—"Is there anyone to carry the coffin?"

For me, Beta is still alive; that word, 'coffin', knocks me to the floor.

## 11.

I won't talk about the funeral. It's beyond me. I got through it somehow, but how – words fail me.

One thing I will say, though: Gamma didn't show up, and I carried the coffin, and once again—for the last time—we were "Alpha plus Beta."

Gamma had a bout of high blood pressure. I guess that explains his red face – his blood flows to his head.

Beta went off somewhere down below, and then, probably, into the skies. As we were coming back, the crematorium chimney was dutifully belching thick, greasy smoke skywards.

## 12.

The fate of Beta's violin came to light suddenly and unexpectedly.

When he heard about Beta's death, the conductor at the House of Scholars orchestra took a bad turn. Later, I realised why: he was used to seeing her right in front of him; she sat in the first row, after all.

The conductor was a notable fellow: Leonid Piatigorsky, brother of the famous American cellist Gregor Piatigorsky. There was a third musical brother, too, who'd taken the surname Stogorsky, which literally meant a man from a hundred mountains, whereas Gregor only had five of them in his surname. However, as someone once joked, quality doesn't depend on how many mountains you have! The existence of a legendary émigré brother created a certain aura around Leonid, who was, after all, merely the modest conductor of an amateur orchestra. It gave him a mysterious, romantic air. He had a limp, too, but not just a slight one, like Lord Byron; he limped quite noticeably. He had some serious illness and had been told he would die young. But he was still afloat. He was an extremely talented musician; it was only his illness that kept him from becoming head of a top, professional orchestra. Did he feel a failure? Maybe, but be that as it may, this was one reason for his irritability.

And when he called the orchestra together two weeks later, he was in a particularly furious mood. I was there, too – someone called me, and all of a sudden I managed to get myself together. To my own surprise. I can't say I'd already regained my senses, but at least I could function, albeit mechanically. Piatigorsky ranted and raged, yelled at everyone. The first and second violins were playing *piano*, he shouts: "What are you scratching there?" and then added angrily, looking at someone, "New violin doesn't help, then?"

I pricked my ears. When the rehearsal was over, I approached the concertmaster, the old man Kron, and asked who had a new violin. The hinges of squeaky Kron's rigid professor's torso turned, he fixed the blind lenses of his rimless glasses on me, and finally waved his bow into the distance: "Marianna."

I knew Marianna. We all did. Not because she played well – no, quite the opposite. But she did her best. This plump, squat woman always gave everything her best; she bit her lip while she played, and beads of sweat glistened on her brow. And that's exactly how she'd tried to get herself a husband, too, not long ago, with the whole orchestra judging every twist and turn of the plot. At last it happened. But Marianna didn't get on so well with her husband; they were always either fighting or making up.

Hearing my question about the violin, Marianna poked her head up and said coquettishly:

"Oh, so you already know… Seems you can't keep your eyes off me…"

"Mhm, but who did you buy it from?"

"From Beta," she said, hurt. "The day before… What's the matter? I paid for it in full!"

Excusing myself, I headed for the exit. So that was it: she and her hubby had made it up again, and he'd given her money for a violin. And she, poor thing, thought that with a better violin, she would suddenly start playing better, too…

But what about Beta… Why had she sold it? Did she need the money? Or was it that the violin brought up painful memories of her mother? And why hadn't she told me anything about it?

13.

Oh, and where is the money, by the way? Auntie Manya didn't find anything in the flat. Surely Beta hadn't managed to bank it already? That wasn't like her – you could hardly call her the prudent type. But she wouldn't have lost it! I can't understand it. Or maybe I don't want to?…

I'm living somewhere inside myself, following my habitual daily routine. On Sundays I go for rehearsal and practise with Vassa's Vasya. I don't feel pain any more – how can you feel pain when you consist entirely of it? When your whole being is made up of it, one hundred percent?

One day—more than a month since (I have a new way of marking time now, or rather, non-time)—Vassa asks:

"So, I expect you've sorted out what happened there, then?"

"No," I say.

She gives me a long look and asks:

"You mean you don't know how it happened?"

"I don't understand."

"Oh, but you do!"

That night, having got home, I give myself a straight talking to before I fall asleep: actually, I do understand. I understand that I can't get it into my head: I am completely convinced that, after that terrible incident, Gamma *went through the flat and took the money*.

14.

But I can't accuse him of that! No matter what he's done, I can't.

But still, when I next see him at rehearsal, I can't stop myself:

"Listen, I want to talk to you."

"Go on, then," he says with a jaunty smile.

"About money."

He is surprised: that was the last thing he expected to hear from me, unmercenary since I was a kid, since those three roubles.

     

"About Beta's money," I add.

He gives me a long look and agrees:

"OK, let's talk. But not here."

"After the rehearsal."

"No. We can only have that conversation in one place: Beta's flat."

Now it's my turn to be surprised.

"You'll understand later," he explains.

I tell him we'll have to get the key from Auntie Manya.

"Get it. I'll give you a ring."

He is remarkably calm, almost serene. Except for his crafty smile; that's how he smiles when he beats me at chess.

15.

Outward people are not in the least like inner people. External people talk for others, and only listen to themselves. Internal people don't say anything at all, they listen to the wind and the waves, to streams and strings, to hail and harvest, and then they store all that they have heard in the back room. Internal people have another room for words, a front room. Cold words are kept in a fridge there, warm words are kept by the heart. Because these internal people have a heart, you see, a small heart which feels the cold, as all hearts do. The hearth of grand words can warm an external person's heart, but not that of an internal person.

Sometimes the two meet, an external person and an internal person, and others think that they get on well together: the external person can talk and talk, the internal person keeps quiet and listens. The others don't know that internal people are choked by words, unspoken words, and as a result, the little fragile heart in each of them aches.

16.

In the tram, my heart really does begin to ache. Thank God it's just hurting, and not aching incessantly as it did not long ago, after…

I remember how alarmed Beta once was when this happened to me while she was around. That was in the tram, too. Actually, nothing was aching or hurting then, but Beta suddenly asked:

"Aren't you feeling well?"

"Don't think so. Why?"

"Your lips have gone blue!"

"Blue?!" I asked. I listened to myself and felt a certain uncertainty. Maybe something really frightening was happening to me? I grew uneasy.

"They're almost purple now. And your cheeks have gone really pale."

And then pain really did sear through my heart – from fear, probably. I would have looked at myself in the mirror, but there's only one mirror in a tram, at the side, in front of the driver. I couldn't very well stop the tram and ask the driver to let me look at my lips and cheeks.

"And what's wrong with your eyes!" she almost yelled. "Your pupils are all dilated, like a corpse's…"

I passed out onto the tram floor. Some plump lady, a nurse as it turned out, pressed my head to my knees enthusiastically.

"Seems I gave you a fright," Beta said, sheepishly. "Sorry…"

And then she apologised again, profusely.

## 17.

There's another story connected with the tram, too. I can hardly remember it now; hardly surprising, I was very young. It wasn't long after my parents had got divorced, and I hadn't started talking yet – still gathering impressions, I suppose.

And there and then, in the half empty evening tram, I suddenly broke my silence, and loudly pronounced my first historic words:

"My Daddy hits people with chairs. It's not good to hit people with chairs!"

The passengers giggled, trying to restrain themselves. Shocked by such family reminiscences, my mother hurriedly put her hand over my mouth and dragged me off the tram at the next stop.

And thus I began talking. And that is how my tendency to denounce people was born, too, a tendency which Gamma had had to face for a few unpleasant moments earlier that day.

I suppose my parents' divorce was inevitable. My father was a major with the green trimmings of the KGB on his cap; he had to be, of course, to conquer a dissidenting lady, but how can you put up with a bad character when your own is just as bad?

   

## 18.

That night, I dream of Beta, again. We are travelling together. She brings rain with her wherever we go. And gives me lessons in bravery.

"Do you like this weather?" she asks me.

"I do," I reply, sleeking back my wet hair.

There's a flash; lightning strikes the oak we are sitting under.

"And do you like it now?" asks Beta.

"I do," I respond, through the ringing in my ears. "I love sitting by a fire." And it's true, the oak in front of us is burning down.

Beta smiles her new, brave smile, throws her head back and lets down her long golden hair.

Thunder roars with such might that our little plywood house collapses.

"Don't you feel sorry for it?" Beta asks.

Green sparks shine in her queer eyes.

"No," I reply, since there is no other reply.

"Then let's go for a walk on the storm clouds," Beta says and jumps onto the nearest cloud.

And so we walk together in the lowering sky for so long that I lose track of time. And then I lose track of her, too, behind some cloud.

I search for her in the heavens and on the earth, but I cannot find her. Then I wake up and remember: Beta was a terrible coward when she was alive.

## 19.

If only I could muster some courage… How am I going to talk to Gamma? Accuse him right to his face? But what if I'm wrong? No, no, I'm not wrong, Gamma knows something. I can tell by that smile. He knows something, and he's keeping it to himself, holding it inside like a balloon. Like a big, rosy-cheeked balloon… I suppose there's no need to burst him, I could just untie him, and then I'd know what kind of air he holds inside…

That's how I talk with my room, where the light is on day and night. During the day it seems yellowish, at night it's bluish. And a currant bush peeps in through the window.

I remember how an artist friend of mine gave me a picture, how I carried it home, carefully planning each step. My steps were tiny, timid – walking is not easy when you are carrying Beauty! Beauty lived in that painting. She was bright and sunny, and I carried her into my room with its north-facing windows and thought I was bringing in the Sun itself. The real Sun never looked into my windows; it wasn't interested in what went on behind them, I suppose. Ah, but such a lot went on – on paper!

I shuffled the picture around, getting a better grip on it, carrying it in front of me now, like some kind of shield. It parted the flow of people, like a breakwater. The artist had framed the picture, put it under glass, and I thought: quite right, let it always stay just as it is, and never come into contact with a world deprived of harmony. With the world in which Hindemith had still had the audacity to unearth some sort of harmony, "Die Harmonie der Welt"... There were already fewer steps to home now. I wonder, I thought as I stopped to catch my breath, why did he tie it up with string? And I set off again, carrying the picture like a briefcase, by its string. And I nearly lost my treasure – one of the knots the artist had tied undid itself and the picture began to fall. I managed to put my foot under it, grabbing the top of the picture at the same time. Nothing dreadful had happened; the corner of the glass merely grazed the tarmac. My heart belatedly skipped a beat: something irreversible might have come to pass!

I retied the knot, firmly, but now I no longer trusted the string and carried the picture in front of me again.

My block of flats, at last. The main entrance, and my own front door reluctantly opened for the new tenant. The strings are off, the nail is in the wall, and the picture is already hanging above the piano...

Yes, the picture settled into its new home. It looked around right away, searching for the sun, but, not finding it, the picture absorbed the white rays of the lamp instead. Then the picture took on a new hue and decided: "I shall keep this."

I took a few steps back, examined the picture and was amazed: it was evening there now, not sunny midday.

   

20.

Tired of trying to fathom the mysteries of eternity, I talk to myself about tomorrow. But once again the sphinx towers up in my dream, plying me with unspoken questions. They split the silence like flip-flop soles slapping on a marble floor. I am like a grain of sand under Time's feet; I have given up hope of finding any answers. All I want is to get far enough away from myself, and I roam the sun-kissed desert amongst the cacti and question marks. Another dark stone sphinx looms in the distance, and I know it is no mirage, and maybe even no longer a dream.

The next day comes. Noon, albeit a sunless one. It is time to call Auntie Manya.

"What are you going to do there, in Beta's flat?" Her question is quite reasonable.

"Talk. Maybe I'll find out what happened to the money."

Auntie Manya is a practical woman, much more concerned with money matters than matters of friendship and betrayal. I meet her at the metro, and the key is mine.

I call Gamma.

"I've got the key. Today?"

"No, I'm not ready yet. Tomorrow morning. At ten."

I agree and hang up. What's he not ready for? I thought he was always ready for anything, ready for any eventuality. And he always comes out unscathed.

21.

How should I talk to him? I don't like conversations like this, and he's not my favourite person to talk to of late. Actually, it's not a recent thing. It happened much earlier, a long time ago, when his reason parted company with his heart.

Not counting Beta, there was never really anyone I could talk to, not like I talk to myself, without pretence. For me, a person's character is a mosaic. I see people as cracked amphorae, and they all are shattered into smithereens, some of which can be very beautiful: it's pleasant to talk of books with one; to keep silent about music with another; to play a game of chess with a third, and with a fourth, to head off to the ends of the earth. Sometimes I find myself waiting for someone to arrive, someone who has all the qualities I appreciate. But no, that never happens. Yet still I hope, and one day I will see that someone. People have a name for this being who embodies the conglomerate best: God... Or maybe Buddha, after all?

## 22.

A quiet, sunny morning. Moscow is floating on poplar fluff. I sit in the playground in front of Beta's block of flats and try not to look at the window, at *that* window. The swings are broken, no seats, and I try to figure out whether you can still swing on them. You probably can, if you grab hold of the metal chains…

Gamma comes up silently, touches me on the shoulder.

"Let's go?"

We take the lift to the tenth floor. I'm struck by the familiarity of the door.

There's no dust; Auntie Manya must have come to clean not long ago. The sun has streaked the walls, the cupboard, the piano, and lit up the face of the wall clock which, no doubt, stopped long ago. It's unbearably stuffy, and Gamma opens the window.

We sit ourselves down at the table. Beta always used to cover it with a white, embroidered tablecloth, but now there is no tablecloth, and the bluish mark of an iron shines right in the middle of the round, brown varnished table top.

Gamma puts a bottle of Borjomi mineral water down next to it; it's almost the same colour. He opens the bottle with the edge of his key, and I fetch two glasses from the kitchen.

"So, now we can talk," Gamma begins. "Actually, I think I know what you want to say. You think I took the money."

I don't reply, but I suppose the look on my face speaks volumes.

"Prepare yourself for a surprise," Gamma goes on. "You want to know where the money is? It's here. In the flat."

"We didn't find anything," I protest.

"You didn't know where to look."

And so saying he goes up to the piano, opens the little door at the bottom, above the pedals, rummages right into the heart of the instrument, and brings out a plump brown envelope.

     

"Here it is," says Gamma, putting the envelope right in the centre of the table, next to the bottle of water, so it is between us. And then he calmly begins to brush the cobwebs off his sleeve.

"How did it get there?" I ask, somewhat bewildered.

"I put it there, of course. I didn't want to take any risks – what if some stupid policeman took it in to his head to search me?"

"So you wanted to take the money?"

"It's for me. Why do you think Beta sold her violin?"

"The money's for *you*?"

"That's right. I want to buy a car, I don't have enough."

"And Beta came to the rescue?"

"Well, not exactly. I told her my mother's ill and I need money for an operation."

"You tricked her!"

"That's right," he agreed readily.

I don't say anything. Seems I'm drumming my fingers on the table.

"Why are you telling me all this?"

"You wanted to know about the money."

"You're not pulling my leg?" A doubt crosses my mind, and I take the envelope from the table.

It's not sealed, and I can see it really is full of banknotes. Lots of them.

"No, I'm not pulling your leg," Gamma says with a smile. "She really did die because of this money."

23.

I really can't understand what he's saying for a second. Then the realisation slowly dawns on me, not yet a fully-fledged imprint on my consciousness, like the mark seared into the table by the scorching iron.

"How did she die?" I ask at last.

The envelope burns my fingers; I throw it onto the table.

"What difference does it make? Let's say, she was sitting on the window ledge and lost her balance. I'll give you two possibilities: either she just lost her balance, or I gave her a helping hand."

"You killed her, you bastard!"

I leap up, wanting to smash my glass into that round, smiling, rosy-cheeked face, but Gamma somehow manages to catch my hand.

"Sit down!" he orders, and I do sit down; that last outburst has sapped all my strength. "Are you going to report me?"

I say nothing.

"Yeah, well, there you are. You won't. No matter what I've done."

"Jesus, why are you such a monster?! And why did you do it? You already had the money…"

"A convenient opportunity. She really was sitting on the window ledge, and I thought: what if I didn't have to give the money back…? If she just makes one careless move…"

"No, I am going to report you. Right now. I'll go and do it. Don't think you've robbed me of my last ounce of strength."

"That's not what I think," says Gamma with a disarming smile. "Go ahead, report me. You can do it right now – I'm on duty."

And he pulls a little red book from his pocket, waves it about, and the golden crest paints a little shiny stream before my eyes.

## 24.

I pour myself some mineral water and drink half a glass. This was unexpected, I must admit.

"Don't worry, the water's not poisoned," Gamma makes a little joke.

"Who knows… But tell me, why are you with Them? Your Mum's a linguist, you're from an intelligentsia family…"

This finally gets him riled.

"Yeah, and look where that's got her! She lived her whole life in communal flats, taught school kids for peanuts. I wanted something else. I wanted power, influence… The country is ours now, not yours, and it'll be that way for a long time, if not for ever. Do you think we only have country bumpkins and polytechnic dropouts? No, there's call for brains everywhere, especially here… Why do you think I joined the orchestra?"

"I've no idea now."

"Just think about it. It's the House of Scholars' orchestra, isn't it? So what do you think, aren't we interested in what scholars are talking about?"

"Ah, so that's it…! And no-one in the orchestra figured it out…"

          

"Beta did. She asked me outright that day when she gave me this money."

So that's why she died, I realised. Beta would have told everyone, and then…

"Why are you telling me all this? You think I'll keep mum?"

"I hope so. Me and those two down there will make sure of that."

I walk over to the window. The playground has acquired two men. One is reading a paper, the other is inspecting the broken swings. They both give me a friendly stare when I appear at the window.

And suddenly Gamma attacks me from behind.

25.

I can't say I wasn't expecting it. When he'd announced yesterday that he wasn't ready to meet me yet I sensed something was going on. Of course, there are the witnesses, ready to confirm that I threw myself out of the window. Gamma wouldn't even have to declare his presence; when I'm lying there on the ground, he'll just leave, as if he had never been here. They'd wipe the place down for finger prints later…

All these thoughts whirled in my head as we fought, grappling each other by the open window. It wasn't that I particularly wanted to live, but to die at the hands of this scoundrel? No, I certainly didn't want that. I struggle instinctively. Or rather, my body struggles. When he grabs me from behind, I wriggle out automatically; automatically, I grab him by the shoulders.

But he is stronger than me. He's pushing, pushing me towards the window ledge and now I'm already squashed up against it, my head is outside, I can see the ramparts on the roof and the sun is blinding me. Gamma is sitting on the window ledge, too, tugging me, trying to lift my feet off the floor. Just a bit more and…

And the phone rings. Gamma seems to slacken his grip. It's obviously a reflex: listen. Yes, he really is slackening his grip and even loses his balance for a second, grabbing at thin air… now he grabs at the window frame, and now he's going to do it, he's going to throw me out of the window. And I push his shoulder—ever so slightly—away from the frame. He tries with all his might to reach it, misses, and then his grey trouser leg shoots past my eyes, and his ill-suited brown shoes. With a wild yelp he plummets downwards.

## 26.

A loud thud, and the yelping stops. Meanwhile, I manage to turn myself around on the window ledge. I'm no longer looking at the roof but at the ground below. Gamma is lying on the tarmac, spread-eagled, as though he is trying to embrace the whole globe. He's not moving. Neither are those two, they are in shock. They don't understand what's just happened. There is no-one else about. The telephone is still ringing. Ringing and ringing...

And then, as if jumping to command, everybody begins to move. The two operatives run to the body, I close the window and rush out of the flat. Without thinking, I grab the envelope of money on my way out. I slam the door and take a few steps down the stairwell but then stop short: the operatives are out there, I can't go down. Where can I go?

I run up the stairs to the next floor, then the next. Should I ring on someone's doorbell? No, they're sure to check the flats one by one and find me. So I keep going up. Now I'm on the top floor, just below the attic, and there's the door fortified by tin panels leading into the attic.

Surely it's not locked? I give it a push, then another. It gives way and swings open with a squeak. The attic is vast. It's empty and smells damp. There are small narrow windows on the far wall, light is coming in through them, they're like arrow slits. I close the door behind me. But they'll find me here, too! If only I could barricade the door from inside! I examine the door. It opens inwards. I notice a broken catch without a bolt. It would be broken, of course, who needs to lock themselves in the attic...? Me! I need to! But how?

I look around. Broken bricks, dust, sand. Ah, there's a nail. Crooked, but... If I could only find a thicker one... And here it is, a thicker one, and it's nice and straight, too, no need to straighten it. I put it in the catch in place of a bolt and try to open the door. It holds! They can kick it in, of course, but they won't break it down immediately! Seems I've gained myself a breather.


## 27.

I sit down on a broken crate by the wall and try to stop my hands from trembling. A thought comes: I've just thrown someone out of a window. But for some reason my conscience doesn't nag me. Turns out I have avenged Beta. Surely that primeval law 'an eye for an eye' isn't sitting somewhere deep inside me?

I wonder who phoned? Probably Auntie Manya. Or someone dialled a wrong number. Whoever it was, they saved my life. Though probably not for long. If those two find me up here, they won't be taking me down to the police station, they'll kill me.

I go back to the door to check my makeshift lock once more, but I can hear voices on the stairs. Very close.

"He's not here. Maybe he's in the attic?"

And someone gives the door a shove. In the nick of time, I throw my whole weight against it from the other side, and it holds.

"Hmm, doesn't open. What do you reckon, it's locked?"

"Let's try together."

This time the shove is stronger. The wood cracks; one more blow and it will give way. But they give up trying to open it.

"Call the caretaker and get him to bring the key," I hear. "Meantime I'll knock on the flat doors."

Seems as though the immediate danger is over. I creep away from the door and decide to examine the attic. It's a big block of flats with many entrances; maybe I can get to another stairwell from here?

I head right. Yes, there are two doors, but they are both locked. I come back and set off in the other direction. As far as I can remember, there are eight entrances in this block of flats, so that means I have another five doors to try. Three of them turn out to be locked, but the fourth isn't there at all! The doorway is blocked with plywood. I smash a hole through – and I'm already on the stairs. I call the lift, but then decide it's probably still dangerous, so I run down the stairs, gradually slackening my pace. I pause on the third floor – somebody's smoking on the second-floor landing. I look at my clothes – not too dishevelled? Seems OK, I've lost the top button on my shirt – it probably flew off while Gamma and I were fighting. But it's a hot day, maybe I just didn't fasten it? I knock the sawdust off my trousers, put on a business-like face and go down. A skinny teenager in a blue Dynamo Moscow replica shirt is smoking a cigarette on the landing. He takes no notice of me whatsoever. Evidently I'm far enough away from the scene of the crime: the commotion hasn't spread this far yet.

I go out onto the street. The sun is blinding after the semi-darkness of the attic. At first I'm not sure which way to go. Onlookers have already gathered by Beta's entrance, a police car is pulling up. I turn in the other direction, taking a roundabout route to the bus stop. I wait, then finally decide to walk, but just then the bus arrives.

I make it to the metro. The clock says twelve thirty. But to me, my time in the attic seemed an eternity! I take the metro home, thinking: I only have 15 minutes to pack.

At home I change my shirt, throw on a jacket, thrust some money in my pocket—the royalties from a book, received just recently—toss the bare necessities into a suitcase, and then bethink myself and pop the score of *The Flying Dutchman* on top.

## 28.

I have to get out of town, quick. Everyone who needs to know already knows who threw operative Gamayunov out of the window. And they also know where to look for that person. I'm on the clock.

I lock the door behind me. Farewell, musicologist Konstantin Borisovich Alpheyev!

I have one more task to do on the way. I call in at Auntie Manya's. She lives in an old block of flats, and the letterboxes are fixed to the doors in the old-fashioned way. I toss the envelope of money in—I had already put Beta's key inside—and ring the doorbell. But I don't wait—no time—I just run back down the stairs. From down below, I hear the door opening. I hope Auntie Manya won't take offence, that she'll understand. She always did understand me. I hope she and Beta's grandmother will have the sense to look in the letterbox…

Yes, they did. Out on the street, I look up and see Auntie Manya at the window, envelope in hand, waving it in a farewell gesture. Soon, today, she will find out what happened. They'll call her when the police want to examine Beta's flat, there's no way around it.

I'm in the metro again. Half past one. I decide to get on a local electric train, not at the main station but on the outskirts of town. I buy a ticket to the very farthest station. It's more than a two-hour ride. But it won't be too late by the time I arrive, I'll still have time to travel further out into sticks and find shelter. I walk up to the ticket office, being careful to keep my face out of sight.

There's the electric train. Half empty. Five minutes, and I'm already beyond the city's limits, beyond Moscow's boundary. Quite interesting, if you think about it: where will my survival instinct take me?

29.

There's hardly anyone in the carriage. I talk to myself as I ride. In silence.

"You're running away, aren't you?" I say to myself. And go on: "Running away is pretty unbecoming. Who are you running from?"

"From bad people."

"There are plenty of bad people."

"From the worst people."

"But are they so frightening, those bad people?"

"They're scary, if they are in power."

"Authority is always in the hands of bad people. So should everyone run away?"

"Those in authority aren't always bad people. And even if you're right, bad people are not always given the freedom to commit evil."

"How can you run away from the authorities? They're everywhere."

"I'm running into myself. I'm running away into nowhere."

"Then you'll have to become no-one."

"I already am No-one."

And I bid farewell to my previous name. Beta and Gamma no longer exist. Alpha will no longer exist, either.

A and B sat on the wall.
A, then B, had a great fall.
So who is left upon the wall
If A'n'B aren't there at all?

When the young rosy-cheeked hooligan Ga-Ga heard this children's riddle he guffawed coarsely, and then treated it to one of his puns and giving his own reply: K-G-B.

30.

A shabby-looking threadbare salesman had spread himself out on the seat next to me. He has a see-through plastic bag bulging with matrioshka dolls wrapped in cellophane and he's nursing it on his lap, protectively. The carriage lurches over the sleeper junction and the matriohskas knock against each other with an eerie wooden sound.

Matrioshka – now there's an interesting symbol: tomorrow lives in its belly. But inside that tomorrow there is not a real personage but just another matrioshka. And in that new doll—the dream of long, boring days—there is less substance but more meaning. Sometimes the clothes vary, sometimes the age varies, sometimes even the gender varies. As the days pass, the meaning thickens, condensing into the small genderless doll, a small, wooden saint, which cannot be opened, and which no longer needs anything except prenatal peace, for she is the end product of all activities. The doll cut from a single piece of wood looks at its master with empty, badly-painted eyes. Maybe she wants to say that she doubts a different time will come? The severed halves of the matrioshkas of yesterday lie scattered around. They can be re-assembled and given to someone else, someone who has not yet reached that great final truth and has not yet experienced the wooden terror of despair.

They say that people have matrioshka-brains. But the state is a matrioshka, too, that inner doll which thinks: I am the state. And the doll is right, you see, each state is only as good—or as bad—as the person who represents it. Because it is the state which decides what that person is permitted and what he or she is not permitted …

At the next station, someone gets on and takes a seat opposite me. A man of my age, black-haired, looks the Jewish-intellectual type. I can't put my finger on it, but I feel I know him. Could we be acquainted? Surely not? Or am I just imagining it? I glance at him from time to time.

Finally, he says with a smile:

"No, we don't know each other."

"Maybe we met somewhere?" I venture.

"I doubt it," he replies.

"I don't understand… we have something in common," I say, thinking aloud. "Don't you agree, we have something in common?"

"Yes, we do," he says. "We're both wearing a yellow shirt."

# PART 3

## Adagio

### 1

A ship breathes with its sails. There is a ship with a dark red sail, parchment embossed with writings nailed to its mast. Writings chronicling a good life…

But the good life had long since gone South – or more precisely, West, according to the map. It had seeped through the dotted line, off to the West, over the state border. And what's left? Square metres, transparent litres, the pennies of a cash advance and non-essential dates – dates of non-being. Ships and toy ships sail the streets, sail into stagnant harbours, kiss the silt or knock their sides against that same dotted line through which you can seep, but not sail.

So many sails. On every balcony. Yellow, white with blue-eyed spots, pink for a wedding… They aren't all for sailing, although you can certainly sail with the red and burgundy ones, and your ship will be fearsome, more fearsome than a stranger's tragedy, for wherever you go, their tragedy will be plashing beside you.

### 2.

Another day came in on the sails, and once again he had to find himself something to do; he had built a self-disciplined life, and it was holding course, moving ahead, so now it simply sailed up and gazed reproachfully at him with its anchor eyes.

N. sat himself down to write. He fancied writing a fairy-tale, for the child inside him. A notebook turned up on the shelf. It had absorbed the yellow of the evening sun slung low under the ceiling, 40 watts strong. Turning to a clean page, he wrote the words: "The Kingdom of Starry Eyes." And he was immediately transported there.

*In the Kingdom of Starry Eyes, the Wind counted flowers every evening. If they were few, the Wind grew angry and snatched the hats of the passers-by one by one. So the passers-by grew angry, too, though they couldn't devote themselves long to their burgeoning rage – they had to catch their hats, you see!*

*The Transparent Princess was the Wind's only friend. No, it wasn't her clothes that were see-through, it was her thoughts. Take one look at her, and you can see what is on her mind. They called the princess Blanka, which means luminous, just as her future should be.*

*The King, her father, dwelt in the palace, under the cupola which was also home to a huge telescope. The King would observe the life of the celestial bodies, and he counted himself among them, one of their kind, no worse than the rest. So he did not concern himself with the lives of those around him. Deep in his heart, the King never doubted he was a true scientist, all the more so since his subjects readily confirmed this.*

*The King sewed stars on his garments, donned a tall pointed hat and came to be known as the Astronomer King. His subjects conjectured he was more likely of the heavenly realms than of the earthly ones. This flattered him – who wouldn't like to be thought of as a heavenly body while still alive?! Sojourning somewhere in the heavens, as a young man he had nearly let slip the royal throne, only just managing to take it in time. It is known on good account that the King had descended to earth on at least one prior occasion – when he married a foreign princess visiting his realm.*

*An incompatibility between the couple soon came to light, however: the queen was not in the least interested in astronomy, she collected sounds and smells. Once a year, on the most important holiday, her collection of scents was opened to public sniffing. The most popular smell was The Scent of a Good Dinner, the second-last in her collection. Visitors were offered The Scent of a Trouble-Free Retirement as a snack, and the effect was so dramatic that they tottered from the palace on unsteady legs.*

*The very best phonogram of the collection wafted over the town on those festive days. It was called: "Exclamations of Youth in Abundance." Unaccustomed to any sort of exclamations, the townsfolk were delighted by such an energetic expression of feeling. Two things were forbidden during these Compulsory Celebrations: working, and not smiling. If someone was caught committing one or other of these felonies, they were awarded the honorific title 'Knight of Labour' and were sent to the stone quarries to justify this epithet.*

*One day, right at the height of festive smiles, the travelling violinist Pimpinello arrived at the palace. Never and to no-one did he deny he was the world's best musician, and that is probably why so many agreed with him. He played for the Queen—of course!—and sniffed her scents – of course! On that occasion, she uncorked The Scent of Local Culture.*

*The violinist was brought before the Astronomer King, too. Pimpinello glanced into the telescope, but since his eyesight differed from that of the King, he saw nothing but a cloud of fog. The virtuoso did not confess to his deviant vision, however, nor did he ask for the apparatus to be corrected. Instead, he advised the King to point his telescope higher and study the farthest worlds – might he not find something useful for his people out there?*

*And from that moment on the virtuoso could rest assured he would always find favour in the palace: the King loved his 'people' and considered himself their benefactor. Pimpinellos's advice to observe far off worlds found its mark – the King detested advisors who sought to convince him to aim his telescope downwards and examine the lives of his subjects. In such cases, the Astronomer King would reply that it was not for him, the King, to know the lives of his subjects, and anyway, the telescope was most particular and could not be trained downwards.*

*That day the Wind was trying to circumvent the palace. Although the King had nothing against the Wind – after all, the Wind could shake neither the telescope nor the stars he saw through it, the Queen took a different approach. The least draft could destroy her carefully constructed mosaic of smells and sounds; thus the Wind had been declared the palace's worst enemy. Only the Transparent Princess would leave her window open a crack – and the Wind would bring her the silence of the woods and the rivers' silvery glint.*

*The Wind was not Princess Blanka's only friend; she also befriended the flowers, and her heart overflowed with music. Not the music of Pimpinello the Virtuoso, but the music of kind eyes. The Princess longed to look into the eyes of the people, all at once.*

*And so while Pimpinelllo the Virtuoso soothed the palace-dwellers with the most sophisticated passages of his compositions, followed by his rather stuffy humour, the Princess did something which was categorically forbidden: she went to her father's observatory and, turning the heavy screws with difficulty, managed to train the telescope downwards…*

*At first she couldn't see anything at all. Then she realised that the dark spot in front of her was soil, and for an instant she observed its tiny antlike life. Adjusting the screws slightly, she could see the people. They were walking along the city streets, their faces lit by smiles – not forced, festive smiles, but real smiles. And their eyes… Blanka let out an involuntary cry, for she suddenly realised why their country had such a strange name: the people had shining, starry eyes!*

*Courtiers rushed over at her cry, the telescope was hastily trained upwards once again. The offending Princess was taken to her father.*

*"What did you see through the telescope?" the Astronomer King asked, curious.*

*"I saw the future," replied the Transparent Princess.*

*"And was I in that future?" the King grew alarmed.*

*The courtiers, too, wanted to shout out: "And me? And me?" but they wisely held their tongues.*

*The Transparent Princess could not hide the truth, nor did she try.*

*"I saw all the eyes of all the future townsfolk," she said. "I did not see your eyes."*

*"Then you shall await your future under lock and key!" declared the King angrily, and ordered the Princess to be imprisoned in the farthest tower…*

And from that far-off tower, or from elsewhere, well-earned writer's sleep overcame N.

3.

Yesterday's words are always boring. Having reread what he had written, N. decided not to continue. But then he told himself: it's not good to give up half way through… And as a result of all these musings, the following lines appeared in the notebook:

*Many years later, I found myself once again in the Kingdom of Starry Eyes. What had become of the Princess? Had her friend the Wind come to visit her in her captivity? Had her father's rage lasted long? I did not know. They say that not long ago an actor began to grow a cape which covered the whole of the country's capital, but it snagged on a TV tower and ripped. After that it was turned into pyjamas. That's one cut – pyjamas with pockets full of memories. Just the job for cases like this.*

*Now there are neither Kings nor subjects here, there are only beautiful men and women with starry eyes and bright countenances. I enquired as to which of the women was the former princess but the townsfolk merely smiled and changed the subject. To flowers, for instance: there are so many of them here now, and the Wind never gets angry or snatches the hats of the passers-by.*

4.

On the following day, the words are boring and things are grubby. There's nothing you can do about it, even if you make new things. Their grubbiness is predetermined, like the boredom of words.

The washing machine in a village home is a bucket, some foul-smelling household soap and raw, red human hands. It's a machine with three components. It makes dirty clothes less dirty but more crumpled. And that's OK. But there is no machine which can return words, boring from day one, back to their primeval state. There is neither bucket nor household soap for words, only hands – to cover your mouth before it's too late.

The whole of the terrace facing the police station with its spyglass was now festooned with sails of shirts and sheets. The wind gave them a thorough shaking, till the window panes rattled.

Neutralised by many sails, the spyglass turned away, disappointed.

N. went out into the garden and took a sidelong look at the house. It replied with a proud flutter of its sails. Atop the mast piercing the porch swayed an orange cape. Who knows how it had got there, or who had washed it. It was spick and span, like a flag.

5.

The garden kept him for itself awhile, penetrating his every pore. N. stood under a tree and absorbed the universe. It was hard to leave, even though there was no need to go anywhere.

And then it rained within the rain. Rain-dust seeped surreptitiously from the whitish sun-lined haze… And suddenly a hard, slanting rain pierced that dust, falling from gloomy, low slung clouds.

He had to go back inside. N. glanced at himself in the porch mirror and saw a strange, broad-brimmed hat perched on his head. When had he donned it, and where had he got it from? Well, the peculiar objects in this house had long since ceased to surprise him.

N. took off the hat, brushed the rain drops from it and hung it on an antler branching from the wall.

"Antlers may look like branches, but they rarely blossom," another of his quirky thoughts arrived from their breading ground. "Although the horns of Cernunos, the deer-god, are the tree of nature, so they sprout buds, and green leaves in summer."

Closing his eyes, he saw the god Cernunos patrolling his domain. The god tossed his young head, he was well aware of his own importance; in that, he was almost human. And like a human, Cernunos loved to observe the path he had trod. His horns sat firmly on his head, the leaves fluttered green, little goats licked them tenderly. Summer had not yet drowned in autumn, and as yet no-one concerned themselves with the twilight of the gods, when the leaves fall, antlers snap and divinity trickles away over the ground with the rainwater, stripping you down to the body nature gave you. Or is it the nakedness of moral greatness?

But as yet Cernunos was unshakeable in his magnificence. As yet he was a god, touring his domain – the realm of reason. His subjects followed him closely: lion, wolf and snake, submissive spectators for now. Waiting for their day to come.

6.

Take the person out of the picture and you get a landscape. Take the landscape away, and you are left with bare canvas, and then you can draw whatever you like with the bushy brushes of your imagination.

That evening N. opened his notebook. It was yellowing reproachfully. He began to fill its pages, thirsting for ink, with a tractate on the idler's role in history. The idler is a joker, he wrote, a joker who can take the place of any card. At first glance, the joker seems a good guy, neat, with a cheery grin. But he is not a card, he is an empty space, and cannot do a damn thing. When you need to go somewhere, or do a card trick, or gather the harvest, the joker lies down like a stone which doesn't roll, and that stone presses everything to the ground with its weight – the sprouting grass, anything which can think, as well as the various non-thinking, insect-like beings. Jokers—i.e. stones—like to finish monarchies, and in that case, the jokers have loud nicknames and numbers: Louis XVI, Nikolas II. Empires sometimes end with jokers, too, but they are smaller fish. Like Marshall Grouchy... But what if another joker emerges after that one, and then lies down, gazing heavenwards with naive eyes? After Nikolas II, a certain Monsieur Kerensky, with a knave's moustache or a king's royal beard. Two jokers, that makes for a minor game, a game of small fry cards.

And so we gaze heavenwards, gentlemen, and convince ourselves that the blue we see is the sky and not the back of some card, heavy as stone and decorated with self-awarded gold medals.

7.

The blue waters of sleep called him unto them. He jumped in. And landed with a thud. The sea, it turned out, was merely drawn on canvas.

The dream ended, and the dream within a dream began. Somewhere in the far reaches of his boundlessness, N. was sitting reading a certain *Book of Meros*. And he was marvelling at the fact that not only had he read it before, but had even absorbed it, all without his slightest participation. It was that kind of book.

What do we know about the mysterious *Book of Meros*? A papyrus scroll, found in due course in the Desert of the Unthinkable, a book which rendered the occupation of chronicler superfluous. Down the endless coils riders gallop, chariots whirl, swords clink, cities crumble. The scroll consumes everything which has happened since the dawn of creation up to the movable "now." The *Book of Meros* grows ever longer, the memory of generations ever shorter. The manuscript will soon catch up with time, overtake it, most likely, and people shall read in the morning what they are destined to do during the day. What they will do once they know this remains to be seen!

His dream caught up with the flow of time, too, and, bang on midnight, the sheen of the orange cape loomed large. Or maybe it was the gingery ray of tomorrow – or rather, today. The ray of a sun dreamt up in darkness… Actually, it was neither a reflection nor a ray, but a ginger fox. After stretching himself out comfortably on N's seat in the corner of the room, carefully curling his tail on the floor, the fox gave a salutatory bark.

N looked at him carefully, but kept mum. Instead it was the ginger fox who spoke:

"Hello!"

N. stared at him, amazed, and said:

"But… don't you speak Russian?"

"Oi do," drawled the fox in a thick foreign accent. "Oi spik Russian with an English accent, and Oi spik English with a Russian one."

"A bit like some of our émigrés," said N., smiling.

"Everyone emigrates somewhere," the fox barked with fresh enthusiasm and with no trace of an accent. "Some emigrate to their own stomach, some lower still. Others emigrate to a purely mental life, without any body below."

"Ah, that's exactly where I'm headed," N's reply was unpretentious.

"I knew it!" yelped the fox gleefully. "I have a nose for such things. And I also know that we all bunker down wherever we are. Take yourself, for instance, wouldn't you like to move yourself elsewhere?"

"Well, it's not so bad here," N. said pensively. "But it may be better somewhere else, of course."

"Of course, of course. And I know just where."

"Not in the grave, I hope."

"We all find peace and comfort in the grave," intoned the fox. "But that is not where I meant. I mean that it all depends on you. Why do you need to rush along, headlong? Repent, make peace with evil – and then, maybe, you'll also get a piece of life."

"Even if I wanted to make peace, I've done something they won't forgive me for."

"Go slowly, be gentle. Just find someone you can talk to, then, maybe, everything will be forgiven. Just look at your recent acquaintance, much has also been forgiven him. He might even be able to suggest the best one to talk to."

This reference to Poro made N. wince – he felt an actual physical aversion, even in his sleep. Almost waking, he thought it would surely jerk him out of bed, but instead he merely rolled over. And began dreaming that he was an aeroplane, flying under the wind's mocking whistle: "Ginger fokssisssss, compromissessss…"

But it got easier. How easy it is to fly, he thought gleefully, how marvellous it is to bore through the clouds by yourself and come out into the wondrous blue of sunny palaces! Yet so many people mistake the clouds for the sky, having seen nothing else!

But his flight turned out to be short-lived. He hit the ground, and woke in a cold sweat. A voice was by his side. A beloved voice.

And a conversation got going:

"Why aren't you asleep?"

"I am asleep,"

"No, you're not, you're talking to me."

"I'm only listening."

"Do you understand everything?"

"Yes."

"You have no complaints?"

"None."

"We'll see each other soon,"

"Where?"

"Look."

And a tiny green phosphorescent ship sailed into his line of sight. It was the size of a sheet from his notebook. Wherever he turned his gaze, the little ship was there bobbing before his eyes. He tried to pick it up, but the glowing green wonder slipped through his fingers, and a starry green light was left on his palm.

8.

N. woke early, meeting the dawn on the garden bench. The mast was directing the orange ball towards its destination.

"A hapless man's morning," N. said to himself. "The fortunate ones are all asleep at this hour. But how easy it is to plunge into misfortune here in my homeland… 'The Kingdom of Wintery Blizzards' tosses people out; rubbish bins are put out for them. And, worst of all, these bins are full of 'life that goes on everywhere.'*

_______________

* The title of a famous painting by the Ukrainian artist Nikolai Yaroshenko (1846-1898).

N. took out his notebook. The Flying Dutchman sailed over the lines of both score and notebook. "Work saves," he said to himself after a short pause. "But who will save the fruit of our labours? Take this, for instance, for whom is it all written? I'll be put on the black list now and no one will publish my work…"

Chasing these thoughts from his mind, he continued writing. Turning over the next page of the score, he found a page of notes. A message from the past, to himself:

*This is where I lived. And here, too. And in that house there. I glance up as I walk by the windows of my former home. But I'm not there!*

*So where am I? I am somewhere I do not want to be. Because it's teeming, because it's noisy, because a private tête-à-tête with myself is too crowded.*

*And, pencillessly, I draw the house where I would like to live, the garden around it, the spring with a lion's head, the grotto laid out with stones, and the mozartesque andante dissolving into the blue yonder…*

*And I am there, too. There's the house, I'm heading towards it. People on the street pass me by, their gaze upturned for some reason: slow, lyrical people are hovering in the air.*

*Why are they hovering so? you ask. Because how can one live in this land without writing about flying people?*

9.

"Yes, there is flight, and there are the windows where flight begins," N. continued his conversation with himself. "A special kind of window."

N. had discovered such windows as a young boy, when a 16-year-old fell from a window on his stairwell. He had sat on the balcony as a dare, dangling his legs high above the street – first one leg, then the second. Maybe he was pushed, maybe he was drunk… It was a fourth floor window, and they took him to hospital to heal his fractures. And it wasn't long before a lift appeared outside the block of flats to hide the stairwell window, but N. now knew that such a window existed: a window where flight begins.

He had often dreamt of flying from his bedroom window – looking up from the street he had worked out it was the nearest to *that* window. But whether or not it was a window where flight began remained to be seen, although he later noticed other such windows, too. An old lady threw herself from one; her landing was immortalised on a grave slab of ideal proportions. And a musician fell from another, after a concert; he took it into his head he could fly.

"Well, maybe now he is indeed flying somewhere amidst the stars and the sounds of his own perpetual melody?" N. pondered. "We launch into flight, the book remains unread, the dishes unwashed, and life unlived. Well, no matter which window I look through, it is always a window from a life unlived into non-life. But it wasn't I who launched myself into the flight which lasts but a second, a second more lasting than eternity. And where's the sense in thinking about landing? Maybe non-existence is waiting down there, or maybe otherly existence, but either way: oblivion. And that is where I'm flying. Folk with spyglasses glue themselves to my window, even if I am nowhere to be seen. They also know my window is a window where flight begins."

## 10.

The orange cape has vanished from the wardrobe. Did it walk off? Did something else come to take its place? Wouldn't it be funny to discover a wardrobe within the wardrobe…

Instead, N. found an old crucifix in the bottom drawer. He picked it up. The cross was made of mahogany, bronze casting…

"The cross doesn't care who is crucified on it," N. said to himself. "It doesn't ask whether the crucified or the crucifiers are Christian. But it hurts when the nails are driven in and pulled out. It's soaked in blood. It's fed up with the setting sun, it wants to be free. It doesn't even want to be a cross. Going back to its historical roots, it falls apart into two wooden beams which then rest on the building site of time. They are waiting for their glorious and inglorious past to blaze like the bonfire spawning the warm dawn of new misconceptions.

N. was about to move the drawer when he realised there was something else inside. Delving deeper, he pulled out something large and round. A head. The carved head of a woman. Time had darkened the wood but the austere, almost masculine beauty remained. So when female beauty borders on male beauty, is it degeneration or not? Things are clearer the other way round: male femininity is rarely met with sympathy. He remembered Gamma's joke from the old days: it's when, in days gone by, a nobleman had four sons, one was a gambler, one was a drunkard, and the other two were girls. "But can we say deviation from the gender standard is degeneration? The carved head is so beautiful…"

There was a crack under its chin. N. thrust his hand inside and felt some paper. It was old and crumbly. Unfolding it, he saw it was a page from an ancient book, the portrait of a knight with a caption in Spanish. N. had once studied Spanish, he had taught himself – back in days long gone when he had written a monograph about Manuel de Falla. Now the forgotten words began to return and the pieces of the half-guessed phrases gradually revealed their meaning.

*Don Miguel was a great warrior, bravely fighting the clock hands. He would ascend the clock tower, grab the long hand and hope time would thereby slacken its pace. It took them a while, but they talked him out of it, and he froze in the '6 o'clock' position: feet together, arms by his sides.*

*"This person managed to halt time," was inscribed on his tombstone cross, the crossbeams of which were suspiciously akin to clock hands.*

## 11.

The hunter runs toward the beast, the shop assistant to the non-customer, and the customer to the non-shop assistant. N. had not managed to tidy the head away, back into the wardrobe, when someone gave a hurried knock at the door and proceeded to walk in without waiting for a reply. Poro. Long time since he'd shown up!

Catching sight of the head on the table, the guest was stunned; it took him a while to regain his senses. But when he did, he grabbed the head and began looking at it from all sides, dousing it with emotions, like varnish. He clearly hoped never to part with it again.

"It's not mine," N. declared curtly.

"Whose then?" Poro's eyes lit up with a child's greedy passion at the possibility of buying it: it would be a most prestigious purchase, and prestige resounds loud and clear with children and collectioneers alike.

"The landlord's, probably."

"I'll have a word with him when he returns. Such a beauty!"

"He's so attuned to beauty," N. said to himself, shaking his head. "So why is he a gerontologist, studying old folk? To bring harmony to the feeble? Or is he just like the rest of us, busy doing something he doesn't like because he has to? He probably has some safety valve he's corked – but what with? Himself...?"

And the safety valve revealed itself. Poro invited him to a musical soiree. That, apparently, is why he had come.

"The well-known bard Bagriuzha is coming," his guest informed him. "He's giving a concert in the forest, not far from where the book sellers meet, just a bit further."

"And what does he do, this bard Bagriuzha?" N. asked curiously.

"He sings and plays the guitar. Using poems from good poets – Akhmatova, Mandelstam."

"Does he write his own music?"

"No, his friend does, he's an amateur composer."

"Hold on a minute. The lyrics aren't his, the music's not his… so what's he got to do with it? Is he a professional singer or guitarist?"

"No, no, he's a man with a complicated fate. Been behind bars and so on. He's a plumber, actually. But he has good taste in poetry."

"Well, probably quite different from my taste."

"You mean you're not going!?"

"No, I'm not." N. declined firmly.

"Your loss. There'll be a very intellectual audience."

"Seems our pseudo English gentleman has fallen prey to 60's spleen, though he's no protester," N. smiled when his guest had left, pouting childishly. "Ah, our poor old generation! A generation which didn't create a positive aesthetic and can only struggle. But not with itself. Why? Because if you struggle with yourself, you might win, and it will be your gain. Otherwise your negativity might win, and then…"

12.

Poro's appearance reminded him of their bike ride and, maybe, that is why Beta came to him again in his dream, saying:

"Let's take a bike ride, right through the whole city!"

He replied with a smile:

"Let's go!"

They spent all day putting the bikes together – they were folding bikes, and the tyres were missing. The cupboard was full of tyres and inner tubes of all sizes, but the latter were all punctured. It was midnight before the bikes were finally ready. They strapped rucksacks on the back and set off.

The city he was dreaming of seemed to be Moscow. Maybe it was even called Moscow, too – when they set off, at least. By night, the city was like any other city and like many other things, too. Even like a wolf curled into a ball, sleeping in a cage. From time to time the wolf growled sleepily with the rumble of lorries. People were sitting in them, people with batons and baseball bats, singing nasty songs.

Beta gave him a sign and they turned their bikes onto a more secluded street. Barricades were being thrown up here; sometimes they had to dismount and go through the backyards.

When they rode past the Kremlin, power had already changed hands. The ruby stars had been hurled from the towers and the metal fences were being dismantled for lances. When they rode past Government House, power changed hands again, and the government was being drowned in the river. The wolf was now evidently wide awake.

They rode past the Borodinsky viewpoint. Another lively panorama opened up in the nearby streets: the battle of Krasnaya Presnya, even though Krasnaya Presnya itself was far behind them. Peddling under the Triumphant Arch, they gathered speed and rode non-stop, further, further, further West.

"Moscow is big," he said to Beta as they cycled into Warsaw.

Just then, he woke in a different dream. Beta was with him again, and also – their young daughter, who had never existed. The three of them arrived at the stadium and walked up to the tourniquet.

"Take your souvenirs," the cheerful young people said to them. "Hats. A black one on your ticket, and red ones for the lady and the little girl."

"Can't we get in without any souvenirs?" N. asked, although the little girl was already tugging at his sleeve; she didn't want to part with the hat.

"No," replied the young people with their unmistakably Russian rosy cheeks. "These are compulsory souvenirs."

The three of them took their places in the stalls and watched the gymnasts who were led into wheels, instead of hamsters.

"Hamsters are more interesting," the little girl said.

"And now let us all don our hats as one!" A joyous female voice rang out over the stadium.

                    

They dutifully donned their paper headgear.

A march struck up. Their stalls appeared on the big screen, and they saw a huge sign spelled out by their black and red hats: "*Sieg Heil!*"

## 13.

Nightmares have nightmares of their own. Sometimes elemental, sometimes cultivated, well-matched, comfortable. But terrifying ones, too, of course, frightening us with their humdrum reality. Contradictions collide, but two nightmares do not counter each other out, as you may expect; they merge, becoming a single grey bottomlessness where no-one wants to be, yet where someone finds themselves nevertheless. A nightmare sometimes overflows into reality, tries to drown it. And if the nightmare doesn't succeed, it fences itself off from reality, founding its own gloomy citadel, which it proudly invites you to visit. Dreams – they are windows from nightmares into non-nightmares. Poems are, too.

Closer to dawn he dreamt about the river of dignity flowing *il tempo di adagio*. Observing eddies behind the weir, an aged and dishevelled man announced solemnly: "I think of the water's ordeal, of its screams and moans. And please don't tell me that it gives us light and heat."

N. was woken very early by knocking. It was not loud, but unmistakable. It sounded like a knock on the ceiling. Still sleepy, and subsequently ill-tempered, N. went to discover the root of this evil.

There was no-one in the attic. The knocking was close at hand, somewhere to his left. N. went to look, but that was the outside wall. He peeped out of the little window – no-one outside, either. But there were some new panels among the old cladding. They were not painted, just white squares on a green background…

The knocking jumped over to the other wall. They were doing a good job, efficient. But who were they? No one knows. N. smiled: he remembered a poem in the book by Ivan Elagin, published abroad, in Germany:

"It's being built somewhere, it's being built somewhere,
A house for me, a house for me.
Just around the corner, the corner of light,
Just around the corner, the corner of the day."

A thunderstorm kicked off later, rather reluctantly. Someone ripped through the sky's pillowcase and thunder boomed down. A strong wind got up. N. went to close the windows he could reach and had almost closed them all when he found himself in room he had never been in before.

Furniture was absent. Gloom reigned. A flash of lightning lit up a complex geometrical pattern on the floor. There was a book lying in the centre. N. tried to enter the pattern, but it wouldn't let him. He began circling it, and finally managed to enter – from near the window.

The book turned out to be very heavy, but N. managed to pick it up somehow. And he started: a flaming triangle blazed under it. There was no title on the heavy leather cover.

N. took the same route out of the pattern, then out of the room. "What sort of pattern was that?" he mused. "A circular square? A squared circle?"

14.

In the corridor the book lightened a little. On the sunny terrace, it was completely light. Seating himself at the table, N. opened the book. The title page declared: "Catalogue of Suicides."

*"For he that seeketh non-existence, this tractate shall be their calm companion on their last journey, their guide to the land of eternal rest. It is never too late, nor too early, to depart for that land; quite simply, existence here, on this side of the invisible barrier, must have become unbearable. Knowing this life and the people who inhabit this world, there can be little doubt that it has already become thus to many…"*

There followed a discourse on the pros and cons of poison, nooses, blades, firearms, falling from windows, death under the wheels of a moving carriage, on the battlefield and in the jaws of wild beasts.

There was also a section entitled "Slow Suicide." It included: work, idleness, family life, solitary life, drinking, abstinence, pleasures of the flesh, eschewing the flesh.

And there was a section entitled "The Slowest Suicides." It contained but one word: "Life."

15.

Wherever we go, we take our language with us but it slips between the words and sinks into the silence of the fields. Curious children will pick up a few broken syllables and play with them.

We travelled across the realm of the unborn; we'll ramble on the other side of the unthinkable. Life that can be described on a single page is but a shadow dance in the starlight; story that doesn't have to be told more than once is but the clinking of wind chimes.

Chic plush drapery of the past conceals a corridor of mirrors, with its icy breath and a milky glimmer at the other end.

That day N. busied himself with thoughts about continuance and with excavations in his suitcase. He had barely touched it until now. He came across a brown oilcloth notebook. Actually, it had no right to be in his suitcase, and the handwriting was not his, either…

And suddenly it dawned on him: this was Irina's dairy! She was Beta's best friend who had suddenly died of a heart attack at forty something. Beta had handed him the diary to read, saying:

"I sometimes think music is like the Minotaur."

"You mean, the one from Crete? The one who demands offerings of maidens?"

"If it were only maidens… but yes, them, too. Here's a good example," she nodded at the notebook, now already under his arm. "Here the sacrifice was brought early but accepted late."

"Once the Minotaur had already availed himself of her gifts…"

"Precisely. It's just a shame a talented person couldn't develop her potential. This sacrifice could have been more meaningful… less pointless."

"As if there is some point in sacrifices…" he had said wearily. "Though of course, there are involuntary sacrifices, since you never know when the Minotaur will lunge out from some corner or other…"

"And in whose guise… By the way, you know the hero of this story, it's your friend, you wrote the essay on Wagner's *Lohengrin* together."

"Ah, that's who you're talking about," he said, a bit taken aback. "I can't really picture him as a Minotaur. But who knows... Interesting. I'll read it, definitely."

But he still hadn't read it; he had got the diary just before... well, before... And then he had buried it in a pocket of his suitcase.

Holding it in his hands now, he noticed the oppressive smell of casein glue. "Every single person in this country has their secret oilcloth notebook," N. said to himself. "And later they are all found and published as historical documents. So the next generation will know what we lived through, how we killed ourselves in our attempt to survive. Killing ourselves with life. The slowest form of suicide..."

He began reading. The first entry was dated Summer 1964.

## 16.

It's my entrance exam for Gnessin College, the correspondence course. We're milling around in the corridor waiting for the teacher. The history of music exam is about to begin. The teacher shows up at last. Introduces himself. He's called Sergei Borisovich.

I can barely remember what the exam was about.

"We were very pleased with your answers," I was told.

So that must mean I've been accepted. I blush, I expect. I usually do in such situations. Sergei Borisovich is sitting there, his legs crossed. He's smoking, eyeing me up. When he turns round, I examine him surreptitiously. What is it they say about men like him? 'The interesting type.' But does that mean he is interesting as a person, too? I'll have to wait until he turns sideways so I can see his profile. If you want to know what to expect from someone, think up some excuse and ask him or her to turn sideways. Their profile will tell you far more than their words.

## 17.

Winter. An exam on the music of Handel and Bach. We take our questions, gather our thoughts. S. B. is examining a different group, in the same hall. They play the students music, and they have to identify it by ear. It's Schumann's *Carnaval*. I guess which theme it is straightaway, and before I can stop myself, I whisper aloud: "Chiarina." It echoes round the room: "Rina… Rina…" Since then, S. B. calls me Rina. Strange name…

I look at the piano, and my thoughts carry me into worlds with other harmonies. Unexpectedly lost in thought – farewell, reality! hello, unknown land where dreams come true and people do what they are born to do! The legendary writer Kozma Prutkov was right: what's stopping us from inventing water resistant gunpowder?

I don't remember how the exam went; seems I guessed all the pieces correctly. But what I did remember, for a long time, is the look S. B. gave me. He put his whole self into that look, all his inner substance. But just what was that inner substance?

In Yermolova's class:

"We had a staff meeting yesterday. My, how Sergei Borisovich praised you, how he praised you! 'We've nothing to teach her!' he said."

But someone can always teach us something, and that someone is Life. You are walking resolutely along in the world you know, looking out at it from your clever, educated eyes, when suddenly a certain manual in the guise of a lorry comes roaring round the corner, and just try to get out of its way…

S. B. is playing us Beethoven's *Appassionata* sonata. I'm leaning against the piano. It's my favourite place; vibrations on my back. S. B. is playing *appassionato*. The land of water resistant gunpowder is calling me once again to its dreamt up expanse…

A young woman pops her head around the classroom door. She's quite pretty. S. B. stands up, goes out into the corridor.

Artem whispers:

"Now that's what you call a wife!"

She's pretty, but her face is ill-tempered, with narrow features. Like that little snake, "the lady of the Copper Mountain" from Ural fairytales.

Nadia leans over to me:

"Isn't Sergei Borisovich like a tomcat?!"

I stare at her, dumbfounded.

"Like a tomcat who roams the rooftops at night," she explains.

I don't say anything. I look at S. B. The resemblance is, in fact, striking. He wears pale suede boots, he walks silently in them, like a tomcat. Those boots, by the way, are far from small. A brawny, out-and-out tomcat!

Maybe this cat-like-ness is just a question of his primal pedigree? After all, there is such a thing as ape-like-ness, some kind of incarnation of original sin, *ab ovo…*

Someone nameless fell out of time. Time rolled far away, and disappeared behind the horizon. Someone was floundering in earnest, until they finally felt solid ground under their feet.

With a sigh of relief, that someone seemed about to nestle down on the beach, when a nosey passer-by showed up, out of the blue.

"What came first, the chicken or the egg?" the passer-by tried to egg him on.

"How should I know?" the someone yawned and tucked his head under his wing.

"Well you should know, you're a chick!"

"So?" the chick replied, nodding off; he really was a chick. "I'm not asking you what the monkey you descend from did first – made some descendants or called himself Adam."

18.

I'm sitting by the grand piano facing S. B. The Hungarian Embassy is across the road, it's very pretty. The lesson's not started yet, I'm looking out of the window – and find myself thinking about someone I loved long ago, when I was young. They are sad memories. What is love? Essentially, it is when you love another person the way you imagine them to be; in other words, you love your ideal of that person, i.e. the ideal as you imagine it. Another's imprint on yourself. In other words, you love yourself. No matter how much you toy with the concept of sacrificial love, love remains egotistic. But whatever it is, it is better than the incapacity for love. Even unrequited love is better than nothing, since every block of flats should have a window, even if there is no door and no-one can get in, or out…

Just then I sense S. B.'s gaze on me. Attentive, studying. Is he looking into my inner substance, too?

 

In our next lesson, S. B gets us to listen to excerpts from Wagner's opera *Lohengrin*. He tells us about the romantic duet, about the scene with Elisa and Lohengrin. 'It's vital to trust the one you love,' he says. 'That's why Elisa lost Lohengrin, she didn't take him at his word and began extorting secrets he couldn't share with her.' But first S. B. had asked us all to sit closer to the piano, to facilitate our discussion. Many of us did move closer, but I stayed where I was, until he spoke of trust, at which point I moved over to the piano, too. Who hasn't been caught, like a fish, hanging your soul on the little steel hook of sweet words, the hook which is not yet there at all but which will nevertheless appear and pierce you…

19.

We're studying Ravel now, and S. B plays us some of his music.

And suddenly the simple Pasha bursts out:

"So what if he is Ravel! Just a miserable chauffeur! Call this music?!"

S. B. says nothing, but I feel sorry for him. I happen to know he's a fan of Debussy and Ravel, so quips like that must hurt him.

When a very self-confident visitor enters a fragrant rose garden, sniffs around and announces he only detects a faint smell of melon, well, all one can do is praise the Lord that one's own nose is tuned somewhat differently.

I am sitting very close to S B., throwing him sidelong glances. He's so old! I notice the crowns on his teeth, the plethora of wrinkles on his face. Then I turn my gaze to the wall, so that S. B. will not notice he is being scrutinised. The wall is old, too, coated with olive green oil paint. Cracks and cobweb line drawings are crawling over it. God only knows how old they are. Life has already been played out among these props, my dear, and you have missed it, so now you have to repeat those who have left the stage and their half erased roles.

20.

I dreamt I was talking to my cat Mashka.

"Don't wheedle!" the cat said to me, rubbing against my legs.

"And you? What are you doing?" I smiled.

"I can't help it," she announced. "That's how I rub against the bench, too."

"Then rub against the bench," I said, pulling my leg away in a huff.

"You're softer than the bench," said the cat by way of explanation. "And you might give me some chicken grizzle later, too."

"Take your grizzle then," I sighed and gave her what she was asking for. "I thought love was supposed to be selfless."

"Of course," purred the cat. "But love somehow flows better with grizzle."

I woke up thinking she was right. If only I knew who to save that grizzle for!

The next day I'm on my way back from the music school where I earn a bit of pocket money. It's out of town; I'm taking the metro home from Paveletsky Station. I'm tired, cello in hand. A tall man is standing by the change machine at Kropotkin station. I have the feeling he's waiting for me and no-one else, he stares at me and my cello so fixedly. Then he gives a decisive nod of the head, turns around and follows me. He disappears not far from my block of flats. Reality can dissipate like a mirage, too…

It was as though the man had been asked to spy on me, to check something, and he had done so. He'd spied me out, sniffed me out. When we think we are looking at the world, actually, it is looking at us. The hounds have already slipped the leash, so don't hide behind the mask of your face – run! But the hounds already know where you'll run to…

21.

I'm reading a textbook quietly to myself in my room when suddenly I notice a head in the window of the block opposite. It looks very much like S. B. The man is sitting at an angle, not looking at me. Finally, the head disappears…

I had never paid any attention to who lived there before. It was enough to know that, well, someone lived there, someone hypothetically uninteresting who, thank God, was not at all interested in me. But I was mistaken: there is no-one who goes by the name 'someone' and that hypothetical 'someone' always turns out to be some non-hypothetical one, and maybe even someone you could never imagine.

 

Our flat is being renovated. My mum and I are living in the lounge, all our furniture is here, too. There's a wardrobe at the window. I get changed as soon as I get home. And suddenly I'm aware someone is watching me from the window opposite. I can't see anyone, but the net curtain twitches slightly. I open the wardrobe door and hide behind it, getting undressed out of sight. But the gaze seems to penetrate the door. Now changed, I leave the room. Mashka the cat follows me, regal, in her grey fur mantel, tail erect, a sceptre.

One of the teachers comes into our class and talks to S. B. about some book he should have returned. S. B. apologises:

"I didn't bring it today, it's at my other flat."

Surely he hasn't really rented the flat opposite mine and is watching me? Unlikely, but it seems so. As W. H. Auden wrote:

*The Inevitable is what will seem to happen to you purely by chance;*
*The Real is what will strike you as really absurd;*
*Unless you are certain you are dreaming, it is certainly a dream of*
*your own;*
*Unless you exclaim—"There must be some mistake"—you must be*
*mistaken.*

## 22.

I graduated from Gnessin college specialising in cello, and joined the fourth year at the same college, specialising in theory of music. I decide to see if I can get a place at the Gnessin Academy of Music, as a cellist.

As you would expect, we rehearse with the accompanist. I'm talking to someone in the corridor after one rehearsal. S. B. walks by, announces he is now teaching history of music at the Gnessin Academy of Music and that's why he's abandoned our class. After that I somehow no longer felt like applying for a place as a cellist there.

A few days later, I was late for an exam and played reluctantly, without any feeling. They barely asked me to play anything anyway, just a few bars from Bach's Partita and the beginning of *Pezzo Capriccioso* by Tchaikovsky. I got a D. On my way home, not in the least upset, I bought myself an interesting book—*Obermann* by Senancour—which I spent all evening reading.

That is probably the joy experienced by a steam locomotive which finally leaves the siding and is running along the rails being chased by other trains, running from his past to his future – if he has one.

I am going to class – when I catch sight of S. B. at the end of the corridor. He's heading in my direction, biting his lip as he goes. He looks very upset, and I feel sorry for him. I want to stop, to talk to him, but instead I just say 'hello' and walk by. Maybe something dreadful has happened and I suddenly bounce up with my stupid, unasked for pity? No, I won't do that. Love, or let yourself be loved, but never, ever pity anyone nor let yourself be pitied. He who comes with pity dies of pity.

I enter the classroom. The lesson has already started, I'm late. Ratner growls angrily, but I have tears in my eyes, I barely hold them back. My unexpressed moral support has to suffice. Why does everything connected with him touch me so deeply? To paraphrase Saint-Exupery: we are responsible for the men we have tamed!

I come home that evening, walk along the gloomy Gogol Boulevard. The maple trees are whispering with the elms, bringing order to the chancery of their leaves. Finally, I come out onto Ostozhenka Street. A rather tall man is striding ahead of me. His suede boots are all too familiar. Is it S. B. or his double, my thoughts manifesting into real time and space, between the parked blocks of flats and the semi-detached cars?

He stops, uncertain. I duck behind the newspaper stand, waiting. He crosses the street at last and drops into the off license, exiting my personal space, which is little more than a metre in circumference; how little a person is given to separate himself from the crowding of foreign bodies, although no-one can prevent less bodily objects from crowding in – shadows of his prejudices for instance, or phantoms of his preferences.

23.

With college behind me, I enter the Academy of Music. My main subject is the same: theory of music. Later I discover I finished top of my class. We hold on, keeping afloat!

I bump into Pasha in the corridor. We stop and chat. Seems he just can't graduate from college.

"I take exams, but they don't let themselves be taken," he says. "Like soldiers in the Red Army." And then he adds, irrelevantly, like a red herring. "Come on, let's go and look for our unforgettable."

He doesn't give the name, but I know at once who he's hinting at. "What for?"

"I'm broke, I'll borrow a rouble from him."

"If that's all, then here, take a rouble and relax."

I give him a rouble.

24.

I'm in my second year at the Academy. It's the musical literature exam. Berg fell ill at the last minute, S. B. is conducting the exam alone. Vika is in front of me.

She finishes her exam, comes out, shares her impressions.

"He literally stripped me! Grilled me, wormed out everything I know, everything I love." Then, turning to me, she adds, "Just don't clam up – the main thing is to say something. He listened so carefully to everything you said in class, he obviously fancies you!"

I really don't know how she figured that out. Actually, we all live in shop windows and try to sell ourselves for the highest price, but we have to pay the price of standing on show for hours and hours. For idleness has eyes and boredom has eyes, too, and these eyes are unblinking, lidless, and their gaze is dead, yet still too lively, like those of people in a photograph. Or the eyes of the black-brown mink on the collar of my mother's old coat. Open the wardrobe, and there it is, that glassy, yellowy curious and at the same time indifferent gaze.

During the exam, S. B. asks me about Beethoven's third symphony. I talk about the musical development in the first part – and remember that our orchestra performed this symphony not long ago at an anniversary concert in House of Scholars. I had felt the gaze of someone in the audience staring at me throughout the whole concert – surely the omnipresent S. B. couldn't have been there? Or maybe only his gaze was there, separated from its owner, living a life of its own, flitting through the musical empyreans like the Cheshire Cat's grin?

25.

At the end of our second year, Vika says to me:

"Why don't you ask Sergei Borisovich for tutorials? He's a good teacher, and he obviously likes you. Talk to him."

Her advice seems sound. I ask S. B., he replies evasively:

"Actually, I've already promised to take on two students. I should know in a day or two whether I can take on a third. Ring me at home, here's my number. Just don't leave it too long, I'm going away soon."

Damn it, I can find neither pen nor paper. So I say:

"I'll remember."

"It's not easy: 222 59 74."

Not so tricky, I think to myself. Three twos, that's simple, then the next four digits are Beethoven's quartets' opus numbers.

"I'll remember."

I see a smile spread over S. B.'s face, from ear to ear. I don't like that smile – it's unpleasant, nasty, as if he wants to say: "See, I got one over on you!" What's he grinning about anyway? There's nothing funny.

I ring a few times, but he's never home. So finally I decided to ring in the morning, before I set off for the Academy. Engaged. I dial again, then again. Always engaged. OK, I think, one last time. I get through at once. A woman's voice. I ask for S. B. Silence. Then I hear an argument – and someone hangs up. I ring back. Engaged again. This makes me mad: "Give me a ring! Give me a ring!" Well, you try and give him a ring! It's degrading – trying to get him, especially after that grin.

That's it, I'm not calling again, I'll apply for it. If it works out, fine. If not, so be it. I'm not going to beg him, even if for the simple reason that every stage has a back door, so why not wriggle out of your designated role, all the more so if it is not your role!

26.

I fill in the application form and post it. The term ends, there's still no reply, and everything is gradually forgotten.

But then a month later I bump into Rachmanova in the corridor. We call her Old Lady behind her back; she's from blue blood. She was supposed to teach us Soviet music a while ago, but she just read one initial lecture, gave us a reading list and that was the last we saw of her. We would show up to her classes, wait hours for her, but she never appeared. It went on like that for six weeks, then someone snapped and went to the office of the head of studies to complain about her. Rachmanova came to the next class and caused a real old Pearl Harbour: she had taken such pains with us, cared about us so much, and what did we do, we ingratiates? Had the nerve to complain about her!! Who did we think we were?!

But she still didn't teach us, nor was she reprimanded in any way. But we still had to buy her an expensive bouquet of roses at the end of term, otherwise Tshushima would have followed on from Pearl Harbour! I later discovered that Rachmanova, Ratner and S. B. were close friends, and rumour had it these two women had S. B. wrapped around their little fingers.

Now the Old Lady runs the department. High heels clop, she comes up and says:

"You're just the person I need. I want to talk to you about allocations. Follow me into the classroom."

I follow her.

"It's like this: I have your application here, you are asking to be allocated to Sergei Borisovich's class, but I'm afraid I can't do that. He has already given his word to two others, and cannot take on a third. I can't reach him now – he's not in Moscow. So you have a choice: you can either go to Skvortsov, or to Berg. You can choose. Like a bride."

Her last words and the tone in which she pronounced them grated on me. I sensed something between the lines.

"Can I think it over?" I ask.

"I can give you until tomorrow. Make a note of my phone number."

I walk home, unable to make up my mind.

At home I agonize over it: surely S. B. could have made room for me before he left town? Skvortsov had! Was this his way of getting revenge: I made a pass at you, now it's your turn? Not going to happen – wouldn't want to see him after that, let alone study with him.

Who should I study under? Berg is a fussy old biddy like my Jewish relatives on my mother's side. I had taken a dislike to her from the day we met at the entrance exam. So it's Skvortsov, then. But he fancies me, too. If I join his class, it'll be the same old furtive glances and suggestive conversations. I'll have to be on my guard all the time. S. B. all over again! I'm so tired of it!

Maybe I should go to a different department? There's a great teacher in the harmony department, for instance, I studied with him in college. But I don't want to specialise in harmony; I don't know it that well, either.

And suddenly it dawns on me! Denisova from the solfeggio department! She knows me from college, too. She's exceptionally clever and witty, we'll get along fine. I phone her straight away, and she immediately agrees to take me into her tutorials. So I phone Rachmanova straight back and tell her I want to move to a different department altogether. She's curious: which one? Then adds disdainfully:

"Oh, so you've decided to become a *solfeggiste*!"

27.

In spring I'm told S. B. has accepted Vika into his tutorials. So he did have room for a third student, after all!

But then I got to thinking that maybe S. B. is not only to blame – who knows, maybe he took her on at the last minute, by chance. Anything could have happened… We always try to justify the other person's behaviour, to look on the bright side of life and all that, all the while bearing in mind the likelihood, even the probability, that things may be quite the opposite.

Vika did her utmost to worm out of me why I had suddenly decided to study solfeggio.

Now I find it difficult to say a forced hello to S. B. as though nothing had happened. I try to avoid him, although I don't always manage it. Has his attitude towards me changed? I don't know, but it's clear he's vexed. Now he's like a general who, having fired all his guns at the enemy, only showered his own vanguard with shrapnel and cannonballs. He's ashamed of himself, and, worst of all, unable to shake the thought he has made a catastrophic mistake, a mistake no university can teach you to avoid; you can only learn about it at one college, and that's the one he hasn't yet graduated from: where they teach you to walk straight.

  

28.

The third year. They are both lecturing us – S. B. is teaching contemporary music, Skvortsov, Russian music. I find it hard to see either of them. I had, of course, offended Skvortsov – he can't understand why I refused to study under him.

On the eve of the exam I'm sitting in the Lenin Library revising the score of Gershwin's *Porgy and Bess*. I'm singing something under my breath. Suddenly Ratner comes along, strikes up a conversation. Although she doesn't say anything in particular, I don't like talking to her: her words are gilded with lemonade but they taste of pure bile. There are well-wishers who wish only themselves well, and as for what they wish you, well, obviously nothing good, so it's better not to ask.

I'm taking my exam. It's Nadia's turn next. She walks into the classroom. S. B. appears and looks me straight in the eye. His stare makes me uncomfortable. The exam over, I go down to the library and start revising again – I have to prepare for my next exam. But I can still feel that gaze on my back and I have a strange sensation, my ears are burning, my eyes watering – or maybe I'm about to drown in that water, maybe the whole charade was no use to anyone, least of all to myself?

Strange thing, human emotions and preferences. So you (hypothetical 'you'!) want to be with me, and I want to be you. Yes, yes, you, with your knowledge and lightness of being. But I don't want to be with you, not for anything, and don't even ask, because soul-mates, well, that is a first rate fairy-tale, the epitome of the absurd, and we love what we hate and we hate what we love, and it is hard to love, we don't want to, hating is easy but it's boring, so we don't even want to do that...

Finally, the last exam of the third year is behind me. I'm soon home. A continuation of the cat theme: a hungry Mashka meets me at the door and winds herself around my legs. Most pets are low maintenance creatures. A cat is a cat even without a diploma, a bread bun is still a bread bun without any filling, only a person needs filling. Without it a person gets stale, browned, turns crusty and crumbles, then the birds come and peck it all up and—behold!—an empty space, as though nothing had ever been there.

29.

It's my fourth year at the Academy. S. B. is giving a course on contemporary music. I look out of the window. I can see the Hungarian embassy from here. I make notes mechanically, then turn my gaze to S. B. He's still talking, but he's facing the window now. He's looking at the Hungarian embassy, too, and the Hungarian embassy is looking back at him, and quite innocently at that.

After the lecture, Vika and I bump into Rachmanova in the corridor. With a contemptuous half-smile she looks me over from top to toe:

"You've lost weight!"

Vika tells her:

"We're studying in the same group now."

Rachmanova, to me, spitefully:

"Still with Sergei Borisovich?"

"No, with Denisova."

Vika adds:

"It's me who's with Sergei Borisovich."

Rachmanova's smile transforms into a fastidious grimace. The Old Lady cuts the conversation short and turns her back.

30.

The exam questions on Soviet Music are announced before the winter term. I think: can music be 'Soviet?' or 'British?' It can be Russian or Ukrainian, Tartar, English, Scottish, but if it is 'Soviet' or 'British' then it is not music but something else altogether. Yet many people consider Prokofiev and Shostakovich to be Soviet composers. How naive! Take the never-ending, rubbery Anthem of the Soviet Union, for instance, stretching out like gum, cobbled together by some distinguished puncture-patcher from the country that occupies one-sixth of the world's land surface – that is Soviet music, the music of an empire, maybe because listening to it you want to lie on a patched inflatable mattress and float off into extra-historical dreams from the fountain reservoir in Pushkin Square.

          

I dreamt of the laughing room. A man was standing by the door. There was a notice on it: HERE WE LAUGH.

The man enters.

"Yes, yes, people come here to laugh," the receptionists reassure him. "That's what this room is for. The walls are covered in black canvas, and plaster masks grinning from ear to ear loom out against the blackness. Look at them and have a good time."

But the man begins to cry.

"What are you doing?!" a huge commotion breaks out. "This is the laughing room!"

"May the laughter rest in peace," utters the visitor, wiping his eyes.

## 31.

It's ten days to graduation. Vika is telling me about her tutorials with S. B.:

"He loves me! He holds my hand!"

Her voice is strange: she's boasting, of course, but she seems to be pitying me, too. It's a particular kind of pity, the pity a specimen which has learned how to jump from tuft to tuft shows towards a fellow specimen which is forever sinking.

By night, strange, never-ending dreams from the land of unattainable hopes and sunny wintry days in the middle of summer, the cloudy eyes of the morning skies and measured steps of approaching night. And this is how we tumble into a dreamlife – or into a dream of the life we dream. Every now and then I dream of S. B. – talking, following close on my heels, walking right into my flat. I'm making the bed, I turn around to fetch the bedspread from the sofa – and freeze on the spot: he's standing behind me, stark naked! I wake in a cold sweat…

As Macrobius said, some dreams are but dreams. If only we could fathom reality…

Temptation is an unfamiliar neighbourhood in a familiar city. It is dark there, destinies can comfortably be made. Myriads of stars twinkle there, bright as during a lunar eclipse. Between the plentiful green twinkles, you glimpse the black and white streets of dream and you foresee what you'll do – go right to the border, whatever that border may be, and then kiss the cellophane. Kiss the cellophane.

Kiss the cellophane. Even if you don't go to the bitter end, you still have to kiss the cellophane.

How complicated everything here is, by the way, both the temptation and overcoming it. You overcome one thing, but then another appears, just as alluring – can you step over that, too? They speak of temptation and overcoming it in church, too. Essentially, everything depends on the person's capacity to think, to defend their own viewpoint and stick to it. Otherwise witch hunts ensue, then the witches begin to hunt those who are hunting them, i.e. everyone else, all of us, and how can we get away, pray tell? It's like a Hindemithian 'concert of angels;' but look closely, and they are not angels at all…

32.

Finally, the long story-less story ended – in nothing, as I had suspected. Still, any completion is cause for celebration, even the completion of life itself. And completing university – well, that is the celebration to end all celebrations! Although the reward is merely a diploma in my bag, a sheet of paper in exchange for all those years!

S. B. couldn't even muster up enough courage to say a few farewell words to me. He had tormented both me and himself for so many years, for what? How he had aged: gone bald, stooped, seemed shorter… My attitude towards him had taken its toll, too, of course. He was used to being admired; deep down, he was in love with himself and his "unobtrusive courting." A narcissist, that's who he is. I had seen it in his profile long ago; I had had plenty of time to study it. A longish nose, shortish chin, soft features like those of a perpetual explorer, a hedonist. Nothing suggesting strong sentiments or lasting affection! Sentiment and lasting affection, they are like a text in a foreign language for him. And then he met a woman he had to woo. This was something new for him, but he had evidently decided it would be short-lived, and then everything would fall into place—he would just have to show some perseverance—but only in small, homeopathic doses.

I bumped into him in the metro one day, he started to walk straight towards me, boldly, but he lowered his eyes, abashed, when he came level. He had obviously hoped I wouldn't be able to withstand his gaze, that I would be the one thrown into confusion. But that didn't happen. And when he realised tricks like that wouldn't help him, he wanted revenge.

Narcissi are easily offended. Even the flowers. Don't touch them, or they wither, shrivel. If they don't get their way, they hide their beloved self-image deep within themselves to worship it there, internally. They are so offended they even stop smelling, though their fragrance was feeble, to start with. And as for narcissi-people, well…

"Give me some sunshine," Sun asked of the puddle.

"Help yourself," plashed the puddle, unconcerned.

"I shall," Sun said.

"Already done?" puddle asked.

"Already done," Sun replied.

"Didn't make any difference," the puddle sighed.

"But it did to us!" said the wan reflection of Narcissus, now a-quiver in the puddle.

33.

I had hoped that a joyful vista would open up before me when I graduated – high praise had rained down on me throughout all my years of study! But no offers came my way, the phone was silent in my flat. Vika and Nadia were applying for post grad places – offers were made, help was at hand, and I was certain: they would be accepted. But as for me, I just got a whole load of bubbles. Who knows why…

Actually, I do. Because Spring has to seek admission from Winter, and Summer from Spring. Otherwise there would be neither Spring nor Summer, and instead, our worst fears would come true. You have to beg the masters of another's illegitimacy for that to which you have full right, and they reply with the knock of dry bones seemingly borrowed from a Shostakovich symphony. You pawn yourself not with trifles, but with fragments of yourself, courteously, with ritual bowing and scraping, otherwise they will give you nothing. And when you pull yourself together and realise there is no way to re-decompose yourself, you may be able to start to straighten up. But they did not give me back myself…

Maybe I can't put it down to my independent nature alone, maybe the fact I was the daughter of a former political prisoner also had something to do with it. My father, from Siberia, who had survived the Gulag, was now in the grave but here, the seventies are upon us, the infamous 'thaw' had long since splattered into slush, but then everything froze over again, and life became slippery. All the posters are saying that the one lying in the mausoleum is 'more alive than the living,' the one they have taken out is too, in fact, while the living are deader than the dead.

OK then, let's cultivate our garden and eat what grows there. In my dissertation I posited there are two kinds of people, and they absorb study materials differently, hence the need for two differing approaches to teaching solfeggio. I got top marks for that dissertation; they said I'd made a breakthrough. If only they'd let me continue working on it, too… But no, my dissertation was at the junction of music, pedagogy and psychology, and that is like the blank space on any map. In other words: insignificant territory – or the territory of insignificant existence?

I'm beginning to understand what the future has in store for me. There would be nowhere for me to continue my research, even though that is what I am best suited to. I would have to work alone since it would be impossible for me to find a common language with my fellow researchers. And it would even be all but impossible for me to publish any articles – after all, who is interested in the writings of a teacher in some music school?

Despite all the pep talks in the press, you can't get far on talent alone. There are exceptions, of course, those who have been frightfully lucky. Before giving anyone a position, Napoleon would ask whether that person was lucky or not – but what should the unlucky ones do, or those who didn't catch Napoleon's eye? Give one of the undistinguished ones a chance, and his talent quickens and sprouts into a vast leafy canopy, so now how do you catch scarce sun's rays, stunted and puny as you are?


"Let's go to the May pole," they suggested.

I went to the May pole. Girls were singing round it, holding ribbons fixed to the top.

"It's time to choose the beauty queen," announced the head of my music school. Then turning to me, he added: "You're on the jury."

Everyone began vying to show off their brides or daughters.

   

I shin up the May pole (it's easy in a dream!), take a good look and shout:

"I see her, the beauty queen! She's far away, she won't be here for a long while, but her heavenly beauty is visible from afar!"

Before I could climb down, someone began sawing at the pole, saying:

"Humph! What do we want with heavenly beauty!"

They chose some saucy lass as the beauty queen. The sawn off May pole and I collapsed. June began. And I woke up.


## 34.

In honour of my graduating from the Gnessin Academy of Music—which I did with distinction, by the way—I was fired. There was no place for me in a mediocre, out-of-town music school. Thank you, they said, offering me tea, and kissingly wishing me all the best. I must have done a bad job, you think! No, far from it. My only fault was that I 'noticed': the headmaster had nonexistent people, 'dead souls', on his register, and he took their salary himself.

In college we are taught by those who know how to teach. When we graduate, we are taught by life – in other words, by random people, who cannot do anything, or who can do something you wouldn't thank them for. So now you have to think how to find a job, any job. You are back to square one. Don't go out of your front door, since no matter where you go, you end up going home. And you can't get away from your curse, because, well, you are your own curse.

An art critic dug up an ancient Greek statue in his vegetable patch. It was a magnificent woman with wings on her back.

"What is your name, *la belle dame?*" he enquired.

"Nike," came the reply.

Having examined the statue from all sides, the art critic announced:

"Something about you irks me, ruins the harmony."

"Maybe it's my wings?" the statue suggested.

"No, probably your arms."

The statue grew sad, and her arms fell away.

"Is that better?" she asked.

"Yes," the art critic responded. "It's odd, though – no arms, but a head…"

The statue's head fell away.

"Masterful!" exclaimed the art critic, delighted.

He placed the statue in a museum and labelled her "Nike: Goddess of Victory." And another art lover, who remained anonymous, added in charcoal: "Over Oneself."

35.

It's the First of September, and I am teaching out of town once again, in a different music school. The journey is even more tortuous than to my previous workplace. The same bog-like streets, stray dogs which the cars end up running over, drunkards in the local trains, the shaky footbridge over the tracks. It never ends, it is the cross which you carry and carry until you find yourself hanging from it.

As for my classmates, Artem got himself a teaching post at a music school in Moscow's inner city; Vika and Nadia were accepted for post grads. Vika now hangs out with musicologists, she listens to what they say, remembers it all, writes it down when she gets home and that's how she gathers material for her dissertation. Tanya and Lena got positions as research fellows at museums and publish articles in the *Soviet Music* journal. Even our good-for-nothing party-goer Pasha gets published. And me? Still working out of town, just like before, and I haven't even managed to get anything published yet.

My university teachers told me many times I was brighter and more talented than others, but now I am almost the only one left with nothing. Someone told me potters have a rule: when you mould a woman, first of all you have to break her neck.


I dreamt I wrote a book which was published in a beautifully bound edition. Everyone congratulated me, and I frantically tried to remember what it was about. In our 'happy' homeland, why are people's dreams more interesting than their lives? Even death is more interesting than life.

Life consists of… What does it consist of, actually? You were born (tick). You went to school (tick). You went to work (tick). You went to university (tick). You went to work again and again (tick tick tick).

You got married (tick). Your children got married (tick for each). You took things at face value (big tick).

Your life is made up of ticks. Are you happy? No? But you should be!

Bread is eaten, snowmen are made of snow. Ah, but what would happen, what would happen if snow were eaten and snowmen were made of bread!

36.

Three years have passed since I graduated from university. One cheerless October morning I am walking down Chistoprudny Boulevard to the editorial office of *Supplement to Moscow Evening Standard*. I want to put in an ad, 'cello for sale.' I don't play it now, and I need the money. My mother has diabetes, I have to buy her medicine. The Boulevard is half dead, all but deserted, the dry leaves rustle under foot. Reflections of reflections flicker in the pale windows of the restaurant in the middle of the boulevard, ripples of the morning pond.

I run into Lyudmila on the corner. She's a former student of S. B.

"He's a wonderful teacher," she says. "He should write books, he's burying his talent in the ground."

"Maybe he is," I think. "But where's that ground? Don't ask 'On what grounds?' because the only answer can be: 'Why, here in Denmark.'"

"And he's such an interesting person, too," Lyudmila goes on. "I could listen to him for hours. I still remember his tales of his trip to Paris…"

Ah, some people flit abroad… But they won't let me out of the country, I'm the daughter of a former 'enemy of the nation.' In other words, someone who cannot travel abroad.

I would like to visit other countries, to see the altarpiece in the Isenheim church, for instance, the work of that same Hindemithian *Mathis der Maler*, or *Matthias the Painter* – Matthias Grünewald. It's cramped and stuffy here, in the stagnant pond of a chaotic country with a dull government, but maybe that 'inner life' is a blessing for many of us. Because if you break the dam and open the floodgates, Russia would flee Russia and cast herself on the far off shore like a giant whale, and the ocean would revolt and the small fish would splash frantically.

On Sunday I go grocery shopping, as usual. I go out onto the street, and just then Vika appears on the porch of the block opposite. She's dressed smartly, a fashionable beige coat tossed nonchalantly over her shoulder. She doesn't notice me, crosses the road, smiling. She's obviously coming from S. B.'s place, an expression of sexual satisfaction spread over her face... Well, they share a similar attitude to life. And besides, she needs S. B. so she can use his words to write a couple of pages of her dissertation

I can understand and forgive everything, but why does he invite her—and, apparently, not only her—to that flat which he had once rented because of me? Such refined revenge! He still sometimes waves his curtains at me and spies on me from his window – after all those years...

Good God, how disgusting it all is! He's supposed to love harmony and art, so why can't he create any harmony in his own life? Why does he compose his life so carelessly, so unscrupulously and falsely, as though it were a harmony exercise written by poor simple Pasha?

## 37.

It's seven years since I graduated. My mother has died, I am completely on my own. How strange it is to live in a flat where you don't hear anyone's voice and the silence builds in cotton wool layers! They say that's the silence and loneliness Glen Gould inhabited, and he liked it. Not so strange, incidentally: he conversed with Bach in that thick silence!

Typical chain of events: someone became a living god. The papers first explained why he is a god, then told the tale of how he had become one... Someone wrote maliciously: "He is not a god!" And anyone who still harboured doubts immediately realised he was indeed a god. Then one clever person published an article entitled: "Is he always a god?" And everyone immediately realised that he is not always a god, that he is often not a god at all, and is in fact god only knows who...

So do you think he ceased being a god? No, not in the least! For one who has been a god but for an instant is already a god; one who has been a human but for one teardrop is not yet a human, but close, so close…

A dream: I am in a shop selling success. I browse around, enquire about the prices. I am told, as they tell you in Soviet shops:

"Go to hell."

And so I set off. Walking down the street with a nonchalant air.

"Where are you going?"

"To hell," I reply.

"Don't be rude!" they say, offended.

"I really am going to hell."

"Why?"

"They told me to."

"Ah, well, you have to go, then,"

And so I am going. Going, going, going. And everyone gets out of my way.

Should I write a manifesto of non-life? It would go something like this: "Children, I am a teacher. I love no-one. Nothing and no-one excites me. I have no goals. Nothing brings me true joy. The only thing I can do is work, work, work. Don't follow my example."

And once again, the same old Bruegelesque scene that has come alive: winter, the local electric train, the rickety footbridge over the tracks, child's smiles and the childish pranks of non-children. Still, when I'm among the children I can throw off my "I" for a while, and that is already something… After work – the joyless journey home, my solitary self-confinement cell where I pace back and forth, even though there is no going back, no going forth. Like a wolf in a cage. Like the wolf, I did not choose this for myself. "For myself" – how strange that sounds. I cannot live "for myself," when I'm at work, I live "for others," the remaining hours I gladly emigrate to the world of literary heroes and comfortable destinies. There, you don't have to live for anyone, which is fine by me… Such a difficult task, to live out your life; no matter how, just live it out.

# PART 4

## Grave

### 1.

Before us, it was the *voloty*, giants, who inhabited this world. After us, it is the *pyzhiki*, dwarves, who shall come. According to the old believers. And as their yardstick they take themselves – i.e. all of us. Folk who are neither big, nor small.

And that is precisely how N. thought of himself, neither big, nor small. He chose the most ordinary, *the slowest* form of suicide: life.

"I am alone," he said to himself.

"Ours is a country of lonely folk," he answered himself.

"The price of declared collectivism," his two inner interlocutors thought.

But the papers thought otherwise. As to what the people thought, well, only the people themselves know that…

A knock at the door. N. opened it. No-one to be seen. He looked down.

A mad thought dashed through his mind: "The dwarves! They're already here!"

But his guest was alone, and, as it happened, hunchbacked rather than short. He was dressed quite flamboyantly, and his rags had a theatrical flair. His bent back formed a letter 'r' while his head, adorning the horizontal bar of this letter, hung out at waist level. His gaze was tenacious, staring out from under his brow.

"Some food?" N. asked.

"Some water," replied the hunchback grumpily; his retort seemed rehearsed, the whole episode playing out like a well-directed drama.

The hunchback got some food as well as some water, of course, along with sympathetic glances and the chance to vent his anger.

"I'm a poet," the visitor declared. "A former intellectual."

N. cautiously expressed his doubts as to whether one could in fact stop being an intellectual.

"You can," the visitor replied. "If you want to."

And he had wanted to, when his teacher was imprisoned then exiled to Siberia while he himself, the day after daring to speak up for this teacher at a meeting of the Writers' Union, was beaten by hooligans and strangers with iron pipes, none of whom were ever found by the law enforcement agencies. The result: his hunchback, his tramp's lifestyle, lung disorders and universal rage. Quite understandable.

"There's no call for intellectuals now," the hunchback declared. "It's 'workers for art' they need now."

"Who are these 'workers for art'?" N. was curious.

"They're the ones the House of Workers for Art was built for."

"So they opened a House of Culture, that's a good thing," N. decided to tease his guest.

"As if there's any culture in the House of Culture!" his guest muttered gruffly.

"Wait until we have a more humanitarian regime here, then there'll be a place for culture here, too."

"Do you really think there'll be a humanitarian regime here in the foreseeable future? In a country like ours?" the hunchback asked him, amazed. "And how long do you think it would last? I'd give it nine months, the gap between the two revolutions in 1917."

"That's pretty pessimistic."

"OK then, say we give it a few years. But then someone in uniform will come, for sure – or at best, someone with a bunch of medals on his chest."

As a 'thank you' for the food, the visitor began reciting his poems.

"These are old ones," he said, clearing his throat. "I don't write any more. No point."

Fish tanks and flutes of crimson wine smashed against stone floors in his poems, freaks from the cabinets of curiosities danced stripteases on the shards of glass, bouquets of poisonous flowers rustled with dull cellophane. The hunchback smacked his lips with every word, as if each one were a juicy olive. N. was particularly struck by a poem portraying the souls of the dead as bats flitting above the earth.

"Do you really believe that?" N. asked.

"Well, they're not still registered in their flats now, are they?" quipped the hunchback sarcastically. "Yes, that's what I believe. And I believe we can communicate with them, too. And that you shall one day, too."

With these words he began to stuff his knapsack with the remains of food from the table.

"You can live here, if you like," N. offered. "There's plenty of room."

"No, the likes of me shouldn't pair off. It's tantamount to nesting, conspiracy, grounds for arrest."

## 2.

His visitor disappeared into the night, letting some of it into the house on his way out. N. began playing Beethoven's seventh symphony, the finale, on his imaginary keyboard, i.e. the table. His fingers begged for sound, but there was only a hollow knocking.

"What will remain of me?" his thoughts rambled on. "Will the Minotaur swallow everything? Will music remain? But I don't compose. Love? It will be effaced together with me. And what will remain of my love for Beta, for music? Just somebody else's music, nothing more."

The knocking of his fingers on the table was accompanied by a determined rustling somewhere in the house innards. It went on all night, hindering sleep.

Overcoming it at last, N. penetrated the world of dreams. He dreamt he was reading a newspaper, a rare event in his waking life. An announcement caught his eye: "Become a figure in a famous painting!"

Having consulted his inner voice, he decided it was not such a bad idea.

When N. finally tracked the artist down in his country studio, the latter was inexplicably clad in the white coat of a medic.

"So, which picture shall we transplant you into, then?" he asked in a cheery voice.

"Do what?" N. was confused.

"You know, resettle you. I copy famous paintings, but put in other faces – the faces of my customers."

N. looked around. The paintings were indeed famous: "The Napoleoni Family Crossing the Alps." "Locksmith Saturnow Devouring his Son." And even "Detective Inspector Libertin Leading the People."

"How about The Three Musketeers?" N. ventured hesitantly.

"Good idea!" Delighted, the artist painted N., himself and the minister of culture as the musketeers.

The painting went on show in the Tretyakov Gallery.

"Now, that's what I call real intellectuals," one art critic declared at the opening.

Slightly disgusted, N. left that dream room – and found himself in another. It was not so much a room as a huge hall which housed a shop called "Guest of Honour." At the entrance, N. was given a trolley on wheels, which he wheeled around easily – while it was empty.

Uniforms with epaulettes, dinner jackets, cocktail dresses and jewellery were on sale in the aisle nearest him. A window with medals and insignia took him by surprise at first, but then he thought: "Why not? Maybe I'm just behind the times."

He turned into another aisle. The goods here were somewhat unusual: all kinds of positions were for sale, from the lowest to the very highest – civil servants, generals, presidents. Appointments with blank spaces for names were laid out in open caskets. You could even buy Nobel Prize certificates!

He resisted the temptation to place one of the caskets in his own trolley; he didn't think himself worthy of such distinction. But he was soon seduced by a diploma with the words "Master of Style," and a casket appeared in his trolley after all.

"If you have a casket you must have a dinner jacket and a cape," smiled a shop assistant, appearing out of thin air.

N. popped into the changing room, removed his nondescript clothes and donned a white shirt and bow tie topped with a dinner jacket. The shop assistant draped a long purple cape over his shoulders. It came right down to his ankles.

Coming out of the changing room, N. all but bumped into a pompous, purple-faced old gent struggling to push a heavily laden trolley. The old man was aspiring to become a general, and an academic, and a writer. "I wonder why he didn't help himself to a presidential casket, too," N. wondered. "Age limit?"

Clad in his cape, N. pushed his trolley towards the checkout. The old man got there first. "Can he pay for all that, I wonder?" N. thought.

The cashier greeted the old man gushingly. The caskets from his trolley were laid on the counter. The cashier brought out an antique mahogany abacus and set about making calculations. N. strained to take a closer look. The beads on the abacus were shaped like skulls.

At last the calculation was complete. The old man was ushered into a booth near the checkout to pay. With its brocade curtains, the steel-framed booth on wheels reminded N. of a fitting room. The cashier disappeared inside with the old man, the black curtains closed behind them.

Overcome with curiosity, N. surreptitiously lifted the edge of the curtain opposite to watch. The cashier helped the old man off with his cape, and he was left wearing a black dinner jacket. Moving the stool towards him, the cashier said:

"What you have chosen weighs three lives. Sit down, please, I need to check whether you can bear that weight or not."

The old man sat himself on the stool. The cashier clapped his hands – and the old man suddenly disappeared. The cashier took a black rug from the stool and, hanging it over his arm like a towel, put the stool back in its place. The contours reminded N. of a human body, and it suddenly dawned on him: the rug was in fact the old man, or rather, what was left of him. The cashier carefully wrapped the rug in the purple cape.

N. had been watching all this with some alarm through a crack. Exiting the booth from the other side, the cashier looked around:

"Where are you, my friend?" he called. "I am at your service."

N. started. Grabbing the casket, he rushed into the aisles. The cashier was hot on his heels, and would probably have caught him, had N.'s cape not slithered from his shoulders and tripped up his pursuer.

N. put the casket back in its place and hurried on, tearing the jacket and shirt off as he ran. Leaping over the aisles desperately, he dashed out onto the street in his underwear – and the dawn sun splashed free gold in his eyes. As a result, the street curled up like a snail and disappeared, to be replaced by the walls of the room, lit by that same inescapable sun, as they fanned out like a pack of cards in a morning game of patience.

     

N. woke fully, at last – and smelt the pungent smell of tar. He had a terrible headache. He went down the steps into the pensive morning garden and looked back at the house from a distance. It was tarred and caulked, like a ship in the dock.

3.

Who knows what will remain of each of us? Of thoughts – poplar fluff. Of deeds – wind in the birch leaves. Memory is short and capricious, the eternal fades into eternity, the transient transits into the vanished. Eternity belongs to the actors' guild, and it mocks the audience who are not even given the chance to watch so much as the first act. But eternity needs no applause; it performs for itself alone.

"What remains…" Having traced his thoughts full circle, N. returned to yesterday's reflections. "One thing for sure – the manuscript of *The Flying Dutchman*. My book's finished, and, good or bad, I don't want it to fall into unfriendly hands. What shall I do with it? Post it to the publishers in Moscow? Will it make it, or will it live out its days in some Lubyanka cellar? I can but try…"

Remembering the 'fish post,' he smiled: that would come in handy now! If only I knew how to summon the postal fish…

But he had to avail himself of the most ordinary of postal services; he set off for the village post office early in the morning. The sun was rolling its flaming August ball over the treetops and N. was glad of the landlord's straw hat he had found in the cupboard. The hat made him look like Chekhov's Uncle Vanya on the stage of a provincial theatre – but who cares?

A covey of sounds corkscrewed out of one of the houses as he passed by: "Roll over Beethoven."

"That's brave. Rock'n'roll is more 'forbidden' than 'permitted' here. But what does it mean, anyway – "we roll over Beethoven"? Blockheads – it's Beethoven who rolls over you, squashing all your pop songs and cheap tunes…"

Suddenly someone's deep-fried deep voice rumbled out:

"Hey you, jerk, turn off that crap! Who do you think you are, the village fop? We knew just what to do with the likes of you in Stalin's day."

The music shut up at once.

"Has Stalinism encapsulated itself in some of our fellow citizens, like a festering sore?" N. shook his head.

The post office stood with doors akimbo. N. mounted the crooked provincial steps and found himself in a room divided by a counter. Someone's feet, clad in huge sandals, were making themselves at home on it. Ankles covered in flaxen hairs gleamed gold in the sunlight. Nothing but those legs was to be seen.

"E-hem," N. coughed in a serious professorial way.

The feet withdrew themselves at once, and a bespectacled blond head covered in freckles appeared.

"Trampin. A student. A simpleton," N. remembered the shop assistant's words.

"Oh, sorry," said the head. "Normally no-one ever comes here."

"And precisely No-one has come," smiled N.

"So you designate yourself as an absent element of society?" the student remarked, curious.

"The urge designates itself as a chance happening, a coincidence … Didn't Hegel say that?"

"Well, Hegel simply said that all coincidences are well-founded. The rest is your own… Are you a philosopher?"

"No, a musicologist," N. responded automatically, but immediately thought: mistake!

But Trampin the student was the very picture of innocence. N. relaxed.

"I want to post something," he went on. "But I need an envelope and stamps, too."

"We can fix that," smiled the student. "You won't believe it, but I have everything shipshape here. I hide it well, though."

"Hide it? Why?"

"The Hamlet principle. In a society like ours, you have to keep your intellect hidden from those around you. I am completely at home in my role as a simpleton-cum-student who was all but thrown out of uni."

"Did they really nearly throw you out?"

"What do you reckon? Suppose they'd think twice about throwing someone out after they found him with Nabokov's *Invitation to a Beheading*?

"How careless, my dear fellow."

　　　　　　　　　　　　

"A friend ratted me out… And that's when I began acting the fool. It works a treat, by the way."

"Yes, I can believe that," N. said, unable to check his smile. "It won't work for me, though… But back to business. I want to send a manuscript to Moscow… Tell me, do they check the post?"

"Not here," replied the student. "But they may well do at the regional sorting office."

"I didn't put my name on the cover, just in case, but I'm sure they'll work out who sent it."

"Well, I can hand it to the addressee  personally, if you like. Just tell me who to give it to."

"The name's on the card, here, and the address, too."

Actually, N. had written the address on the card for himself since he didn't trust his memory. But it had turned out well – now he could simply give the card away.

"I'll be sure to hand it to him," said the student. "Though it won't be for a while – I won't be in Moscow until September."

"There's no rush. Thank you very much!"

4.

He was thoughtful on the way home. "So, I've lowered the basket into the water, it will float off, baby and all. Who knows which shores the waves will carry it to?" The name and address on the card were those of the S. B. in the diary he had just read.

"There's no-one else," N. tried to convince himself he'd made the right choice. "I'll have to risk it. Funny, he held the fate of a person's life in his hands—Beta's friend—and now he holds… well, not exactly my fate, of course, but the fate of my book. Will he let me down? He takes trips abroad, like Poro. Maybe the Bolsheviks were right about rotten intelligentsia? If so, how can you determine the extent of the rot? I'll just have to hope for the best, there's nothing else to hope for. So my manuscript is taking on a life of its own, and I am beginning a life without it…"

Peals of rock'n'roll burst through the open window again.

"Just you try and ban it!" N. smiled to himself. "Our stubbornness is our last line of defence… That was an interesting story in the diary, by the way. Seems it was the same girl who they say had an affair with a Dutch cellist who took part in a Tchaikovsky competition. A round-faced young man with an open smile, who went home without her, then came back a year later. Everyone thought he'd take her with him that time, but he didn't, and that was the last she saw of him. No-one knows what happened between them, but the general opinion is that he didn't treat her well. She did write in her diary: "I remember someone I loved long ago, when I was young. Sad memories..." Was she referring to the cellist? Who knows... And then S. B. comes along with his silent footsteps, his cat and mouse games, and his quasi-musical quibbles. First one, then another. Really makes you want to lock yourself in a room with a window onto nowhere and play *Pezzo capriccioso* for all the local ghosts..."

5.

He struck a match and lit the sun, took a bunch of keys from his pocket and swung the bell ropes, said the word and rustled up conferences, public poetry readings, prayers, symposiums and book club meetings, from which we can conclude that it is far better to strike a match and take keys from your pocket in total silence, without uttering so much as a single word.

Silence seeped in from every chink of midday. Not feeling like going back inside, N. lay himself out on the bench in a shady corner of the garden. He gradually peaked into the interrupted dream of that morning, or, perhaps, woke up inside his own dream. The blue sky, the house, the attic, the swing and the bronze key all found their way into the dream. The blue sky called him out of the house. He walked on and on, until he walked right into a labyrinth. N. had never been in a labyrinth before—not counting the maze of his own thoughts, of course—and so he decided to proceed straight ahead and see what happened. And he at once came out the other side.

"That's too easy," N. said to himself. He went back into the labyrinth. And walked straight through it again. "Most peculiar," he mused, and decided to go home – and got lost. "Where's my house gone? Where's my attic gone?" These unexpectedly doleful thoughts rumbled around inside his head. Somehow, imperceptibly, he had begun to love this home he had always hated. At last he found his street, and even the spot where his block of flats should be. But there was no building; some gorgeous narcissi were admiring themselves there instead.

"Maybe today is tomorrow in disguise?" his thoughts raced. He decided to go and live in the labyrinth, but he couldn't even find that. Then what one should do in such situations began to dawn on him, and he started rummaging in his pockets just in case. In one of them he found the large bronze key which he always kept in a special box but which he had brought with him that day for some reason.

"Now I'll find out what this key opens," N. reassured himself. And noticed he was standing in front of copper gates, greened with age. He wasn't alone, he was surrounded by a throng of the most diverse individuals clad in queer costumes, from a Roman legionary to a Levantine merchant. The gates were shut and the crowd was seething, someone was trampled on, swearing was abundant and vociferous.

At last a man came out. Shortish, but portly. He gave an apologetic smile, took the bronze key from N. and unlocked the door. The crowd poured down, flowed over the man as if he were a stone, and he disappeared into the underwater, under-human realm. The human river flowed in all directions all at once, unstoppable. Green panels torn from the gate were already floating in it, folk clambered onto them, and stood waving from their make-shift rafts.

"Why are they floating?" N. wondered. "The panels are made of copper!"

And that is why they float, his dream answered him. To remind you how people stood in front of them, like water held back by a dam!

6.

As a child he had stood before the shut gates of the infectious diseases ward. How he had wanted to go outside! He had somehow suddenly turned a sunny yellow, like a lemon. Grown pensive. So then he wasn't allowed to eat anything tasty anymore, but at least no-one scolded him for reading all day.

"You could build the Great Wall of China with all the books I've read." N. was collecting his thoughts like bricks. "As for books I've written, well, that's my age. I'm not forty something, I'm three books. Well, three and a half if you count the two slim children's books on music as half an ordinary book... I like to think like that, but how is it really? The years we have lived dwell inside us, you know, set into a pattern of rings. Then all those rings appear on our necks, multiplying mercilessly. Some agile folk manage to juggle them, but sooner or later they will all come to roost on your neck, and swell with leaden heaviness, bowing us to the ground. If someone were to chop us down, how many rings would they find? Not as many, of course, as in a Moscow blockhead hewn from oaks as old as Pushkin. Blockheads are thick and hardy. Oaks and blockheads are given freedom, respect…"

"As for us, our protestations of innocence have developed into exile. What we kill these days is time; bronze lamp-post lions open their mouths as days flash past. From the heap of unearthed history, we pick the twentieth century: at fourteen, a soldier; at seventeen, a rebel; at thirty-three, an informer and a torturer; at thirty-nine, again a soldier; at seventy, a dementia sufferer. What do we expect of it these days?"

"An unearthly wind—or is it the voice of Chronos?—croons to us in a dusty voice: *Your fathers arrived in Purgatory naked, with bunches of flags; each had enough ghastly memories to fill three lives. Now they discuss whose deeds justify their flesh.*"

The hospital for infectious diseases was on Falcon Hill. There's something about that name… Falcon Hill. Falkenberg. The yellow-faced, grey-haired captain…

7.

"*The more you yearn for happiness, the less happy you are; the more honours are bestowed upon you, the more you want to renounce them,*" wrote N. in his notebook. "*That is how you console yourself, sitting in smothering silence. Not long ago, the City of People Ahead of Their Time called me to live there as a respected citizen, but I declined. I don't consider myself a person ahead of my time. And anyway, I don't like adjectives about the word 'person…'*"

Then he decided there was more emotion than meaning in what he had written. He turned the page and began writing afresh. He spent the whole morning thinking about his night-time visitor, and this time the text in his notebook was given the name: "Treatise on the Human Dimension."

     

*"The gadget known as a 'heightometer' does not measure what you might expect. If a person stands himself in the corner, his intellect grows, and grows… And then a plank is lowered onto his head, a board. And the rest depends on how much pressure is exerted on that board. Thus a person's height is what remains of his height once the board has been applied.*

*The boards differ from country to country. In some places they are made of light linden, in others they are steel or even lead. There are even boards on springs. That's why some tall people are seen as dwarves in their country, and vice versa.*

*The professional measurer is well respected. The height of the state is judged by the head measurers. But no-one ever measured the measurers' height; and hence we do not know how to spot them in a crowd – if, of course, they deign to join the crowd."*

That evening he switched the light on in all the rooms, went into the garden, sat down on the bench and gave himself over to admiring the illuminations. Wouldn't it be wonderful if there were a show in each window…

And in a flash, a show appeared! The landlord arguing with his runaway wife, the gasman who was afraid of pondweed, the hunchback who recited poetry, his own conversations with Poro. And then… Sorry, who is that?

But no-one said: 'Ooops! You weren't meant to see that.' And he began to watch two odd characters. One was wearing a black camisole with a crocheted Brabant collar and turned-down ginger jackboots, the other was in a sailor's cape and worn out boots. This couple—who so obviously deviated from the Russian standard—were standing by the "Groceries" store, with every intention of entering it.

"Interesting scene," pondered N. "But honestly, if the little windows of that kaleidoscope showed me only what could actually be there, well, that would mean I were in the real world. Art begins with a certain deviation: you see what you don't expect to in those little windows."

Rain came and smudged all the pictures.

"Ah! Impressionism!" said N.

He didn't notice young sergeant Vasily Safonov and his binoculars glinting in the wet bushes just in front of the prickliest barbed wire. Half an hour ago, Captain Merinos had dragged him from his regular evening domino game of 'Kill the Bastard' and ordered him to take up the afore-mentioned position.

"His windows are all lit up," declared the captain, clouding over. "Hope it's not a gathering…"

The sergeant tossed his dominoes on the table, spat, and went to his post, having bargained two days off in exchange.

Had N. seen him there in the bushes with his binoculars, he would not be pondering the finer points of impressionism but of socialist realism. Or should it be surrealism?

8.

The picture turned out to be from the future, from the next day: a man in a camisole and another in a sailor's cape showed up at midday right in front of a small building with a sign "Groceries." They stood in the dusty, sunny street of the small town with the strange name VIL, which turned out to be neither Assyrian nor Aramaic but simply the perpetualisation of the initials of our unforgettable leader, Vladimir Ilyich Lenin. What happened next was repeated over the next few days in all the local shops. The odd couple entered and asked to buy tarpaulin. As much as possible.

In some places they were offered deckchairs, in others – tents, and in some they were told everything Russian shop assistants hardened in verbal battles with consumers should say. The couple listened to all this patiently, bought tents and deckchairs and even rolls of tarp, if they were to hand, and then disappeared with their goods.

Two days later, our very own shop assistant rushed once more to Captain Merinos.

"Foreigners!" she gasped. "Foreigners!"

"Whe-ere?" the ginger Captain ether yawned or hiccoughed, having drunk a lot the day before.

"Here! In our village! They came into the shop, bought a deckchair."

"Tourists, most likely. From the Baltic states, I'll bet," Merinos drawled lazily. "But where did you get deckchairs from?"

"I gave them mine. They kept on at me… and this is what they foisted off on me in exchange."

And a yellow coin with the image of an unpleasant-looking hook-nosed man was soon weighing heavily in the Captain's massive, sweaty, freckled palm.

     

"Gold!" A glimmer of reason finally flickered in Merinos's insipid green eyes. "Found treasure, did they? They should hand it in to the police if they did, they're only due a percentage."

"Gold!" gasped the shop assistant. "I thought it was false."

"Where were they staying? Did they say?"

"Why, no."

"Ok then. Phone round the other shops, find out if they were there. If they weren't, warn them. If they see them, tell them to call the police."

The shop assistant rushed off, all in a tizzy.

"Well, well," sighed Merinos, fully awake at last. And began dialling.

9.

At night the rain powered up, pouring into the blue skies of sleep where tiny ships were scurrying hither and thither. The little boats were not registered in any port, each sailed blithely on, over the ocean, or by the shore, and the shores opened to them.

And the man in the moon looked on approvingly, though many believe him to be a mere splodge. "Maybe he really is a spreading splodge?" Milkiness overflowed into N.'s thoughts. "It's not easy to be forever watching the life of others from your own existence in non-existence."

In the morning the rain, which had paused at dawn, came down again. Uncalled-for August rain. Uncalled-for indeed: it arrived from autumn, summer would not admit it, yet still it seeped in, and everything was soaked: it was damp in the attic, there was nowhere to sit in the garden, and it was chilly even in the house. Autumn? Too early.

N. was lying under two blankets. A small round heater glowed red, alone; midday was approaching, but he didn't feel like getting up.

"Maybe I'm low on inner energy?" he asked himself. "Energetic folk bounce out of bed at 6 am, do some exercises, go off somewhere. Some even go to power…"

But then it occurred to him that it's not so easy to rise to power. Ordinary folk don't. "Power to the People" – just an empty slogan. The people don't need power, ordinary folk don't know what to do with it, they shun it, even fear it. If someone's shouting: "Power to the People!" you can bet they want that power for themselves. What does a revolution boil down to? Swapping one elite for another, sometimes less barefaced or less greedy, which may justify the revolution and similar acts. Folk like me would never get to power, nor even the likes of Poro – they position themselves close by, so that something comes their way, but then they can even pride themselves on not having completely sold their hell-bound selves to the devil. But – there are other types of people…"

N. picked up his notebook, wrote the heading: "Silence" and began listening to that very silence. Then the notebook received the following text:

*"I am lying in bed. Silence. I know my family is in the house. That they love me. There is a cup of hot tea on the bedside table. The phone is there, too. I can ring my friends. Silence. I fall asleep.*

*And find myself in the ocean. Silence. The sun shines tenderly. There is nothing and no-one around. Miles and miles of emptiness. No birds, even. I try to swim, but where to?*

*Summoning my willpower, I wake up. I am lying in bed. My family is in the house, they love me. Silence. I fall asleep. I am in the ocean once again. The dream is relentless now.*

*And one day it all changes. I am in the ocean. Silence. The sun shines tenderly. There is nothing and no-one around. Now, when I close my eyes, I dream of the house, my family, the telephone by the bed. I open my eyes. Miles and miles of emptiness. No birds, even.*

*I spot a huge, white ocean liner on the horizon. It sails proudly by. Distant music, dark specks on the decks – people. I wave, try to swim, but the liner slides away, slowly and inevitably. I remain alone in the silent blue smoothness…"*

10.

Finding a needle in a haystack is not so hard. The police will find it for you; it'll prick them but they'll find it. It's harder to find a straw in a haystack or a needle in a sewing kit, especially if you don't know which needle you are looking for.

The police found a whole handful of gold coins—the shop assistants had brought them right to them—but the people who had handed out those coins? Well, it was as if the ground had swallowed them up.

      

"Where can they be hiding?" This very reasonable thought popped into Captain Merinos's head.

And an attempt at an answer popped into young sergeant Safonov's: "In the house by the river?"

And a visit was paid to the house by the river. Though this time Captain Merinos did not take the ex-'gasman' with him.

At that particular moment, N. was engrossed in a most prosaic activity; he was peeling potatoes. And so he made a rather odd impression when he opened the door, dressed in a checked pinny and brandishing a knife.

"Are you alone here?" asked the captain from the doorstep, eyeing the knife.

"Physically, yes. Metaphysically, I'm not so sure," replied N. watching with fascination as semicircles of sweat spread out from under the armpits of the grey-blue shirt the policeman had only recently donned.

"Physically, metaphysically..." muttered Merinos, thinking to himself 'bloody smart arse.' But aloud he said: "Can I take a look around the house?"

"You can," came the reply, "If it lets you..."

"If who lets me?"

"The house."

"Nutter," thought the captain, and proceeded to stamp his boots through all the rooms which opened themselves to him.

"Hmm, interesting mirrors you have," he said pensively as he came back out on the porch. "There's a lot of crockery, I see, and a lot of clothes in the wardrobes, too... There's no-one else living here?"

"No, no-one," echoed N., realising suddenly that No-one did indeed live there.

But they didn't let him play the role of No-one for long. Merinos suddenly bethought himself on his way out:

"Do you have papers, by the way?"

With a sigh, N. took his tatty passport from the jacket hanging on a nail.

"Aha. Alpheyev Konstantin Borisovich. Hm. Moscow, number... A-huh. Staying long, are you? You'll need a temporary residence permit if so."

"'Til the end of summer."

"Well, summer's nearly over, just a week left."

"Really?" N. was surprised. "Then I'll soon be…"

"Seeing as you'll soon be leaving, I'll overlook the permit…"

And the captain walked right out into the drizzle. On his way back he tried unsuccessfully to banish the image he had glimpsed in the room with mirrors: himself, in his old age, grey, wizened and unloved.

## 11.

The rain welcomed N., too, as he walked out of the house. The house which, at least for a time, had been no home to him, no protector of his anonymity. The rain surprised him by its inevitability, its confidence in its own rectitude.

"I don't know where to go, but the rain does," N. said to the sound of the rain. "The rain trusts its own gravity."

Evening came. Lilac mists rose from the river. It would soon be September. Autumn. Hard to imagine.

"Will that autumn be within me?" N. wondered. "And will I be within that autumn?"

Closing his eyes, N. saw the moon-faced tree of death, glazed in blue rubbery dampness. Its sharp tip pierced the night silver, its branches shed their lustrous leaves patterned with milky veins, its roots ensnared the planet, quivering like an egg in a fowler's pouch. The moon-blue shadows of the tree had long since chilled his skin, in his dreams and in his daydreams.

The rain, tired at last, knocked off. Darkness fell. N. wanted to go back inside but the river smelt of cinders. He decided to take a look. Following the narrow path, his trousers brushing the wet grass aside, he went down to the riverbank.

Fires were burning right on the sand. The yellow flames lit up huge cauldrons. Something was boiling in them, spitting evilly. There was no-one around.

N. approached, covering his face with his collar, and peered gingerly into one of the vats. The liquid was burgundy. Bits of some strong cloth were floating in it. *Sailcloth.*

That evening he opened his notebook and wrote the heading: "The Symphony bids the Conductor Farewell." Nothing more followed, except a symphony of silence. The window called to him. He went, and gazed for a long time at the dark, troubled trees. After a while, writings did appear on that page:

*"Before we leave, we bid farewell to things. They reply, albeit imperceptibly – with the wave of a blade of grass barely glimmering in the moonless night. Things have long since grown accustomed to the inevitability of parting with us. They have grown accustomed to their farewell gestures going unanswered, too. As we leave, let's answer nature's eternal farewell."*

## 12.

In the morning, a sluggish Merinos once again bore down on the telephone, bearlike, stuffing his fat fingers into the dial.

"Alpheyev. Aleksandr, Leonid, Peter… Yes, that's right. He's called Konstantin Borisovich. From Moscow. Run a check, just in case."

They promised to ring back the next day if they found anything. And indeed they did.

"Seems the KGB gang have their eye on your Alpheyev. He's on their books, apparently."

"Really?" Merinos was surprised. "What's he done?"

"I don't know. Anyway, expect visitors."

And the phone rang again almost immediately.

"Faddey Savostyanovich?" his name echoed hollowly in the handset as if it were coming from the toilet. Merinos hated to be called by his name and patronymic; he winced silently. "I'm calling from the Komitet Gosudarstvennoi Bezopasnosti. Which Alpheyev do you have there?"

"He is called Konstantin Borisovich."

"Getting on?"

"Middle-aged."

"What does he look like?"

"He doesn't smile. He can't."

"That's him."

Having received the order to keep vigilant watch over the house by the river's resident, Merinos handed a cape-cum-tent, a sleeping bag and a Primus to sergeant Vaska, who duly signed for them. Safonov was sent to take up position by the barbed wire fence and: keep watch.

"Make sure he doesn't sail away in a rowing boat," fretted the captain.

"He won't sail away from me," Safonov reassured him. "Do I have to keep watch for long?"

"'Til tomorrow. Seems they'll take him off our hands tomorrow."

## 13.

The river burst its banks the next day. Mustering all its might, it flooded the floodplains in the night. Feeding on more rains, in the morning it was already licking the grass by the house. The porch facing the river was soon submerged.

The house had been restless all night. Heavy steps could be heard, voices came from somewhere. It was as though the invisible residents had gathered together, maybe for a counsel, maybe to join forces in some shared task. N. had slept badly. The bed was shaking under him; the whole house was a-shudder, rocked by light tremours. A figure loomed beside his bed.

"Are you Death?" N. asked, only his lips moving, unsure whether he were awake or dreaming.

"I am not Death since I cannot come close to you."

"So I'll wake up, then?"

"You will wake if that is your wish. If not, you will remain in this dream."

"But if you are not Death, who are you?"

"I am Love."

"True. Love can no longer come close to me."

"I am your love for earthly harmony, your acceptance of being. And I am taking my leave of you."

"You're leaving me?"

"No, you are leaving your earthly shell."

"Yes, but what comes next?"

"Next? Whiteness."

And the figure swished the hem of its cloak – and the dream became blindingly white.

     

14.

And yet he wanted to wake up. The rain's drumroll called him… The panes were tearstained once again, and the house seemed to be rocking.

N. walked over to the window. Something warned him: *today*. He was already in that no man's land twixt life, music and literature, which is actually literal, the border between water and dry land in the sea, or rather, neither sea, nor dry land but 12 hours at sea, 12 hours on land, and stones, stones, stones… Water was under the window. Water was under every window. Under the floor. A flood.

"Flee?" N. was on the point of making up his mind when he decided: don't flee. He had coalesced with this house now; he was a house-man now. *Che sarà, sarà.*

The river poured itself out, grew to fill the whole world. The river world replaced all others.

"What if my inner world were to come out and replace the outer one which now reigns?" N. quizzed himself. "Oh, then a mad life would begin! But at least it would be filled with music…"

But even thoughts of music seemed out of place. There was a flood outside, a natural disaster of universal proportions. What would come bursting out? Silence? Cries? Conciliation? If only…

15.

'Don't rule out a prison cell; a begging bowl may come as well,' as the saying goes. But who actually goes to prison? Whoever does not share an abundance of himself with the state. The state abhors emptiness, but it adores abundance, smacking its iron lips with a triple value 'mmm': "For me, too!" And it gets what it asks for – how can you refuse? Naturally, those whose 'self-abundance' has breached the bounds of the solar system are excluded from this law for they, well, they are the state…

Later that morning a black Volga pulled up at the police station. The police were not flooded. The police are unfloodable.

The car rid itself of some stinking exhaust fumes, then of two men in mousey jackets with unmemorable faces. The couple exited the car simultaneously, the doors banged in unison, too. They were simultaneous types.

The corridor proved wide enough for the visitors to walk two abreast. The door to Merinos's office presented some difficulty, but, somehow circumnavigating it smoothly, the coupled flowed into the room. Simultaneously.

"Good day, Faddey Savostyanovich," they cooed in a dovelike duet.

Looking at them askance with one eye, Merinos answered rather fastidiously and with military precision:

"Good health to you."

Actually, these two were, in fact, abundantly healthy.

"How is our charge?" they inquired sweetly.

"He hasn't drowned yet."

The visitors, who had driven here over roads which were wet and muddy but far from flooded, were so taken aback by this reply that they lost their synchronicity for the first time.

"What do you mean?" one asked, just as the other gave a sudden cough.

"Take a look at what's going on here," Merinos said, leading them to the window in the corridor, the one from which young sergeant Safonov so loved to watch his surroundings.

Water could be seen from the window. It began just about twenty paces from the police station and spread out so far that it seemed endless. Safonov had returned an hour ago, soaked to the skin, and announced: the water is flooding everything and has almost reached the level of the barbed wire fence. The young sergeant, now changed into clean and—more importantly—dry clothes, was warming his stiff body by the heater in the far room.

"But the house is still standing?" the visitors asked, their gift of synchronicity restored.

"Yes. There it is."

The distance between the station and the house seemed to have shrunk, swallowed by the watery desert pierced by the odd treetop. Other trees, growing down by the water, were passing themselves off as low shrubs.

"And how do we get there?"

"How? We row," Merinos replied.

   

16.

And a rowing boat was knocking at the window. Or rather, a human hand, stretching out from the boat. The water had already reached the window ledge.

N. woke from his reverie and popped his head out of the top window. A man was sitting in the rowing boat. Poro. Clad in a tarpaulin sailor's jacket, he looked like a conspirator in a play.

"Can I come in?" he asked.

"You'll be able to sail in soon!" N. replied.

"Yes. I'm playing the role of Grandpa Mazay from that Russian poem, the one who used to save hares. I've come for you, actually. Take on the role of one of the hares, if you would, and take a seat in the boat."

"Why?"

"I'll ferry you to a safe place. Certain people have expressed an interest in you."

"Someone is always interested in me."

"You don't understand. They've come from Moscow, just for you."

"Ah, so it's like that…" N. drawled pensively. "In that case, here I am. Let them come, if they're so interested."

"Don't you want to run away?" Poro was amazed.

"There's nowhere to go," N. said calmly. "I can't sail with you to Finland now, can I?"

"No."

"Then there's no point in trying."

"Is that your final word?"

"Yes, my last word."

The rowing boat, which had been moored like a horse, took its lone passenger in once again.

N. stood by the attic window and watched as Poro worked the oars clumsily.

"Wonder where he's headed?" N. was anticipating some entertainment. "Here it is, the moment of truth. Did I misread him? Is he any better than I thought?"

N. picked up the spyglass to check. Slowly but surely, Poro was making his way towards the police station.

# 17.

Ruptures occur in time, in space, and in thoughts. Essentially, our life is a rupture in non-existence. Our journeys are ruptures in the untrodden, and our philosophy, a rupture between the beginning, which is a creative act, and distant consequences. Each one of us is a distant consequence. So is our era. We try to detach ourselves from our era because we don't like it. And we don't like past eras, either. We only like the future, and we don't even want to entertain the thought that it is not our future but someone else's. We feel at home there, in that stranger's future, because, actually, we are never there. Were we to find ourselves there, well, that would be science fiction. If we are living in a former era's future which is in fact our present, then that is called reality. Were we to bid farewell to this present, then who would hinder us constructing some other present for ourselves, within the constraints of our house, our flat, our room, our Diogenes' barrel, keeping the mundane at bay? No, really, who can stop us? Only the mundane itself.

And so N., having first donned his woolly grey sweater just in case, opened the windows on both sides of the house. And the wind whirled out the air of the mundane, left there by recent uninvited guests. It was replaced by a fine drizzle, the smell of sleepy pines and the spice of dank leaves. Two hushed words flew in and took over the whole house: *summer's end.*

# 18.

We don't know what we should do. We were told we should read Tsvetayeva and Nabokov, and so we do. People were only told to listen to Bach one and a half centuries after his death. And we listen to Bach. But they didn't before.

Now we are told we should believe in God. And we believe. Before we were told we should believe not in God, but in the five-year plan, in the guidelines and the moral code for Builders of Communism. And we believed in all that, but also in God, too. Just in case. But God wrote three words in the sky for us: *not every believer.* Without so much as a footnote. The words hung in the sky, but we saw them not. Only the babes and sucklings cried: "Look! Such pretty aeroplane trails!" We finished our important task and looked. But hazy clouds were dissolving in the sky.

Poro was told what he should do. He tried his best, but did not succeed. So he returned with a hurt expression, like a child who has been promised ice-cream but then, at the last moment, is told: when I get paid.

19.

"A man who doesn't know he is a fool is a fool." With this heavy epithet, Merinos stigmatised his messenger when the rowing boat returned, even though it was said in such a way the latter could not hear it. After thinking it over, Merinos decided that the secret was so great it should not be disclosed to anyone.

Now the two Muscovites climbed into the boat, simultaneously, from either side. Young sergeant Vaska climbed in, too, taking the helm. Merinos stood atop a hillock and watched this odd water chase. The shop assistant rushed up, too, to ogle at the strange spectacle. The autumn rain poured down on them mercilessly.

The simultaneous men decided to see where they were sailing to, and simultaneously crowded over to starboard, as a result of which the boat all but capsized. A thought flashed through Merinos's mind:

"No good will come of that plan."

"But then what's so tricky?" he countered. "Just row there and back!"

The boat was already halfway to its goal when something happened: the house, sticking out of the murky waters like an island, gave out the low but unmistakable sound of snapping ropes. And the house lifted in the water, as though an anchor had been raised; it looked even more like a boat now. Caught by the current, it slowly passed between the trees poking out of the water.

"He's mended the boat!" Merinos exclaimed.

"You mean it was a boat?" asked the shop assistant, dumbfounded.

"I don't know. They say it was an old river barge that had lost its nose."

The rowing boat was no longer gaining on the floating house.

"He's getting away!" cried the policeman in despair.

But the house turned out to be unseaworthy. It sat ever lower in the swollen river: it was obviously taking in water. And indeed, water was already at the windows.

"That smart arse had better get himself out of there right now," said Merinos under his breath.

But nothing happened, no-one appeared at the windows. The house slowly sank. Water poured through the windows, and, like a dying beast, the former barge spun on the spot.

"He'll drown!" squealed the shop assistant, distraught. Throwing off her shoes, she waded into the water.

"Stop!" Merinos barely managed to grab her by the arm.

Now nothing was visible above the water; only a whirlpool revealed where the house had gone underwater. The rowing boat pulled up as close as it could, but there was no-one to rescue. Nothing floated to the surface, not so much as a splinter.

Rain poured into the grey water, bewailing the man who had so loved this rivery dampness, this spicy smell of the quiet heart-wrenching rapture which sometimes floods a lonely soul. On the bank, the shop assistant was sobbing, her head in her hands.

20.

The doors opened and in walked a sailor. The genuine article, with ragged clothes and worn out boots. A ray of sunshine sloped in with him.

"Good morning, Captain. We await your orders."

Waking from a deep stupor, N. stared wildly at the man who had come in. Then, pushing him aside, he rushed outside.

N. found himself standing on the deck of a large 3-mast sailing ship. His eyes were dazzled by the blazing sun.

"Three cheers for our Captain! Hip hip, hoorah! Hip hip, hoorah! Hip hip, hoorah!" they cried from the decks. "Greetings, Captain Falkenberg!"

N. looked down at that motley crew dressed in the most outrageous garb.

"Am I the Flying Dutchman?!" he thought. "You're all out of your minds! I'm no captain – I'm a typical house mouse, a bookworm, I can't tell the topgallant sail from the staysail. I do have flying thoughts, though, of course…"

"We've found the fairwater, Captain."

　　　　　　　　

In his black camisole with its embroidered Brabant collar, this fellow looked as though he had been painted by Rembrandt… Surely it can't be Dirk Slothem? Such devotion shines in his eyes…

"The passengers want to see you!" he says, handing the Captain his peaked cap and throwing an orange cape over his shoulders.

21.

Ah, the sun, the sun, I can't see anything for the sun. Who is that on the poop deck? Why, it's… yes, the hunchback, and next to him… Beta! It can't be! And her friend Rina is beside her, with his own long-dead parents. Everyone, everyone on this ship is saved! And in the distance, there is Gamayunov, alive and kicking, smiling his crooked smile, and next to him some quite mythical figures are gleaming with dirty-bronze glints – surely not Wagner, Hamsun and Goebbels? Really, everyone is saved. Maybe that was the plan – to save *everyone*? So that "death in life" would not differ so greatly from life itself? And do I alone captain this ship, or is everything much simpler, and they greet all newcomers by granting them the rank of captain? Where can a ship like this sail? But there will be time for all this later, later…

Paying no heed to his own doubts or the dim figures on the far side of the ship, he threw himself at his loved ones, and remembered nothing more. Meanwhile, the 3-mast ship sailed smoothly into the golden haze and the dark red sails carried it over the water. And the era sailed away on that boat, too, even though glimpses of it could be seen for a long time, behind the trees. Europe's last empire loomed on the horizon – collapsing and rebuilding itself, glass and concrete gnashing. The ship turned its carved female head in that direction, but then took the other tack, and the gigantic grey cubes were left somewhere to one side, while the bowsprit now pierced the very heart of the sun.

A man with a hooked nose stood at the helm in a black cape. He was smiling, too. King Philip the Second, from the old Spanish portrait, once masterfully drawn by the court artist known as Juan Pantoja de la Cruz.

*Moscow, Dublin, 1997–2010*

*Translated from the Russian by Carol Ermakova*

# THE RED CANALS OF MARS, THE AMBER SPOKES OF VENUS

*Notes from the Early Twentieth Century*

From a lofty mountain peak we see a distant star, from the heights in far off lands we see our native shores. Gazing into the unseen is not wearisome, gazing with the aid of mechanical devices piques our curiosity, yet a glance into the mirror brings us back into our nauseatingly familiar reflected world.

From here, from this microstate of San Marino, Italy seemed a boundless mega-land. The air there kept me afloat, not because of its density, but, on the contrary, because of its rarefication. A true holiday for my asthmatic lungs…

A certain Professor Percival was staying at the same hotel as I was. A philosopher and a naturalist, he existed within the aura of his own unusual astronomic theories, and this aura preceded him like a small but elegant cloud. Percival was approaching sixty, streaks of grey had confidently captured his coiffure, but his moustache stood proud like ears of wheat in a windless field; or maybe despite the wind. His eyes looked out trustingly, even guiltily – was he ashamed of his knowledge? Was he a modest man? Well, he was obviously a high society man, a man of the world – in the sense that the world in its entirety  lived in him, and not the other way around.

I was introduced to him. I didn't ask where he was from; he spoke English with an American accent which gave him away as a native of New England.

The professor was in the early stages of scientific enthusiasm – a trait particular to all those who come to the exact sciences from another discipline: he had trained as a social anthropologist. Musings about the cognoscibility of the world—or even of other worlds—would occasionally trickle down from his little cloud.

"Riddles have a nice, untroubled life in this world, Professor. Better than people," I told him.

"Well, we sometimes trouble them," Percival smiled. "Riddles stir up our imagination."

"And imagination is the mother of new riddles," I said with a shrug.

The sun's rays folded themselves into a little prism-house. Something ungainly, like a tongue-twister, could be read in its windows: from crucial to excruciating, from vital to vile, from meticulous to metaphysical. The spiral of perception laid out its loops, as in a shop front, improper and imperishable.

Meanwhile, the professor switched topics with the agility of a leaping grasshopper.

"We should build an observatory here," he announced. "There is an unparalleled view of Venus from up here. Mars is best observed from the Arizona desert. And that's precisely what I was doing last year..."

 "Build an observatory? Where?"

"On Monte Titano. The higher the better."

He fell silent. For two days.

Then his verbal spring gushed forth once more, and there followed a second attempt to spark my interest. Cozying up to me at dinner, the professor announced:

"I must confess something to you. I have already set up a makeshift observatory. In the old fortress on the hilltop... Well, they call it a mountain here... The facility is no great shakes of course, but it's better than nothing. I have set up a telescope there. Tomorrow Mars will go into opposition. I can take you with me, if you like."

"Yes, that would be intriguing," I replied.

"By the way, you can help me with the telescope. It's rather complicated to set up, a second pair of hands always comes in handy."

I examined San Marino's medieval architecture that day, and it examined me. In the evening the professor delicately clawed at my door.

"Time to set off."

Since I had already completed several mountaineering expeditions in the Apennines that year, my equipment was at the ready. But to head into the mountains in the dark – well, there was something oddly unnecessary about that.

However, the professor announced no equipment would be needed since we would be following a path as wide as a farm track most of the way. He fetched two powerful torches from his room.

"They may come in handy up there," he said. "Though the brightest nightlight has already been lit, of course – the moon!"

Indeed, the moon was full. She led herself along the long lane out of the town into the darkness, into the bushes' dark clouds. The quiet evening noiselessly crooned the lingering strains of an Italian ballad. The smell of strong tobacco and cheap food dogged us like a nagging companion.

The hotel completed the town and, from there, a stream spun itself out into the valley. The moon turned the olive branches silver and poured her whiteness into the stream. The path rolled itself into a ball, unravelled itself again, rolled under some bushes and imperceptibly rolled out onto the foot of a low mountain.

We were walking straight up to the moon herself, but she was running away from us, darting behind trees, silvering our hair. Ah, now we were already high up. The path, previously as broad as a country lane, narrowed; somewhere there, above our heads, the summit hung.

When he came level with a huge boulder split off from the cliff and blocking the road, its jagged point jabbing skywards, the professor stopped.

"Seems there has been a landslide here. Not long ago," he remarked. "We'll have to go around."

A few trees grew by the boulder, ringed by some brushwood. The professor pushed a branch aside and disappeared; but he reappeared again in next to no time.

"It's fine, there's a way through."

A cavern yawned open beyond the brushwood. We strode ahead, the torches lighting our way. We were trying not to make a sound as even an echo could call down another landslide. At last the moonlight shone out in the distance.

We emerged from the cavern and stopped. The mountain's slope seemed lifeless over here. The professor informed me there was no other way to reach this place and that he himself had only been here once.

"You can get to the old fortress from this side, too. Let's go up. But don't stray off the path."

The path was quite narrow, the light from the torches grew ever more feeble, and I was already regretting Percival had roped me into this. We were still clambering up the slope when the professor suddenly stopped me.

"There's a mountain lake below us. Well worth a look," he said, sounding like an Italian *cicerone*.

The cloud which had temporarily hidden the moon was drowning in the lake's dark waters. The surface was perfectly smooth, unruffled.

And finally, here she is! The moon came out in all her glory, glanced at the lake, preened herself in its mirror and then hid herself in the cloud again as it swam up.

"The summit is beyond that crag," said the professor, finally coming to and remembering the reason behind our nocturnal promenade.

The mountain, Monte Titano, had several summits; this one was flattish, and not the highest. Above the summit's sandy yellow hat loomed the fortress, not so imposing as the famous Guaita, but quite grand nevertheless. Percival unlocked the unpainted door.

Cold, dank air threw itself at us as though it had long been gathering its strength, readying itself for this moment. The telescope turned out to be relatively small. We uncovered it and wheeled it over to the inner courtyard.

"I had wanted to bring better equipment here, but I didn't have time for it. The landslide could be dismantled, by the way, or even blown up if need be, and then the track would be passable again."

The evening generously poured its cool, airy streams down from on high, holding nothing back, but it was easier to breathe outside than in the crypt-like air of the fortress. The telescope's shaft was soon straining skywards and the professor plumped himself down on the metal seat. Having fiddled with the telescope for a long time, he finally pulled a notebook from his pocket and set about painstakingly drawing what he saw.

"Hmm, they change their contours each time, but the structure is always the same," he muttered. "Must depend on the angle you view them from…"

  

Then, finally, he lowered himself down to my level and began to explain:

"I'm talking about the canals on Mars, the ones which Schiaparelli described all those years back. I'm trying to map them ..."

Some fireflies arrived and created their own map of the universe, a constantly shifting world swaying with a mysteriously phosphorescent green glow.

The drawing complete, the professor leant back with a flop, all but losing his balance.

"Would you like to take a peek at Mars?" he asked me.

I did not need to be asked twice; in the blink of a few swift movements I was already peering into the oblique cloud.

"Adjust the focus with this screw here..." came the advice.

And everything became clear. A reddish, cloudy ball floated into the viewfinder, its dark streaks faintly discernible.

"Can you see the canals?" the professor asked impatiently.

"I can see some kind of lines..."

"Here, take this sheet of paper. Draw. Then we'll compare."

I transferred what I saw onto the sheet of paper.

Percival took both sketches, gazed at them for a few moments, shook his head in amazement and asked:

"Did you really see what you have depicted here?"

I nodded.

"Take a look for yourself," he said, handing me the sketches.

They bore some resemblance to each other, but the lines connected at different angles, and the alignment within the viewfinder was different, too.

"Mmm, strange, most strange... I would like to keep your drawing, if I may, I need to mull it over... I'm planning to publish an atlas of Martian canals."

I didn't object, but now I in my turn had a request: would he show me Venus? A spider-like web of lines was visible on her amber sphere, too, reminiscent of some elaborate hieroglyph. Were these canals, too?

"Yes, the structure is similar," said the professor. "It all has to be studied. That's why it's essential to build an observatory."

I don't know what became of that project since I returned to Rome the following day.

But the professor did indeed publish an atlas – I came across it six months later lying on an optician's table in Rome. I had paid the optician a visit to replace a cracked lens in my glasses. He was an Italian who had practised in London at some point and acquired a passable knowledge of English.

"What do you make of this?" I asked him, pointing at the book.

"Very interesting. Now everyone will start writing about the ancient Martian civilisation."

"And do you believe it existed?"

"I believe one thing: I believe Percival did indeed see what he drew."

"So it's true, then?"

"That's not what I said."

"But if he observed it…"

"The question is: what did he really observe?"

I told him that I myself had recently looked down Percival's telescope, but had seen a somewhat different network of canals.

"Precisely!" said the optician. "It all depends on the observer."

"But what about objective reality?!"

"Well, of course, objective reality exists. But the question is, how can one distinguish the objective from the subjective? Or in other words, distinguish what the observer sees from what really exists? Percival used a twenty-four inch telescope. In his book he writes that he made his best observations of Venus' network of spokes when the ocular aperture was less than half a millimetre. Do you know what that reminded me of? We opticians use that adjustment when we study the characteristics of a patient's eye, or the pattern of the blood vessels on the retina: with a narrow ocular aperture, the shadows of the blood vessels become visible."

"You mean…"

"No, no, I don't mean anything. I just gave you the facts, you can draw your conclusions yourself."

I sat on a bench in the park by Piazza Vittorio Emanuele opposite a picturesque ruin. The children on the neighbouring bench were diligently licking *gelato*, not forgetting to leave their mark on the sound palette of that pre-evening hour, too. My thoughts ran thus: could it be that Percival had been studying shadows cast by the blood vessels in his very own eyes for all those years, supposing they were canals on Mars and Venus? All those sketches, the atlas of the two 'planets'... nothing but a celebration of wasted labour... Even if he himself realised what had happened, he would banish the thought, just as we banish the thought of death. But what will the next generation think of him? What will be said of his labours at the voiceless court of time where the future is our arrogant prosecutor and the past our timid, absent-minded public defender? Besides, aren't we all sent to fetch time from somewhere or other sooner or later? And so we go in search of it, scooping up as much as we can carry, only to lose it along the way as it slips from our watches like plums plopping through a net bag. "The quest of your life..."

And what if we try to find some higher meaning to this tale? Well, what is there to be found? Nothing, except, of course, the blatantly obvious: no matter what we look at, we are always looking inside ourselves.

# A SYMPHONY'S FAREWELL

Voices past and future live in our heads. But they feel cramped there, uncomfortable. Their restlessness gives rise to a wind whistling in our ears. You can peer inside someone's head through his eyes, and you will see the blackness of the pupils, a blackness you sink into never to resurface, a blackness in which you hear only these voices which no-one else can hear. What I am seeing, what I am hearing now—before the concert—is tantamount to nothing.

Is it mine, this silence, or did someone bring it with him? A thick silence, not so much as a cough. Well, I suppose one could cough professionally: inhale the Berlin dampness, then, holding one's breath, take one's seat in the concert hall and triumphantly let rip that throaty eruption to be recorded for posterity, engraved in the gramophone's vinyl. These almost professional coughers only appear in autumn or spring; in summer they disappear into the depths of some soundproof cocoon, maybe a mental one.

A little light shines over each music stand. Hintermayr has done his best. Having invited the electricians, now, most likely, he feels like the Creator in one of Blake's etchings. That's how it's done in America, or so they say, for the orchestra's comfort. And what else goes on in America? Hmm, who knows.

*What do you remember about your childhood? Was music important to you then? Why did you take up conducting? Was it by chance? Was your success also mere chance? What do you remember about trains, cars, and steamers? What do you remember about America? Skyscrapers, yellow taxi cabs, ice creams, screams on the streets, wealth, destitution, concert halls, more concert halls, people unable or unwilling to speak English… Do you remember all this?*

Bruno Walter is somewhere there now, or maybe he is touring "the rest of the world." There are two realities: us, and the rest of the world, and these two are at loggerheads. "We" spread over the country, ant-like, and the country instantly became black-shirted, military, in our wake. One intimate rogue even wrote in the papers, in his own name, that he, Wilhelm Furtwängler, would never agree to conduct an American orchestra, and out there, in that other reality, they believed him. Actually, of course, "we" kept him for "ourselves;" his passport has long since been confiscated… If those in that other reality only knew what an empire really is, not to mention the kind of people who represent it – like that Goebbels for instance, the man with sweaty hands. Well, they can imagine it, I suppose…

*What first springs to mind when you think of the thirties? Peaked caps? Hatbands? Shards of glass on the streets? Endless protest letters or letters pleading for someone or other, letters that never helped? Shaking hands, then wiping those same hands off on a handkerchief… You haven't forgotten all this, have you? Do you associate Germany with Nazism or would you say this is a "marriage of coincidence"?*

Yesterday has slipped imperceptibly into today, and now another reality is rejecting not only the collective "we" but also the thoroughly individual "I." And not piecemeal but wholesale. Now we can merely comfort ourselves with recordings, then put our hope in radio waves and music's journey through the air. The true voice is not *his master's voice,* so, hopefully, it will be heard, since "the rest of the world" is already weary of political hollering. That hollering, by the way, comes from another life, as do those politics, but music, well, music is from this life, and there are already listeners, listeners with whom we can communicate wordlessly about humanness and its preservation, especially if one doesn't feel like talking about Ubuntu. Today, 21ˢᵗ June, 1942, is a day dedicated to Brahms's Fourth Symphony. His last one.

*Would you say that you attained perfection in your art? Do you consider other conductors as rivals? What can you say about your sense of time and space?*

Little spots of light burning in the orchestra, valiantly living their own lives. The public does not see them as they push their way through the darkness, but the conductor cannot escape them, although he, in his turn, does not see the public, just senses them behind his back, the back into which all eyes are burning. Something unusual hangs in the air. Is it connected with those little lights, perhaps? Hintermayr has conjured up a Viennese carnival in this Berlin hall. Austrians excel at gimmicks… Haydn once pulled a stunt with candles: a candle burned on each musician's stand, until, one by one, the players blew them all out and left. "Farewell Symphony"… And to what, one may wonder, was Haydn bidding farewell? To his Kapellmeister's stipend? After this symphony, he wrote another fifty-nine. Brahms, on the other hand, wrote but four, of which this was the last. He couldn't write symphonies after this one. "Farewell…"

*Do you like Brahms? Do you like German music, even after it became shameful to be German? Do you like your soul which is trapped in the tight cage of your chest? Would you like to set it free? What is freedom?*

The first movement. *Allegro non troppo.* Not too fast. Everything begins by itself. A symphony without an introduction. The violins play in octaves, the violas and cellos accompany them with arpeggios, the woodwinds follow with thirds. You just have to gather it all together, hold it on the tip of your baton… But outside, beyond the window, newspaper birds flap in the wind; Berlin is in E minor. Germany is in E minor. And when one country is in the minor key, the whole world is, too; after all, what is there left to rejoice over? Unless, of course, you rejoice over your own neighbour's descent into madness.

*List the objects which surrounded you over the last few years. Tables and chairs, chests and cupboards, shirts and tails, music stands and conductors' daises… It is all coming back to you now, isn't it? Do you perceive the conductor's baton as a phallic symbol? Why do you move your hand in such a strange way while conducting? Was your fall while skiing a mere accident, as a result of which you were unable to conduct at the Nazi convention? They say you damaged your wrist badly…*

Sollertinsky said of this symphony: from elegy to tragedy. But where is the elegy here? Drama reveals itself right from the very beginning, tragedy, too. While Germany, on the other hand, introduces herself to squabbles and wars. Thirty-three was the year of the black-shirts, and as early as the following spring a certain envoy was dispatched, white-shirted and clean-shaven, like a little piglet – doctor Goebbels requests that Jewish music should not be played at concerts: Mahler, Mendelssohn, Hindemith. The white-shirted one came, decreed, and went, and so it was: the concerts were filled with German music: Mahler, Mendelssohn, Hindemith. Later they were banned nonetheless, after which certain musically naive souls inquired as to why he was dismissed. Why this why? Officially, the Music Director General ceased to be the Music Director, and the chill aureole of freedom hovered about his countenance, unseen yet perceived. And illusory, of course. Brahms' fanfares, the fanfare theme before the development…

*How did you feel when you heard the fanfares at the Nazi parades? Did your attitude toward Wagner change for the worse after his music became a symbol for the Third Reich? How do you understand Germany's cultural policy of that time? What does culture mean to you?*

Mahler and Hindemith are not in the repertoire, neither are there any Jews in the orchestra's ranks. Everyone boasts a high pedigree, pure blood. As concert master Shimon Goldberg said as early as 1934: "Germany must suffer for her future heydays…" He could have been talking about himself… He interceded for Goldberg, as he did for the whole orchestra: for the flautist Hannah Liebermann, the violinist Vogelssohn, the trumpeter Sachsenstein… In vain. Goldberg fled the country, the rest are in the camps, if they are still alive. Many cultural institutions are being trimmed that way. By some miracle an agreement was made with Goebbels and he granted special status to the members of the orchestra, including those who were part Jewish. Those in the main orchestra of the Third Reich were left untouched, but as for the Vienna Philharmonic Orchestra, well, they were subject to cruel cleansing. Of course, the newly freed places were soon filled by other musicians. Someone with the right papers always turns up, but the papers are the only thing right about them…

*Did you tolerate anti-Semitic remarks? Have you ever had relations with a non-Aryan woman? What type of woman suits you best? What foods do you prefer? Do you derive pleasure from satisfying your physiological needs?*

Reprise. Theme in E minor, taken from the chorale *Mein Jesu*... Wait, someone is coughing after all, though not with all their animal-throated might. It is already the coda, tragedy. Violin voices cast asunder, a whirlwind and the beat of the kettle drums. It's over, the end of the first movement. Why has it suddenly grown so dark in the hall?

But there is no time to think of that, it's time for the *Andante*. An ancient ballad, Phrygian harmony. Brahms' most Schubertian music, *pizzicato*, like the "Unfinished Symphony." And like the German countryside, space, and echoes fading into the sky. Evil always comes from people, and it has a face, but this countryside is remarkably unremarkable and faceless. Eichendorff could only dream that "the sky quietly kissed the earth" while they, these furtive kissers, always blushed under the people's unfriendly gaze...

*Are you religious? When did you last go to church? Do you speak with God when you conduct Bach's cantatas? What, in your opinion, does God make of Germany today? And past Germany? Will Germany be possible in the future, or will it be some other human conglomerate based on some other idea?*

Brahms heard the kettle drums of fate when he wrote his fourth symphony. In Steiermark, in the summer of 1884. He read Sophocles, contemplated his surroundings, and penned the kettle drum part. Was it thunder, or a volley of canon fire? A man-made and indelible part of world order... Nature, on her part, contemplates the tragedy of existence from the sidelines; and you, well, you rarely see her but from the sidelines: tours, concert halls, nothing else...

*Is domestic comfort important to you? What do you consider 'home'? Your house, your town, or your country? Why do you dislike conversing with others? What is it you mutter to yourself while you are conducting rehearsals? Why is it that many would say you are incapable of expressing yourself articulately?*

There it is: the sun. Blindingly real, brightly clad. The third movement, *scherzo*. A folk fest, the complete opposite of contemplance. Now they are saying: *Kraft durch Freude*, strength through joy... Brahms would have expressed himself like a peasant on this point, unprintably. Whereas these folk, these simpletons, made a forced celebration for some and a life-negating one for others. That's what happens when Germans forget about contemplance and *mein Jesu*. Germans should not be forgetful. No nation should be forgetful. Yet they all are…

*Have you ever suffered from nausea? From indigestion? What does 'health' mean to you – your own personal health, and that of the nation? Are all happy nations healthy, and is a healthy nation happy?*

How dare he, that swine Schmalfuss? Who gave him permission to don a black jacket with SS lightning instead of a tailcoat? The little bulb is burning, the trumpet glints golden in its light, swanking. And then there are those… hatbands. Yes, they found a replacement for Sachsenstein, put this SS chap with "the youth's magic horn" in the orchestra! There's another one, too, the kettle drummer. He's even sporting his SS cap. Who is going mad, me or non-me? And it is so dark in the hall… *Scherzo* resounds in the gloom, the little lamps burn star-like over the music stands…

*Do you consider the world a three-dimensional space with the addition of a fourth—time—or do you believe in other dimensions? Do you agree with the definition of life's perspective as the art of extrapolating long-abandoned spaces over the plane of memory as it disappears beyond the horizon?*

The finale. Passacaglia. Seven paces, the door creaks. Death enters for a celebration of itself. Thirty-two variations on a theme from Bach's cantata, and Death has just as many faces. A circle dance of masks, a vortex of inanimate animas. A person approaches death, but death comes to a country itself, having set the date long ago. And now Death has come to Germany; after all, they haven't taken her name away yet, the country is still called Germany. Death has come now, with the newspaper ink splatters still fresh after the victory at Kharkov. Death rolls in, armadas of tanks rolling over yellow fields. And thus the frightening, hitherto unknown words are born: Stalingrad, Kursk. The circle is closed. The circle dance of ever-spiralling disasters spins on blithely, but the violins are already begging it to stop.

Everything stops. The plaintive strain of the flutes. Ah, how Hannah Liebermann would have played this...! But look, she *is* playing! And Sachsenstein echoes her on the trumpet, while Goldberg and Vogelssohn hold their violins on their knees: a pause for the violins. Where have they come from? Pale faces, little lights, have starred themselves into the hall's gloom. The French horns softly echo the dying melody. An orchestra of ghosts...

*They say you lived your whole life inside yourself. How was it? Was it an ordinary, quiet life, or something else? Did you often venture out from your invisible casing, and if so, how long was it before you longed to return?*

The whirlwind is set a-spin once again. Chaos, horror, starvation, destruction, hopelessness. The walls of the concert hall crumble under the bombs, the wind bursts in, uninvited, and Berlin's autumn rain, seasoned with cemetery spices, patters onto the public through the celestial sieve.

Seven notes affix the seventh seal. *Es muss sein,* thus shall it be, even if it shall not be thus, and the primordial ashes shall surely rise once more. But as to precisely when and what shall arise from those ashes, well, you'd better ask the ash. But now the symphony is without a conductor, and Germany, too, is without a conductor. But really, who needs the notion of a conductor, and why? If ideas die, they all die together, and not one can be saved...

Applause? Yes, applause. Why?

The lights go on. Everything is Aryan clean, white-shirted, black coat-tailed. The uncanny sensation that everything is in order, even if it is far from being in order. If anyone understood anything they would keep mum, be they the silent sphinx or the Great Inquisitor who loves to ask questions while putting a question to him is quite a hopeless matter. The concert master shakes a hand, all but tearing it off...

*Have you ever dreamt you died? That the world ended, stopped, and that from that moment on everything would be as before, no matter what had happened, or that everything would simply cease to be? Have you ever dreamt you are the last person on the last inhabited planet?*

     

It's not raining outside. There are no bombs either, of course. The evening, soft and warm, sidles up for a kiss. As you make your way through the scent of flowering lindens, you ask yourself the eternal question: why? Why this? Why that? Why God knows what? Why am I here? Why am I asking myself these questions? And who will ask the questions afterwards?

*Did you ever wonder what might have happened if you had been born American, French, or Polish? What would you have done with your life? Would you have become a conductor?*

Home. Elizabet, the wife; conversations about the cousin from Dresden, about her little Spitzi, whether to inoculate him or not, dogs are such sensitive creatures, we don't know what to do, poor thing... In one ear and out the other, in and out into the expanse beyond ears, where the fluff of conversations settles windlessly in the depths. Why is she worrying about dogs?! Who cares about dogs? People will soon be worse off. Beyond earshot, beyond earshot... How can one emigrate to that land beyond earshot? The border is crossed with a password, and that password is 'inoculation.' The same word that has got stuck and is sticking out from somewhere beyond earshot. Why this? Why that? Why god knows what? Why the past, why the future, and why don't we want to know what that future will be like? We don't even ask after the present because the reply is already pricking us in the back, or below the back. And the answer... yes, there it is again: *inoculation...*

Wilhelm Furtwängler lived another twelve years. After the war came the court case, accusations of collaborating with the Nazis, acquittal, concerts, more concerts. He avoided Brahms's fourth symphony, though he did include it in the programme on one occasion: a gramophone company convinced him to record it on vinyl. It was 1948, six years had passed since that memorable concert, and he was once again conducting the Berlin Philharmonic Orchestra. The walls of the hall were folding in on him, opening and closing like a book. Then they metamorphosed and became the corridors of his memory, pushing him back into that day when the ancient folds of time parted for a few brief seconds. But a spell only works once, and never again would he attain his 1942 breakthrough.

# BROTHERS IN PENS

1.

While the grass always seems greener on the other side, just remember – when you get to the other side, you may find yourself in the Land Unknown where visitors may be inclined to do things they had never thought of doing. The Other Side may even send you an invitation, a glossy, colourful one. How can you possibly turn it down if your eyes are glued to it?

The writer Swidersky's eyes were glued to a photograph of Lake Geneva. And quite out of the blue, he received an invitation to spend a couple of weeks in a writers' retreat right there in Switzerland. That trip might turn into a kind of diversion, or rather, a distraction from his regular humdrum émigré life in Frankfurt.

He had once translated some poems by a Scottish poetess. They had kept in sporadic email contact, and she had recommended him to the people who ran the house for writers in a small town between Geneva and Lausanne. According to the will of its previous owner, a German publisher, it was given over to writers from all around the world and provided them with a conducive place to work for two weeks every summer.

"Why shouldn't I go along?" Swidersky thought. "It would be no bad thing to spend some time with my brothers in pens."

His plane landed in Geneva. He wandered around the clock-face of this city for a couple of hours, a city where time ticks and tocks and brushes the roofs of the buildings with its invisible golden hands, and then he took a tiny train to the small town of his destination.

'I'm Russian, you know,' said the resplendent housekeeper in poor English. 'My surname is Konobeeff. My grandfather was—how do you say?—White Guard?'

The writer nodded.

'So you and I are both Russian people.' And with that the housekeeper ended her speech.

'I'm afraid I must disappoint you,' said Swidersky with a disarming smile. 'I am a Russian writer, that is true, but it is also true that I don't have a drop of Russian blood.'

The resplendent housekeeper was a little put out.

'Well, never mind,' she said at last. 'Come with me, I'll show you your room. By the way, I live here over there, in that wing of the building. I have a separate entrance.'

They bumped into a shabby-looking woman in the corridor. She was dressed in a grubby, variegated pinafore dress and had sandals on her otherwise bare feet. Oddly enough, her head was wrapped in a waffle towel.

"The cook," Swidersky thought. "She looks busy, probably making lunch."

But Madame Konobeeff gave one of her resplendent smiles and said:

'And here is our first guest. Let me introduce you. This is Madame Alexandra Berkutova, a prose writer from Prague. And this is Monsieur Sviderski from Moscow.'

The prose writer from Prague muttered something incomprehensible or even untranslatable in a French-like tone, after which she headed off into the kitchen without waiting for a reply.

2.

He was introduced to the other guests over lunch.

'We've just been discussing our family backgrounds and have come to the conclusion that we are all Jews,' the writers sitting on the veranda put him in the picture.

'Both my grandmothers were Jewish,' said Swidersky. 'One was from Poland, the other from Germany.'

'There you are, you see,' said an elderly gentleman. 'And my family comes from Ukraine. My father's surname was Katznelson... Oh, I forgot to introduce myself. I'm Gordon Ellenson from Toronto. I live in the USA, in Minnesota, and teach in the local university there.'

A woman with a shrewd face was sitting opposite Ellenson, and Swidersky could only see her profile, but he was sure he had seen that medallion-like profile somewhere on the Internet.

'I'm Lana Freund,' she said. 'From Capetown, currently living in San Francisco. My parents were German Jews.'

'One of my grandmothers was Jewish, too,' said Madame Berkutova, suddenly joining the conversation, and disclosing to the world that she spoke English, too, all be it with a monstrous accent.

The bandage had disappeared from around her head, and enormous tractor-wheel spectacles with orange lenses had appeared instead.

When lunch was over, she began again, having evidently forgotten what she had said earlier:

'Both my grandmothers were Jewish.'

Swidersky realised that since she obviously had grandfathers as well as grandmothers, the conversation would soon turn to them, and this in turn would completely change her ethnicity from what was stated in her passport. So he asked a question he deemed more neutral:

'Are those sunglasses you are wearing?'

The Swiss sun itself was tired of sultriness and was about to take off into the valley, along the little stream and over the bridge, and then find somewhere to lie quietly in the shade.

'My doctor told me to wear these glasses,' said Madame from Prague sternly. 'Otherwise everyone looks nasty to me and I see the world as a repulsive hole.'

A thin, black-haired young woman was sitting at the end of the table; she looked more Jewish than anyone else. But she didn't lay claims to any genetic background.

'Ines doesn't speak English,' said Lana Freund. 'Let me introduce you. This is Ines de la Vega from Bolivia. She lives in France, in Besançon.'

Ines de la Vega gave a frank, heartfelt and purely Jewish smile.

3.

That evening Swidersky stayed up late watching television. They were showing Wimbledon on the Eurosport channel, and he amused himself by following the psychological trials and tribulations of the five sets match. The match finally petered out soon after midnight and the writer went into the kitchen to have his usual bedtime glass of yoghurt. There was a suspicious commotion coming from the corner of the poorly-lit kitchen.

"A rat? Or maybe several?" thought Swidersky alarmed, and began looking around for something to defend himself with. When his groping fingers finally found the light switch, it turned out not to be a rat but Madam Berkutova, who at that very moment was pulling a bottle of Finnish vodka from the depths of a cupboard, and looking very pleased with herself.

'This is exactly what I needed!' she mumbled to herself in Russian, and then, noticing Swidersky, she went on in English. 'Oh, excuse my attire. I didn't think I would meet anyone down here, especially not a man.'

And it was only then that the writer noticed she was wearing a none-too-clean gown of rough, unhemmed canvas which he supposed the lady used as a nightgown.

'Well, it's been a long time since I turned any man's head. Not since I turned fifty,' she went on. 'I was even married once, to someone from Ukraine. He needed a passport in order to live in Prague, and I needed money, so it seemed like a good deal, but once he'd got his passport he swore at me and disappeared. The money didn't last long, either.'

The bottle of Finnish vodka in her hands glistened knowingly and dark blue sparks winked deep within it.

4.

In the morning the sun began its work very conscientiously, and the writers hid in the shade. Madame Berkutova was the only one to spread herself out on a white plastic chaise longue and copiously smear a greasy liquid over every part of her physical mass which was not covered by her scanty swimsuit patterned like an Uzbek dress. The famous orange spectacles covered half her face.

Swidersky helped himself to one of the bicycles and went careering off down the narrow road. Little villages were strung along it like grapes. When a meadow with huge trees laden with cherries raced to meet him, our cyclist realised it was time to take a break.

Half an hour later he had assiduously washed his cherry-blue hands and lips at a friendly wayside fountain.

Far below him lay Lake Geneva, leisurely unfolding like a gigantic fan decorated with reflections of clouds and blue sky before those sunning themselves on the beaches. The purple Alps towered above the far bank, and Swidersky thought he could make out the famous Mont Blanc.

The way back was difficult at times, torturous at others. If his bicycle had been even slightly worse, the forty-year-old writer would not have managed the last stretch at all.

'Not many of our cyclists ride up the mountain,' said Madame Konobeeff. 'They usually walk, pushing the bike.'

5.

The food was indeed excellent. The chefs were not professional, but amateurs, and so they put their heart into whatever they did.

Swidersky's main course was served on a separate plate, as he had warned them in advance that he was allergic to onions and garlic.

'Allergic?' said Madame Berkutova. 'You're not allergic to anything, you're just being fussy.'

'I wish that were so,' said Swidersky diplomatically. 'But alas...'

'Allergies are nothing but stuff and nonsense,' Madame Bertukova went on mercilessly. 'What makes you think such a disease even exists? I can tell you for sure: there is no such thing as an allergy.'

'I respect your opinion, but I am afraid you stand alone against the scientific consensus of the whole world.'

'Huh, science! Those scientists say one thing today and another tomorrow. You can't believe a word they say!'

"Such callous ideas and she calls herself a *writer*?" thought Swidersky. "What sort of reasoned, kind and eternal truths can that ignorant, cantankerous fishwife plant in her novels?"

6.

The evening was given over to football. It was the European Championship. The Bolivian poetess delicately and unobtrusively rooted for every team that played against Spain, usually from the office room, which was next to the sitting-room. She would sit and hammer out copious emails to her French fiancé. Mr. Ellenson and Madame Berkutova, on the other hand, spent hours in front of the television, with an ever-present bottle of Finnish vodka gleaming blue on the coffee table between them.

Ellenson usually dozed in the corner of the sofa; he only woke up when something exceptional happened on the TV, such as when someone scored a goal or missed a penalty. Then he would let out a wild yell: "Thrash 'em, the sons of bitches!" and return to his familiar valley of sleep. Who those mysterious "sons of bitches" were remained a mystery to everyone else...

Madame Berkutova furiously supported the Czechs and booed the Russians. And as if that weren't enough, she did her best to persuade everyone else to support the Czechs, too.

When a small child demonstrates some particular whim, the rest of the family indulges him. As the difficult child of the family of writers, Madame Berkutova desperately needed to be indulged, and the old-fashioned house was filled with writers' whoops.

Lana Freund appeared from somewhere upstairs. She loathed football and everything to do with it. She looked at the screen for precisely a minute and a half, gave a disgusted frown and asked:

'What are you all doing here?'

'We're supporting the Czechs,' said Ellenson, just awake after a doze. 'Collectively.'

'Collectively? Really? Well go on then,' and Lana Freund went off into the vast expanse of her next novel.

As for Swidersky, he was watching the football with interest but did not contribute to the multi-coloured cacophony.

The Czech Republic were playing Germany, and had just scored a goal.

'That was a great goal!' squealed Madame Berkutova. 'Wow, what a goal!'

'It was just a run-of-the-mill header from the corner. A standard goal,' said Swidersky, who had played football himself as a young man.

That was his fatal mistake.

'Standard?' said Madame Berkutova venomously. 'So you think Russian goals are better, do you? Funny how we don't see that many of them.'

'It's nothing to do with the nationality of the goals; it's about their quality,' Swidersky was about to explain. 'Personally, I love unusual, memorable goals.'

But to no avail. Madame Berkutova never bothered herself with the finer points, not even when she was writing her novels for women. And in this case, even the god of the Czechs himself prohibited going into the finer points.

'You simply don't like our country or our people,' she said, winding herself up.

'If I were you I wouldn't be in such a rush to draw such rash conclusions,' Swidersky said. 'I can assure you, I am equally unbiased towards all nations.'

But Madame Berkutova only heard what she wanted to and her malicious grin became the spitting image of one of Notre Dame's gargoyles.

7.

The next morning, drizzle slid off the roof tops and dripped the trees.

Madame Berkutova did the rounds of the writers looking lost and asking everyone if they knew anything about computers. She'd dropped her laptop and couldn't switch it on.

No-one wanted to have anything to do with this lady, so they all said: no, sorry, I'm clueless about laptops. Yet each of them had brought a nice new laptop with them and installed it in their room.

It was Swidersky's turn. He felt sorry for this odd lady and decided to help her.

The rather battered-looking Toshiba started up without any trouble.

'The menu didn't appear properly when I switched it on this morning.'

'What happened to it?'

'I dropped it this morning. My hands were trembling.'

Swidersky didn't bother to enquire as to the cause of this mysterious trembling.

'Can you go into "My Computer" and select the control panel?' he said. 'Otherwise it's all in Czech and I can't understand anything.'

Everything seemed normal.

'Seems to be working OK,' said Swidersky thoughtfully. 'You should be more careful with it.'

'Yo, yo,' agreed Madame Berkutova.

She spoke eight languages, all equally badly. But it was anyone's guess just which of those languages would have claimed that mysterious "yo, yo".

At lunch they found out that the ill-starred Berkutovian laptop was no longer working.

'I'll write in a notebook,' she said, with a face like the explorer Amundsen sitting on a sledge about to cross some frozen gulf.

Swidersky had never had a laptop in his life, nor would he in the foreseeable future. He had always written in notebooks and didn't see anything so dreadful in it.

8.

After lunch he was accosted by Madame Konobeeff in the corridor.

'We have a studio in the basement, you know, where you can work. You have the smallest room and so I'm giving you first refusal of the studio.'

'Can I have a look at it?'

The air in the basement studio was obviously not suited to Swidersky's asthmatic lungs. He couldn't even stay there for five minutes.

'You'd better offer it to someone else who has a small room.'

'That would be Madame Berkutova.'

'Splendid. Offer it to her.'

'And if she doesn't take it, I'll offer it to Ines de la Vega. She's next in line,' Madame Konobeeff thought out loud.

'Can I ask who has the largest rooms?' asked Swidersky, though it was already clear.

'Our guests from America and Canada,' said Madame Konobeeff with evident displeasure.

Naturally, Madame Berkutova did not refuse the studio and sunk her Berkutovian aquila claws into it at once.

But Swidersky's work was going quite well in his room. After all, what does a writer need? A bed and a desk. And if he is fed as well, he will start filling his notebook with scrawny scratches and there will be no stopping him!

He wrote down a poem he had thought up long ago and set about translating some contemporary English poems which he had long since promised a Moscow journal.

There was football on the TV again that evening. The writer sat in the corner of the sitting room and observed the events on the screen from a distance. The Czech lady was sitting in the stalls, taking up a whole sofa. Her fat sausage-feet with peppercorn black nails were occupying another. Mr. Ellenson was spread-eagled on the third, the one closest to the blue-labelled Finnish vodka. The house seemed to have a limitless supply of spirits.

For the last few years, Swidersky had satisfied himself with a couple of glasses of red French wine with his dinner. As for vodka, he never touched it. He liked to joke that he was the only Russian who didn't drink vodka, and that was because he wasn't actually Russian at all!

The events of the previous evening repeated themselves with the precision of a Swiss watch: Czechs, whoops, and vodka. This time the Czech Republic was playing Denmark and they were really playing well. But when you are coerced into supporting someone or sympathising with them, you get a typically Russian urge to show everyone the finger behind your back and support the other side, at least secretly. Which, by the way, is very good for your psychological health. "I don't give a damn about the Czechs one way or the other," thought Swidersky. "But let's hope the Danes win, against all odds." However they didn't.

Madame Berkutova didn't pass up on the chance to throw more insults Swidersky's way.

9.

During the day, curtains shaded the dusty silence of the sitting room from the sun. Swidersky took to watching the BBC news in the afternoons. There was never anyone else there then. News usually left him feeling down, with all that talk of bombing raids and speeches, and speeches against bombing raids, and bombing raids to silence the speeches.

"If you can't act, you observe; if you can't observe, you observe yourself," thought the writer. "Take a look at yourself and you won't have a clue why you appeared on this earth, or what you can do which has not already been done before. Heroes of ancient Greece and villains of Rome, where are your modern imitators? They are even petty and cowardly in their murders and they never kill anyone themselves, as luckily there's always someone else to send somewhere to do your dirty work. Your warriors are brave but your battles are lacklustre, and your anti-war mouthpieces are hoarse, stupid and narcissistic. The real war has been going on since the Middle Ages, and not in the sands of Arabia but in the nearest pub or German *Kneipe*, or in the beer bars of Zamoskvorechye or the *dukhan* inns of the Caucasus. It is not easy to conquer the Middle Ages in your mind as the Middle Ages are completely modern, flourishing and have only just replaced the Stone Age."

Having worked well in the afternoon, Swidersky didn't sit in front of the television that evening but went to the room next door where there was the only computer the writers had access to. He was checking his emails.

There were no European Championship matches that day, and the Czech lady and Mr. Ellenson fuelled themselves with the Finnish elixir in front of a blank TV screen. It seemed they had little interest for what was going on in the rest of the world.

In the morning Madame Konobeeff came bustling over to Swidersky.

'I have received complaints that you are spending too much time on the computer thereby preventing the other writers from using the Internet.'

Swidersky was rather taken aback, but he quickly rallied and said calmly:

'That's not true. I don't spend any longer on the computer than anyone else. I would like to know who complained about me.

'Well, I was talking to Mr. Ellenson.'

'But he spends the whole day sitting on the computer! Not to mention the fact that he could fetch his laptop from his room whenever he wanted to, put it on the next table, plug it into the phone line and connect to the internet. You suggested that yourself.'

Swidersky decided to use the internet later that evening, at midnight, when the lovers of Finnish vodka were already too far immersed in the wilds of that great forest Delirium to find their way to the blue cybernetic space.

## 10.

The morning awaited him with cherries, unknown Swiss villages, a mad cycle ride down and a strenuous ride up.

That evening the Czech Republic was playing Greece in the semi final, and Swidersky decided to watch the match, come what may. The Czechs rained a squall of attacks on the Greek defenders. Madame Berkutova's nerves were so taut that she imbibed almost a whole bottle of vodka all by herself, firing a no less stormy attack of insults and mockery at Swidersky. He decided not to reply. Ellenson, ruffled up like an eagle-owl, sat in the corner of the next sofa pretending he didn't understand his own native English.

Swidersky and the Greeks bravely held their Pass of Thermopylae. They were already into extra time and two zeroes still glowed yellow on the stadium's score board. In the hundredth minute, right in the midst of the strongest Berkutovian attack, at the very moment when "son of a bitch" made the smooth linguistic transfer to "talentless paper-scribbler", the Greeks scored a goal. It was a so-called "golden goal" and it was all over; the Czech Republic was out of the championship.

'Nemesis was born in Greece, wasn't she?' Swidersky said, and then turned to Ellenson. 'By the way, is everything OK with your hearing? No problems recently?'

## 11.

The next morning Swidersky sat down at the computer and wrote a formal complaint, which he emailed to Madame Konobeeff, as well as to two members of the committee responsible for this writers' retreat; after all, Madame Konobeeff was simply the housekeeper, or "manager" as she liked to put it, glorifying her position in the American style.

At lunch Madame Berkutova asked Swidersky something with an innocent smile; he pretended not to hear her.

'Have you developed another allergy?' she mocked.

'Yes, I'm allergic to you,' said the writer. 'What makes you think you can taunt a person all evening and then talk to him about the weather the next day as though nothing had happened? I refuse to speak to you.'

   

The Czech lady assumed a face of wounded innocence.

'Why are you raising your voice?' asked Lana Freund, raising her eyebrows.

'I'm not raising my voice. I am speaking clearly and distinctly because I would like to inform everyone whom it concerns that I will not allow anyone to insult me. You can ask Mr. Ellenson what I am talking about; he was there.'

'I didn't hear anything,' yelped Ellenson in fright.

"Ah, Katz and Nelson, Catty Admiral Nelson. You're a coward and a traitor," thought Swidersky.

'If you don't like it here you are free to leave,' said Lana Freund, adopting the commanding role as usual.

She believed she was one of those women who knew how to organise their life perfectly well, who had everything firmly in their grasp, both inside and outside the home, and whose domestics, if there are any, prance around them on their hind legs.

The charming Ines de la Vega fluttered her eyelashes stunningly, not understanding what the argument was about.

'Of course, if you and the others can so easily reconcile yourselves to the abasement of human dignity so long as it is not your own dignity which is being abused, then I shall do my best to free myself from your company as soon as possible.'

And with those words he picked up his plate with his untouched main course, grabbed his glass of orange juice and went to his room to finish his meal in solitude.

Ellenson caught up with him on the stairs; he seemed to have suddenly developed youthful speed.

'You shouldn't take on so. She's a woman after all,' he began murmuring soothingly.

'Who is?'

'You know, our Czech companion. That's who I'm talking about.'

'I'm sorry, but she is not my companion. Do you think women are permitted to say anything they like?' said Swidersky indignantly.

'She was only joking...'

'You know fine well she was deliberately trying to ruin things for me. And you pretend to be blind and deaf. If someone had treated you the way she treated me I would have done everything in my power to defend you. But you... Do you have even the slightest understanding of morals? Of conscience? What do you teach your students? What do you write poems about – buttercups and daisies?'

Ellenson blinked owlishly and said:

'You take everything very seriously. Women should be forgiven everything.'

His false tone grated on Swidersky.

'She's a coarse shrew and not a woman,' he said harshly and started up the stairs with his plate and glass.

'You do use rather offensive expressions,' said the feline admiral from the bottom of the stairs. But Swidersky was already at his door.

12.

Madame Konobeeff knocked on his door that evening.

'Come in, it's not locked,' he called.

'I have just got back and read your email,' she began. 'I gather you expressed some dissatisfaction at lunchtime.'

'Yes. Funnily enough, I don't appreciate it when people insult me,' Swidersky said with feeling.

'Oh, you are getting emotional, you mustn't do that.'

'I'm sorry, but here in your writers' retreat, a supposed haven of peace and quiet for writers, I have been stripped of all peace and quiet and have been openly abused, what's more. And you think everything is fine?'

'I have spoken to the others and nobody witnessed anything of the kind.'

'I set out all the facts in the email I sent you. In my opinion, you are making a grave mistake to supply a limitless amount of spirits to people who cannot hold their drink, or indeed, who should not drink at all.'

'But they don't drink! There is only one empty vodka bottle in the glass recycling box I put in the kitchen, and it's been nearly a week!'

'Surely you aren't suggesting that when they're drunk to the eyeballs they will dutifully carry their empties to the kitchen and place them in the recycling box? Look around outside, in the nearest bucket or the nettles by the fence.'

'I have plenty of other concerns,' said Madame Konobeeff. 'You are making trouble for me…'

'Me? I'm causing trouble?' Swidersky was staggered. 'Don't you think you are getting the wrong end of the stick?'

'When I first came in, I didn't know who was right and who was wrong, but now I see you are getting agitated and upset...'

'Wouldn't you get upset if someone tried to ruin everything for you? For you, personally?'

'You use very strong words.'

'I am only calling a spade a spade. If you had heard the words which were said to me, your hair would have stood on end.'

'Well, you can't prove it... Personally, I think you should leave, as soon as possible.'

'That's right, of course, punish the injured party. May I say, you have a wonderful sense of logic and a unique understanding of justice... By the way, my stay here ends in six days, and my return flight is fixed. I certainly have no intention of losing money because of you.'

'I will consult with the committee members and we will discuss that matter,' purred Madame Konobeeff. 'So you are overly concerned about money. And you can use the Internet here for free...'

'So much for your famous Swiss hospitality!' the writer said with a broad smile. 'Or is it a measure of your own personal hospitality, cultivated over many generations in your ex-gentry family?'

'Let's not argue. I will contact you tomorrow about the ticket.'

'As you like,' Swidersky said.

'Well, now I have spoken with you and I cannot say I felt entirely safe,' said Madame Konobeeff as she floated out of the room tight-lipped.

'Poor thing,' said the writer sarcastically.

The next morning he discovered a note which had been pushed under his door:

*If you agree to leave tomorrow, we shall buy your ticket to Frankfurt. The flight has already been booked.*

"Well, what would I do here in the company of this sweet flock of hypocrites?" thought Swidersky. "They disgust me."

And he went down to the computer and replied with the shortest email he had ever written: "Buy it."

The ticket was pushed under his door that very evening.

Swidersky took his dinner in his room and then went for a walk in the garden. All was quiet in the common room, no roaring TV, no drunken whoops.

"They're intimidated!" realised the writer.

He walked down from the terraced gardens along a little path between the fields towards the moon which was lighting up the surreally green waters of Lake Geneva with the round arch of its sandy coloured eye.

When he got back, he wrote a poem.

"So I didn't come here in vain," he thought. "I've written two poems, translated a few others, and enjoyed the wonderful scenery. Why do people always have to spoil everything?"

13.

He packed his scrawny hold-all early the next morning and went for a last walk in the village. He came back with two jars of homemade Swiss jam he'd bought in the baker's to give to his friends.

Madame Konobeeff offered to give him a lift to the station in her own car.

"Wants to be sure I've really left," he thought as he went down the stairs carrying his bag.

He bumped into Madame Berkutova on the landing.

'Watch out!' she rasped with dramatic pathos. 'They showed me your email, now I know what you wrote about me. And I have your email address, so watch out.'

'Nowadays it is surprisingly easy to block spam,' said Swidersky completely unperturbed.

'Lucky for you that you lock your door at night. I checked. Otherwise, I have a knife...'

'You should get a part in one of Hitchcock's films,' grinned Swidersky.

He went out and put his bag in the car boot.

Lana Freund was already sitting in the car. She was off on her latest shopping trip and had hired Madame Konobeeff as chauffeur, not for the first time. Lana Freund could make anyone do anything for her.

On the way the ladies talked between themselves. Swidersky didn't join in.

They stopped at the station. Madame Konobeeff got out to open the boot.

'By the way, how come you showed my email to Madame Berkutova?' Swidersky enquired as he lifted his bag out. 'I don't think I gave you permission. Now she knows my email address, thanks to you.'

'I didn't show it to her,' Madame Konobeeff lied blatantly.

"Just like that. Two times two is four," thought the writer. "If you didn't show it to her, then how does she know what it says?"

'One more thing,' he went on, turning towards the car's open window where Lana Freund's medallion profile could be seen. 'Madame Berkutova announced that she roams the corridors with a knife in her hands. I think it might be wise to warn the residents of the house that they had better keep their doors locked.'

'That's just your imagination again,' said Madame Konobeeff, pulling a face. 'Or she was joking.'

'A very funny joke,' Swidersky said, shrugging. 'I would be on my guard if I were you. You have to be prepared for anything when you are dealing with a schizophrenic.'

Lana Freund's medallion profile betrayed nothing, but Swidersky knew only too well: this lady who was so fussy about her health and well-being would now not only lock her door, she would also double check she had locked it properly.

14.

Sitting in the plane he thought: ah, Monsieur Sviderski, you're a lamb, a spineless intellectual. A real Russian fellow would have given that Czech madame such a shove up her arse and kicked all the schizo out of her. But you, you just... And you didn't deal with the others properly, either. They're typical westerners, and you regale them with morals and conscience... They don't even know those words. Learnt them in school and then happily forgot them...

He watched the European Championship final at home, in his tiny flat. Greece was playing Portugal in Lisbon. Swidersky came across a forgotten bottle of Greek Kahors wine in his cupboard.

"After all that epopee, I'm rooting for Greece," thought Swidersky. "The Greeks always knew how to swim against the tide."

The wine was sweet as blood. Greece won.

# RUSSIAN NIGHTMARE

## 1.

A Russian nightmare... But what exactly is it, that Russian nightmare? A bus which never comes, or when you walk along a never-ending fence and nearly fall into a pit, or when you don't receive a letter which may be resting at the bottom of that pit; the trill of a pneumatic drill in the rain, the smell of peat fires from April to August, unfriendly shops, nosy electric trains... You are immersed in all this, and it's like taking a bath in dirty, lukewarm water your neighbours have just washed in. This is what your dreams recall, and what your days spent in foreign towns forget. It would be a good antidote to nostalgia, if only this world were a more hospitable place...

The Russian émigré writer Swidersky was choosing his future – well, at least the next couple of weeks. The day before his German friend said to him, 'Take yourself off to Moscow. To Moscow! To Moscow! You haven't been back to Russia for far too long.'

"It's all very well to say: to Moscow, to Moscow, but where can I stay in Moscow?" thought Swidersky sleepily in the morning. "It's all but impossible to rent a flat for a short time, and my friends live in such cramped conditions there'd hardly be room for me..."

And then Swidersky remembered a student called Georgy Sakovich. Swidersky had been coaching him in his literary studies and before Swidersky left Sakovich had said: if ever you need a place to stay in Moscow, let me know; I have a spare flat.

Of course, there is no such thing as a "spare" flat anywhere, but especially not in Moscow where a flat feeds the family better than work does – if you rent it out, of course.

The writer decided to ring him.

'Perfect timing!' said Sakovich in a fruity voice. 'The tenant has just moved out and we won't be able to find a new one until after the New Year. It's such a joy to be able to welcome my teacher. I'm deeply indebted to you, until my dying day!'

On hearing about "until my dying day," the stylist Swidersky frowned deeply, but thanks to the God of literature, Sakovich couldn't see that down the phone.

2.

The writer was sitting on the Eurolines bus, surrounded by Russian biddies who had successfully married their daughters off to Germans and were now returning to Russia after yet another visit. He was wondering: what is Sakovich so indebted to me for? For trying to develop his provincial taste, for looking over his texts and correcting his mistakes for eight long years? Well, gratitude is a good quality. But that mummy's boy had something else in mind. I recommended him to the Writers' Union, and that nonsense is worth a lot to him. And I got his poems *à la decadence* into a journal. They were surprised there at the journal and asked me what century—sorry, what year—the author was born. But they printed them nonetheless. And under the pseudonym Mandicant, just as he wanted. But he didn't make his way as a poet and earns his living translating. And if he took on a poem to translate, he would always bring it over to me to correct. I expect he's prepared the next batch, and that's why he's invited me. Hmmm, Mandicant. Well, he certainly is a mendicant. Why, for pity's sake, did he choose a pseudonym like that?

One of the Belarus drivers turned round at that moment and yelled at the Russian babushkas:

'Shut up, will you? Or we'll drive you over to the other world!'

The frightened women went quiet.

"I wonder why Europe ends at the doors of a Russian coach?" the writer pondered. "Scholars are still debating the precise location of Europe's eastern border, but here it is! Beyond this there's only barbarism, a heated, swearing boldness alternating with disembowelment. Actually, visitors should be given a vaccine against it all, just as Russians should be vaccinated against the cold climate of European indifference. But they haven't invented one yet..."

By this time the coach had floated over the endless German autumn into the Polish pre-winter and was preparing to dive, as if through an ice-hole, into the depths of the Russian winter. The writer's thoughts were equally unhurried and chill.

People are a means by which they convey themselves towards their own goal, thought Swidersky. There are centripetal carriages but also carts which travel along the byroads. It takes them a long time, but sometimes they creak up to their goal. Then you can listen for hours to their tales of the stones and snags which got under the wheels...

Exactly seventy-two hours later, the writer—rather lost amidst the muffled, downy babushkas—was unloaded onto the snowy square of three railway stations.

3.

The poet and artist Igor Burikhin had once drawn a tortoise over the map of Moscow, and it had matched. It's true, thought Swidersky as he walked along Moscow's streets. This city is a tortoise which is crawling towards the West and has been for many centuries. But so far it has only climbed out onto the bank of the River Moscow because it's sleepy with nightmarish memories, smeared with the mazut of history, gasping through the ill-smelling fumes, and covered in sweat. Coming out of the water, she crushed the eggs she had once laid and now has to drag herself into the future by herself, clumsy and awkward, with a guilty Tartar smile on her high cheek-boned face, nodding her omniscient, thoughtless little head in time to her steps...

Mandicant's flat was not far from Sushchevsky Vallum. The huge streets flowed around the islands of flimsy, rectangular blocks of flats like rivers. They had arranged to meet at the metro station. Mandicant was half an hour late. He showed up bare-headed and Swidersky thought: he's almost bald now, too, even though he's only about thirty. Thrusting his hands deep in the pockets of his sheepskin coat, Mandicant announced that he was not at all late; far from it, he'd been waiting there for ages but hadn't seen anyone. What an odd fellow! thought the writer, but just shrugged and didn't argue.

In the sitting room, there was a black, beetle-like telephone housed on the desk, and the draft of some manuscript lying beside it.

'Those are my translations,' said Mandicant in a bossy tone of voice. 'Sixteen poems and eight articles. It's the first time my work is to be published in a book... Please be so kind as to look through them and make any corrections.'

                    

"So that's what this is all about, the son of a bitch!" Swidersky thought, but all he said aloud was an ironic: 'Yes, I'll be so kind.'

The telephone rang towards evening, when the writer was alone, had sipped his Moscow tea with *baranka* rolls, and was already looking forward to getting some sleep, not the kind of sleep you get when you're on a coach, but the real sleep on an iron bed.

'It's so wonderful you are already here!' gasped the receiver breathlessly. 'I've kept ringing and ringing and thought to myself: when will my beloved author finally arrive? Pop round to the publishing house, we owe you some royalties for reprints.'

'With pleasure,' smiled the writer. 'Royalties are sacred... But how did you know I was coming, and more to the point, how did you know where to find me? Nobody knew...'

'Let's just say we have one department which knows everything about everyone...'

'You mean...'

'You're forgetting, my dear chap, that our publishing house was attached to the Central Committee of the Communist Party of the Soviet Union. I was the director, then, too, so this connection goes back a long time. I have always found the KGB officers most helpful. But that is between the two of us, of course...'

"Aha, Mandicant! So you're under their lense," thought the writer as he tossed in bed, dreaming of a twelve-hour sleep. "They're listening in on you, you nincompoop... Or are you one of them, and it was you who told them I was coming? No, impossible..."

He covered the phone with his coat, just in case.

4.

He dreamt the KGB men were scraping their boots and peering in through his eighth-floor window. They sent him on a course of political re-education in the KGB school, and forced him to write an essay on Stalin. He wrote characters in purple ink with a disposable post-office pen which he had to dip in the ink after every three words. Towards the end of his dream, his essay was handed back to him covered in red ink with a big fat bloody "D" at the bottom of the page. Another "D"! smirked the chalk face on the blackboard. He decided to re-read his essay and realised at once, from the very first line, that he had not written it. Yet the handwriting was unmistakeably his own.

*Stalin was begotten from Lenin's rib. It was a crooked, yellow rib, which is why Stalin came out dark-skinned and with a moustache. The first words he said to Lenin, who had engendered him, were the last words the latter ever heard. Stalin always had the last word, for himself and for others. In his youth he made a living selling ramskin boots, and those boots led those who wore them right down the road to hard labour. Stalin went that way, too, had a look around, and one thought lodged in his head. As he had but one thought, they let him out of the hard labour in order to start a revolution. It goes without saying that he did not succeed; others made a revolution, while he blinked his dull eyes like a ram, which everyone took as active approval. After Lenin was moved to the mausoleum, for a long time Stalin's right hand was irreconcilably contradicted his left hand. The left hand bore the surname Trotsky. Finally Stalin decided to have two right hands and hacked off his left hand with an ice pick. It hurt the ice pick considerably, but Stalin had no sympathy for it. In fact, he generally never sympathised with anything, male or female. He heaped them up in hard labour which was spreading metastases from the single thought in his mind. The hard labour spread quickly over the map like a blot of black ink. It sang, danced and worked in the factories. Having decided he should furnish himself with a second productive thought, Stalin headed off to the other world, to have a peek and see whether or not he could spread that other world over the map in the wake of hard labour. However, those in the other world would not let such a long-awaited visitor return whence he had come.*

"They could get me for this..." Swidersky went cold and immediately woke up, and the morning air in his flat was only too happy to repeat the echo of his dream: they could get you for this, for that, for anything... The nightmare of a Russian émigré who has returned to his native land for a short visit...

5.

Sakovich had a friend called Sakevich. He was also a poet. And that is why Sakovich had become Mandicant. Sakovich and Sakevich had different backgrounds: the former was a Pole, the latter a Jew. For ten years now Sakevich had been seen as a promising author. Sakovich-Mandicant, on the other hand, was always a hopeless case and only fed on other people's promises; he was always on the receiving end.

As for Sakevich, he worked as an attendant in the hospital morgue, and suffered from a strange form of magnetism which meant he was compelled to chase any girl he saw. Walking down the road with him was no easy matter as he was constantly distracted, always saying: "Hang on a sec" and making a beeline for a girl coming towards him. Three minutes later he would slink back with his tail between his legs and say: "OK, let's go." Then the scene would repeat itself just around the next corner, except that he would come back sooner. The tender-hearted Swidersky would always try to calm him down, saying: you'll have better luck next time...

And if Sakevich did have better luck, he would not be seen for two weeks, after which it would once again become difficult to walk down the road with him. All of his girls were called Katya; maybe he renamed them. Some of the Katyas had children by him. He didn't like to talk about Katyas and their children. He seemed to live by a schedule: he wrote two poems a week, he went to work three times a week, and was perfectly satisfied with himself. Yet Swidersky felt sorry for him. He only stopped feeling sorry for him when Sakevich was savouring his own very correct verses on moral themes.

The next savouring, Mandicant informed the writer when he phoned towards the end of the morning, was scheduled for that very evening. The poetry reading was to be held in the former synagogue, oddly enough, which was now the Jewish cultural centre. It was somewhere in the Prechistensky Alleys. It was attended by a lot of elderly ladies; indeed, they were so elderly it was possible they did not realise the synagogue had been moved elsewhere.

Sakevich was late for his own reading. He finally showed up, pale-browed, wrapped in a long black scarf, with his hair standing on end.

'The poet's arrived,' buzzed the ladies.

The poet had of course brought a girl along with him, a tall, thin girl plastered with lipstick.

'Hello, Katya,' Swidersky said in a sure tone of voice.

The girl started visibly and whispered in Sakevich's ear, frightened: 'How does he know?'

'Thanks to his great experience in life,' Mandicant, who was standing nearby, smirked slyly.

The poems were full of lofty morals, as ever, and were delivered lavishly, charming the elderly ladies with their overtones. The end of the evening was drowned in applause.

'Well, how did you like them?' Swidersky asked his student when everyone was already dispersing.

'Yiddish ullalulla,' said Mandicant, twisting his already twisted mouth; he suffered from incurable envy.

'Please, dear sir, express yourself using words in the dictionary. I am not familiar with such words, and do not wish to familiarise myself with them,' rapped Swidersky.

The envious one was quashed.

'Thank you for coming,' Sakevich said to Swidersky, holding his Katya's hand – to stop her from running away, maybe? 'As you know, poets don't usually go to listen to one another here. The journalists sometimes pop in. Have you heard of the famous Motya Kuzkina?'

'I have heard something,' said Swidersky. 'Why?'

'She's here.'

'Really? Where?'

'Over there, in the corner.'

Two young men were discussing something in the corned he indicated, entwined around one another.

'Sorry, but I can't see her,' said Swidersky, somewhat surprised.

'She's one of those two young men.'

'Mmm, "she" sounds rather ambiguous in this case... But OK. Who's the other one?'

'He's her new passion, her *chère amie,* so to speak. He's the right hand man to the head of our Nazi party. He's really good-looking, isn't he, a real blond beast? It's not done to discriminate people because of their convictions now.'

6.

Hmm, other people give performances, read their poems, thought Swidersky as he made his way home. I've got out of the habit of it in Germany. But even if I were to give a recital here, in Moscow, who would come to listen to me?

                                   

Mr. I'm-a-poet-too-I-studied-in-the-Literary-Institute-for-five-years.

Mr. I'm-actually-from-the-KGB-and-I'm-curious-to-see-who-says-what.

Mr. You-are-obviously-catering-to-the-Western-reader.

Mrs. How-can-you-call-yourself-a-poet-it's-immodest.

Mr. We-don't-know-the-new-ones-like-you-where-were-you-in-the-seventies.

Mrs. I-write-tercets-why-bother-to-write-anything-longer.

Mr. How-can-you-be-a-Russian-poet-if-you-don't-have-a-drop-of-Russian-blood.

Mr. But-there-is-no-rhyme-is-it-prose.

Mr. Well-of-course-you-are-on-good-terms-with-the-publishers-that's-why-they-publish-your-work.

Mr. How-did-you-allow-them-to-print-your-biography-on-the-backcover-as-an-advert.

Mr. I-was-just-walking-by-I'll-stand-by-the-door-what-does-this-poet-write-about.

Ms. Oh-men-come-here-too-and-they-are-all-so-intelligent.

Mr. Personally-I-like-it-after-a-shot-of-vodka-and-accompanied-by-a-guitar.

Mr. Can-I-read-mine-after-you.

Mr. What-do-you-mean-you-can't-give-me-a-copy-of-your-book-why-did-I-bother-coming.

Mr. With-your-authority-you-simply-must-support-our-political-party.

Those are the people who will come to my recital, along with a few others. But will I come?

7.

The next morning Swidersky sat down to correct the Mandicant's translations. Still making the same old mistakes, he commented inwardly. Still straining to make it sound nice, but that just makes the language sound unnatural, fussy, bad taste. You can't teach someone good taste, especially if they've never had it. Anti-Semitism – that's the worst bad taste... You can't teach someone to write poetry, nor literature. Anything worth something in literature isn't born by following rules – quite the opposite. In our dim fatherland everything worthwhile arises from going against the flow anyway... And there is no prophet in our fatherland without vice, and there is no vice which is not stamped in the papers with the brand of damnation. And our vices are our true prophets.

Such were the wise thoughts which swirled in Swidersky's gingery head, tousled after his morning bath. Wonderful news had come to him that day glistening like a golden fish: his book of poems was soon to come out in a small town near Moscow. He had given recitals several times in that town, and the last time had been three years ago. He was popular there – they had once offered: give us your manuscript, about 60 poems, we can't promise anything, but maybe we'll publish it here. Swidersky had handed them a folder with poems and quickly forgotten the matter. Poems only come out as books in or around Moscow if someone really needs them to.

But it seems that someone really wanted to publish his book because he had been told it was almost a reality already. It had already been printed, now it was with the binders. We'll try and hurry things along a bit. You've arrived at a good time; maybe you can give a recital here again? And the writer agreed, naturally; how could he refuse if they were being so kind and good and publishing his book? And it was better than giving a recital in Moscow; it was less hectic.

Meanwhile, he visited friends who were curious to see Swidersky-the-foreigner: in a warm, blue, padded German jacket and a red and black Scottish scarf the colours of the glorious Maxwell clan. But Scotland and Germany were like some far-off planets for his friends, planets which were not even part of our Solar system.

'Are you writing there? Are you working?' asked one of his friends sternly. He was a playwright.

'Oh yes, I'm writing away,' Swidersky replied reassuringly, but thought inwardly that he had not written anything all year except some poems and one short story, and was only just beginning to get to grips with his novel now. 'I'm even writing now. I brought my notebook with me.'

'I can see in your eyes that you could have written more. Do you remember who Dante put in the last circle of hell? An artist who didn't work.'

    

8.

Pushing through the morning, pushing through the remnants of a dream, pushing through the noise of a shaver… The phone's ring was all-pervasive, even pushing into the bathroom. It whined and buzzed and rattled and pestered him.

'So you're going to give a recital in that small town. Well, there's a museum of local history there, and they have precisely the documents I need for the essay I'm working on at the moment.' Mandicant fired another round of compound and complex sentences at the writer.

'So?'

'Please be so kind as to make me a photocopy of it. They allow it, I've already rung them.'

Swidersky agreed, although he didn't take kindly to another "please be so kind". He's making a boss out of himself, thought Swidersky. It was a mistake to stay at his place. Ah, the compromises we make as a pennilessness Russian émigré!

But he did indeed go to the small town outside Moscow long before his recital and went into the museum. He introduced himself.

'Oh, we'd be happy to help you; it's just that our colleague in charge of the archives is not at work today, she's taken a day off. We don't have the key. Maybe you can come back tomorrow?'

Swidersky asked to use the phone and dialled Mandicant's number.

'Well, stay overnight and then you can make my photocopy.'

'But where am I supposed to stay, pray tell?!'

'I've no idea, just bring me my documents.'

And the bastard hung up. Swidersky barely refrained from swearing in front of the ladies.

He was just about to leave when someone had an idea:

'Perhaps we could call Anna Yevlampyevna. She might be free and could pop round?'

And so they phoned. And then they told him:

"Wow, you're in luck! She was at the dentist's today and has just got back. She promised to be here at five, so come back then and she says she can do it all for you in half an hour. By the way, are you writing about our town, is that what you need the papers for?'

'No, I promised a friend I'd get them. He's doing the writing,' said Swidersky gloomily, and thought to himself: the word "friend" sounds so unnatural when used about certain people.

And he went off to roam around the little town with its pink-brick buildings. He went to the little market and bought a bunch of bananas and—for the same price—a cassette of Beethoven's *Moonlight Sonata* played by Emil Gilels. Probably a pirate copy.

9.

The bananas successfully suppressed the rumbling in his stomach, and the papers from the museum soon took their place in his writer's briefcase. The rest of the evening was plain sailing, on the wave of eloquence in the friendly hall. The audience was bright: students and young intellectuals – you'd never be able to pull a crowd like that in Moscow, not even if you bribed them.

The reading was finally over, and then came the autographs, and he scrawled the wonky-winged little birds of his signature on the freshly-printed pages of his new book, with his surname, Swidersky, on the cover. The book was called: "After the Flood."

'We've printed five hundred copies,' they told him. 'Leave us a hundred, and you can take the rest. They're yours. They're all in packages in the room behind the stage.'

'Thank you,' said the writer, somewhat at a loss. 'But how can I take them?'

'Call a car. We're not so far from Moscow.'

Actually, the books would have fitted into two large suitcases, but there were no suitcases, so he had to load the packages into the back of the car, and he stuffed them in the boot with difficulty.

The car was a black "Volga" with an antenna for the internal com system. No-one else was going to Moscow that night. There were no taxis and Swidersky, who was trying to flag a car down on the street, was about to despair when the "Volga" pulled up. The driver knew how to drive a hard bargain, but the writer had to agree.

And so there they were, rolling into Moscow, scattering slush merrily as they went.

'You have an unusual car, with radio connection,' Swidersky remarked.

'Yes. I'm an FSB colonel, you see,' said the chauffeur casually. 'The pay is good, but a bit of extra money always comes in handy – I want to send my family to the South. That's why I stopped.'

"As if you don't have anything to send your family to the South with…" thought the writer.

'Tell me, do you have printed matter in those packages?' the driver went on.

'Yes, they're programmes for the local arts festival.' Swidersky decided to play it safe.

He pulled a copy of the programme someone had given him from his briefcase and showed it to the KGB guy.

'Mmm. They do make them look nice nowadays. I expect we'll be sent one, too. We get a copy of all printed materials.'

'And does someone sit there and read it all?'

'Of course! That's what we pay them for!'

'That's a good job. Not too tiring, either,' smiled the writer.

'What do you mean? Come off it? Reading's boring and tiring. It's years since I've read anything. But films, now that's a totally different ball game. I've got loads of videos at home.'

And so chatting, they arrived at the writer's house. The colonel didn't short-change him from his two hundred roubles and even held the black iron gate open as Swidersky carried the packages inside.

Finally all ten packages were inside, at the foot of the stairs. One floor up, three unshaven guys were hanging out near the lift.

'Hey, guys, we don't have enough to buy beer. Could you give us something?' wheezed the muscliest lad.

'Sure, sure,' said the colonel, and turning to Swidersky added. 'They'll help you from here.'

And he beat at a hasty retreat.

## 10.

'Hey, you with the packages,' wheezed the lads. 'We'll carry it all up in a jiffy.'

'It's OK, I can manage by myself.'

'What do you mean?'

And they each grabbed three packages of books and carried them into the lift. Swidersky took the last box. They rather carelessly flung the packages into the lift and squeezed in, cheek to jowl with the writer. And so they rode up to the eighth floor enveloped in the stench of alcohol. Once there, they flung the packages out onto the landing even more carelessly.

'OK, now give us some money.'

Swidersky took the change the colonel had given him from his coat pocket and handed it to them.

'Not enough,' said the ugly unshaven faces, although it was not "not enough".

Swidersky rummaged in his coat pockets and gave the gang around him all the small change he had.

'Still not enough!' growled the ugly mugs.

This was really too brazen. The writer realised that if he pulled out his wallet now, he would never see it again.

'I don't have any more,' he said firmly.

'What? How about at home? We'll carry these packages right into your flat, and you'll give us more money. Which is your flat?'

Swidersky realised he mustn't let these guys into the flat.

'That one,' he said, pointing, 'but I don't have a key. I can't get in.'

'Where's the key?'

'My wife's got it,' Swidersky declared; he hadn't had a wife for twelve years. 'She's out walking the dog, and I can't get in until she gets back.'

'We'll wait,' said the gang brazenly.

'Go ahead.'

And the writer sat down on the packages of books showing to all intents and purposes that he was in no rush to go anywhere.

After five minutes one of the gang said:

'I don't think we've ever seen you here before. Are you here for a short time?'

'Yes,' said Swidersky.

The next question was:

'And what if we rummaged in your pockets?'

'And what if I ring the neighbour's doorbell?' replied the writer in the same tone as the question.

'Go ahead.'

Swidersky got up off his box, went to the nearest door and rang the bell.

A man's voice was heard behind the door a minute later:

   

'Who is it?'

'Call the police, please,' said Swidersky. 'Someone wants to rob me.'

There was a peephole in the door and Swidersky realised he—and the gang he was beset by—was being observed.

'Deal with it yourself,' said the voice at last.

Hmm. Fat lot of good you are, Mister Neighbour. But the gang made no further attempt at violence. Swidersky sat down on his box again.

'What's in the packages?' came the question.

'Books.'

The writer ripped the corner of one of the packages and showed them the bundles of books.

'Boo-ooks,' drawled the faces, disappointed.

Obviously, a writer had more patience than street louts, especially if they haven't had a bottle yet that evening.

The next question followed after another five minutes.

'Where's your wife got to?!'

'Who knows... She's walking the dog in the scrubland. Go and look for her if you want.'

'Nah. We'll wait here.'

'Go ahead.'

After another five minutes they stated:

'She's not coming.'

'No, she's not,' agreed the writer. 'I told you, go and hurry her up. I'm getting fed up of waiting here, and I can't leave everything and go and look for her.'

'What does she look like?'

'She's wearing a fur coat,' the writer used his imagination. 'And she's got a big dog with her.'

'A German shepherd dog?'

'A wolfhound,' said the writer dryly.

'Shall we go, lads?' said the gang looking at each other uncertainly, and, forgetting about the lift, they set off down the stairs.

As soon as they had gone far enough, Swidersky quietly opened the armoured door and began frantically carrying in the packages of books. Finally all ten were inside.

Then he heard footsteps on the landing outside. The writer realised he wouldn't be able to close the door quietly so he just pushed it to.

'Excuse me, you've left your key outside,' said a female voice.

'Damn!' the writer said to himself and opened the door. He really had left the key outside in the lock. Just as well it had been a neighbour in the lift and not that gang...

He thanked the woman and locked the door from inside, then began plying himself with tea. But it was not easy to drink tea; his hands were shaking.

He put a cassette he had recently bought into the old cassette player and let himself be carried away by the Russian pianist to another time and place.

11.

There are poems by the fat and by the thin, by blondes and brunettes, verses written in water, or in blood, dream poems and poems forgotten by morning. And the latter are usually the best. But they are not the ones which get printed...

Still, you get such a thrill from looking at a whole book of your own poems and caressing its cover. If only there weren't any misprints...

Mandicant rang earlier that morning.

'So, how are my photocopies?'

'They've arrived.'

'And your book?'

'That's here, too.'

'Well then I'll drop by.'

And he soon arrived, the balding babe, and began gawping around with his bug eyes the colour of frog spawn.

'Thanks for getting the Xeroxes. Can I take ten copies of your book for myself and my friends?'

'Of course you can.'

'And if you sign books for any poet-friends you don't manage to meet up with while you're here, I'll give them to them. It will give me a chance to meet them. It will come in handy for me.'

'OK, no problem,' said Swidersky.

The balding babe picked up a book, and began leafing through it, praising the poems.

'This here is dangerous,' he said, suddenly jabbing a finger at a page. 'It may create some problems for you.'

'What's wrong? What do you mean?' The writer was surprised.

'Well, you've described our president as: "a lean chap in a mousy-grey overcoat and a policeman's peaked cap." What if he takes offence?'

'I wasn't writing about the president. You voted for him without me, with pre-election bombs... As for me, I was trying to guess who would lead Russia in the nearest future. I wrote it quite some time ago, before this president... Why, does it sound like him?'

The balding babe sucked in his cheeks, which could be taken for a "yes."

'In any case I didn't mention any names, so this is all mere speculation.'

'Of course,' the babe agreed readily. 'By the way, did you have a good journey back with the books?'

Swidersky told him about his adventure.

'Aha, we were all friends when we were kids. They ask people for small change here every other day.'

'And do they always threaten people?'

'Well, no-one's pressed charges so far. And I don't advise you to, either, especially as you live abroad. A suspicious foreigner – that's who you are for them. By the way, you have to fill in a temporary residence document and sign in at the police station every three days.'

'In my own native land?!' The writer was thunder struck.

'A lot of people don't bother and they get away with it. But if you were to come with a complaint, it would all come out.'

'So extortion in the porch is a matter of course for you and the others living in this block of flats, and for the police, too?'

'The police have a lot of other things to contend with. And actually, each of those three lads has had a spell behind bars for petty hooliganism, but that was a long time ago. They say the lads are involved in burglary, but so far no-one has caught them. We all have metal doors, or even armoured ones, and that helps. Everyone in Moscow has fortified front doors now.'

'Nice set of childhood friends you have, I must say,' said Swidersky shaking his head.

## 12.

The telephone woke up in the evening, tearing the writer from the never-never land of his post-television dreams.

'Can I speak to Mr. Sakovich, please?'

'He doesn't live here at the moment. I can give you his number if you like.'

'I know that damn number. He never answers the phone, he always sends his parents and if they realise it's me, they say he's out.'

'Is it something urgent?'

'Urgent? It's always urgent! I need money. I'm Mummy's boy.'

'What?! Who?!'

'Yes, Mummy's boy. Sakovich married my sister a few years ago; she had only just turned eighteen. They had a baby, then they separated. He promised to help out financially, but usually forgets. And it's impossible to get hold of him.'

'Maybe he doesn't have any money himself?' the writer suggested.

'Well, both his mother and father have well-paid jobs, and he earns a fair bit with his translations. Of course he has money!'

'I'll tell him you rang.'

'Please do. When things get really bad, I usually call his parents. They give me money if I lay it on thick enough. But it doesn't happen so often.'

'Let's hope for the best,' Swidersky said, having nothing better to say.

He sat down to work before he went to bed, as ever. He was soon distracted by some strange sounds on the stairs. He swore and went to see what was going on. Peering through the peephole, he saw a scraggy grey rat sitting in front of the famous armoured door and gnawing on the leatherette upholstery.

## 13.

The next day Swidersky popped into the book shop next door. He bought some books or other to take with him to Germany. They had published Nabokov's lectures, Brodsky's essays and Sapgir's prose.

Swidersky also bought newspapers. *The Book Review* mentioned his book in the section on new books, and his name was included in a xenophobic remark made by a certain pseudo-poet on the non-Russian surnames besmirching great Russian literature.

*The Independent* included a brief mention of his book, signed by Ya. Savich. This was obviously not Sakovich but Sakevich. Swidersky thought that most likely another Katya had typed it up before he dispatched it, since Sakevich liked to give them a little task or two. The article began as follows: "This book was on everyone's lips at the Central House of Writers coffee shop." And it went on: "It is gratifying that the generation to which the author of these verses also belongs is coming out on the front line of poetry." I wonder which generation he is referring to? Swidersky thought with an inward smirk. I'm sixteen years older than that pale-browed fellow. And who was he talking to about my book? To his Katya, of course. Maybe he has a new one by now? It seems as though a visit to the Central House of Writers coffee shop was a compulsory part of "the debut stage", as he puts it. Whatever. At least he didn't attack my book.

They attacked him elsewhere. But not in the *Circumliterary Gazette*, where they simply wrote: "poems for western consumption," as though dismissing them, like saying "return to sender". Sounds so simple the way they put it, snarled Swidersky. Makes it sound as though poems are pastries – you eat them where you buy them. Digest Nabokov and Bunin in the West, and Pasternak and Akhmatova in the East. If you try to do it the other way round, they'll curdle and you'll get cranial introversion. Well, we'll sort it out in fifty years or so, and fish out some forgotten ones for you. Then you'll have Nabokov and Georgy Ivanov, even though they themselves are long gone.

A paper with a small readership, *Moscow's Literary Life*, made a serious attack on him. The editor was "M. Kuzkina" whom we have already met. "Mr. Swidersky's new collection of poems was launched the other day. His literary work is of no independent significance. But we do have some excellent writers in our midst. Yesterday, for example, superb texts were recited in the gay club "Arrest and Pilate." The texts were no longer than three or four phrases. Due to lack of space we can only print one example here: "Hey Jumpety-Prigov! So you wanna write a couple of thousand verses? That's cool but outdated. We'll jumpety jump right over you. We'll pump out 22 thousand, and hey they'll be way more refined. So there you go, JP." After the reading, it was announced that an anthology of such texts is under way, which will also include their direct predecessors, miniatures by Turgenev, Gorky and Kharms. So the parallel world of our literature is surfacing and spreading around." It was printed next to reports on two events of supposedly equal significance: the launch of a new book by the famous novelist Makanin and a recital by a young man from a village near Moscow called Malakhovka, who read his own opuses in some local library. He had apparently "rid himself of the perennial fear of non-normative lexicon; his works border on anecdotes."

"Aha," Swidersky smiled to himself. "So the 'parallel world of our literature' is surfacing, but it's a small ice-hole, so other non-parallel worlds may find the way blocked. And someone even asked me why Russian writers and musicians are leaving Russia… Because they drive us all crazy and squeeze us out of literature, out of the country, and then our psychiatrists write books like *The Jump into Madness* and so on about those of us in the West, and then they get rich. That's the collective "jump into madness."

In the evening he made the familiar rounds of literary, half-literary and not at all literary taverns. The end of the evening petered out in Moscow's yellowish neon fog.

At night he saw himself in the mirror, but he was old and dressed in rags. The reflection looked at him disapprovingly, turned out the light and went out.

He followed it. He plodded along this bank of the River Moscow, the reflection walked along the far bank. Then he walked on that bank and the reflection walked on this one.

Changing places yet again, they met at the bottom. The reflection was holding an aquarium in its hands, and a small submarine was sailing in it. The sailors were cheerily waving to the writer and shouting: "Hey, come and join us!" Mmm, the writer thought in his dream, Moscow's lower depths have their own ideas about the dimensions of the individual.

In the morning the phone rang, tearing Swidersky away from the chapter he had just made a start on. It was the stern playwright he had seen briefly early the previous evening.

'How did it go yesterday?' the playwright asked. 'Successfully?'
'Yes. In a garbled sort of way.'

# 14.

He had mentioned his wife, and she turned up. In a fur coat, but without a dog. She had never had a dog. She had had a tomcat, but it had perished in a catly duel. And the cat had actually been called Pushkin. No, the cat had been before his time. Which means it was a long time ago – they'd been divorced twelve years now! But he had recognized her on the street, or rather, as she came out of the metro at "Prospect Mira" station, and he had pulled her out of the crush of the human current. He happened to have a copy of his poetry book in his briefcase, so he swiftly signed it and gave it to her.

'I'll read it and give you a ring,' she said.

'I'll be leaving soon.'

'Then I'll read it quickly.'

And they both rushed off.

But she did indeed read it quickly, was enraptured, and then said: 'I'll help you.'

Well, you have to be a really good person for your ex-wife to help you! Because women have as many men as there are epochs in history or geological periods in nature. A glacier crawls by, then everything blossoms into different configurations of branches, and is resurrected in a different climate. Under different names. And sometimes under different surnames.

'Have you heard the news?' his wife asked him on the phone. '"Motya Kuzkina" has hounded the secretary of the Writers' Union to death.'

'Is that supposed to be funny?'

'It's no joke! It all began with a couple of pogromist feuilletons in his so-called newspaper, and then he showed up at the Writers' Union meeting, stepped up to the microphone after the general report, and poured out such a tirade! That very evening the secretary had a heart attack and popped his clogs – he was no spring chicken. The funeral's the day after tomorrow.'

'Which secretary did he terrorise to death?' asked Swidersky warily. 'Of which Union? We have two of them now.'

'The democratic one, can you believe it?' said his wife. 'He should have torn a strip off some Russian Nazi!'

'Come off it! It's not fashionable to argue with Nazis now, and anyway, what does he stand to gain from it? But here he can promote his own man. You just watch, he'll soon be secretary himself, he's just the type.'

'By the way, he knows how to do more than just attack; he's protecting a progressive journalist who's being persecuted.'

'And who's that?'

'The one who slated you in a xenophobic article.'

'Then he deserves to be persecuted,' Swidersky said.

'No, you don't understand. The progressive journalists of *The Book Review* elected him as their editor-in-chief, but the paper's proprietors didn't approve their choice. The whole of our democratic community is up in arms in his defence. Read the papers. The PEN Club spoke up for him.'

'But he's a fascist!'

'What do you mean? He's thought of as a democrat here! He used to be friends with Yevtushenko. Though lately he mouths off more with nationalist sympathisers. He's been seen more than once at Nazi party meetings, and he was offered the position of party press-secretary. No-one knows whether he accepted or not.'

'I'm starting to like those non-progressive journalists of that newspaper who didn't vote for him.'

His wife laughed.

Swidersky asked her to shelter his books. He wanted to take about twenty copies with him, but he wasn't sure what to do with the rest. The large bookshops don't take any poetry at all. No money in it... Swidersky took twenty copies round to several non-commercial bookshops which were calling themselves salons and book clubs. And that's poetry for you, alias prose – you cart your own books around in a rucksack trying to sell them for a few pennies.

His wife said: I can always find space for books, but I'm redecorating now. How about in two to three weeks? He asked Mandicant if he could leave the books with him for a couple of weeks.

'Books?' Mandicant's eyebrows shot up, and you could see that even over the phone. 'Oh, of course, books. Well, why not, if it's not for long...'

So he could travel off into his back of beyond. And no longer choke in the semi-opaque swamp of Moscow's semi-air, or paddle dirty slush everywhere.

'Would you mind if I came to the station to see you off?' asked his wife.

'Are you taking a taxi? I'll come with you to the station,' said Mandicant.

The next morning they showed up almost simultaneously, and, surprisingly, it transpired they didn't know one another! He had to introduce them.

The taxi he'd booked over the phone rolled up. Swidersky grabbed the heaviest suitcase and a bag of food – he had to live in a bus for two days. His wife picked up the second suitcase. Mandicant brought up the rear, empty-handed.

They came out of the lift. The three infamous louts were leaning against the wall by the rubbish chute one floor up.

'I'll go and say hello to them,' said Mandicant, and was greeted with triple cheer.

Meanwhile the writer and his wife dragged the bags to the taxi and loaded them into the boot with difficulty.

'Ah, you've already loaded up, excellent,' commented Mandicant when he showed up five minutes later. 'Well, let's go then.'

The taxi was sucked into the huge vortex of Three Stations Square, and they barely found a place to pull in.

'Well, I see you are really leaving,' said Mandicant.

## 15.

A week passed. Swidersky was on his way back from a walk in the local park that always seemed to be parallel to itself when a thin little tinkle rang out somewhere deep inside the writer's pocket.

'I have some bad news,' scraped a mendicant voice. 'My flat, the one you stayed in, was burgled last night.'

'Really? How awful,' said the writer, rather taken aback. 'What's missing?'

'I had some valuable things there,' declared Mandicant.

Swidersky recalled the tatty mendicant furniture, but said nothing. Who knows, maybe he kept a cache there somewhere.

'It seems they got the door open without any difficulty,' Mandicant went on.

'With a blow torch?' the writer couldn't contain himself.

'Actually, it seems as though they had a key. The neighbour said you were always leaving the key in the lock outside...'

'You're not blaming me, are you?' said the writer indignantly.

'Yes. You left the key outside,' whined the balding babe, 'and let the drunkards on the stairs into the flat.'

'I didn't let anyone into the flat. That's rubbish!'

'Yes, you did, and they saw the locks from inside. I have suffered losses thanks to your criminal negligence.'

'How dare you?! What criminal negligence?'

'Yes, criminal negligence,' Mandicant went on in a telltale's voice. 'I think you should compensate my losses. Four hundred dollars should cover it. Your ex-wife called and I told her I wouldn't give her the books until I received the money.'

'That's extortion,' said Swidersky in a sweet voice. 'I didn't know you were capable of such a thing. You can rest assured you won't get a penny from me. I don't pay extortionists.'

'In that case I'll destroy all your books. I'll take them into the yard and burn them.'

'The copies of the books you have belong to me. They are my personal property, and if you deliberately destroy them, you will answer for it in court.'

'You think they belong to you?' Mandicant said smacking his lips in satisfaction. 'Didn't you know they have been officially seized? I spoke to the relevant authorities about you yesterday and they were very curious. I told you you'd get into trouble because of your book, remember?'

'Yeah, and I can guess who caused that trouble for me... And how often do you pay those "relevant authorities" a visit?'

'That's my business. Suffice for you to know that the whole print run has been officially seized, and is to be kept in the Lubyanka. But as the authorities trust me, they have left the books which are at my place. So, send me the money or you will never see your books again. The authorities hinted to me that it would suit them very nicely if the whole print run were to disappear.'

'I've already told you all I have to say about the money, so do as you please. I can just imagine a member of the Writers' Union who burns books.'

'No-one will ever know about it. Who cares? So think it over.'

And the bastard hung up.

   

16.

But he didn't know that the writer Swidersky turned into the writer Wrathsky in such situations. No-one will ever know about it?! Well, we'll see about that.

We should point out that the writer didn't like telephoning. There are many different ways of phoning, but silence always lives in the receiver, no matter what kind of receiver it may be. You dial the number and: silence. Sometimes there is some distant commotion of far-off squeaky voices. From time to time the silence cuts off the person you are looking for, saying: he's not here, that number doesn't exist. Swidersky would never forget how he had once heard that silence which no-one has ever heard. He had rung an old writer who lived right in the very heart of Moscow but who wrote in Hebrew. It had been a long time since he had spoken to that writer and as he dialled the number, Swidersky didn't even know whether he was still alive. Once he'd dialled, a biblical silence reigned down the phone. A very particular silence, such as might be heard in the sands of the land of Nod, in the abandoned temple of Jerusalem, in the hearts of the righteous. Swidersky listened to that silence for a long time. It lived in the receiver, spilled over into him, drowning his heart. Then the receiver somehow hung up by itself... And he never dared ring that number again.

But something that you do willingly never feels too hard. Nothing spurs us into action like rage, and the writer realised that, like it or not, he had to break his silence that very instant. And Pfennigs and Marks, light coins and heavy ones, poured into the German phone box. And the people at the other end of the line said: "Oh dear, oh dear! Such goings on!"

And the director of PEN Club said:

'Your student? You have strange taste in students, I must say... You say his number is in the directory of writers? I'll speak to him. Who does he think he is, Herostratus? Taking it into his head to burn books... He'll shame us in front of the whole of Europe. Call me again tomorrow.'

The next day Swidersky was told:

'I've had a word with him. I asked whether he had an official document confirming that the print run had been seized. And if not, then the PEN Club's lawyer wanted to know on what authority he was holding the books. He got cold feet. Said it was all a misunderstanding, that he wanted to hand over the print run but didn't know who to give it to. Did a U-turn. I don't like this story, and I don't like that young man. I've never set eyes on him but he has the unmistakeable voice of a scoundrel. I don't know who he's working for – now everyone's going around saying they work for the Secret Service, and it's considered to be very patriotic.

"Thanks," thought Swidersky. "I didn't expect that, especially after the business about supporting a certain "progressive journalist-cum-fascist", who is also a member of the Writers' Union! But it seems as though our PEN Club protects the interests of writers of every creed and hue, with all kinds of convictions and prejudices."

17.

"Why didn't I notice anything?" thought Swidersky in the evening. "Because he was... not exactly secretive. More like morose. Just kept silent, never said a word, so he could pass himself off as a decent chap. Our troubles begin when we open our mouth..."

The next day he spoke to his ex-wife on the phone:

'He's going to give me the books, after all' she said. 'I don't know how you managed it, but well done. I'm going to collect them tomorrow.'

'Take someone along to help you,' said Swidersky. 'I can ask my friend. He'll come and give you a hand. There are two big files of manuscripts as well as the books. I forgot to take them. One contains the draft of my novel, the other has archive materials, short stories by Fyodor Sologub and Andrey Bely which have never been published. I want to make a commentary and prepare them for publishing.'

'Of course I'll take them,' replied his wife.

The scent of victory hung in the pre-spring breeze, perfuming the air with sweet bread rolls from the baker's next door and with paint from a house being renovated nearby. But it was not only the scent of victory which hung in the air; victory itself was hanging like a ripe pear, about to fall.

'I've already got the books,' said his wife. 'And the files, too. But I've had a look and everything's a real mess. A lot of pages are missing, including the texts by Sologub and Bely. Someone's had a good old rummage in those files.'

'I wonder how that son of a bitch explains that,' said the writer.

'He says the burglars did it. Supposedly looking for money.'

'Mmm. I reckon those burglars are employed by the government and even wear shoulder straps.'

'Yeah, it's a dirty business,' said his wife. 'It's a shame archive materials suffered.'

18.

An uneventful month passed before he heard from her again; this time she sent him an e-mail. There was not much news – a new secretary had been elected to the democratic Writers' Union, instead of the one who had been hounded to death, and now he held evenings of Russian poetry in the Central House of Writers. Tartar and Jewish poets were not invited to read alongside their Russian colleagues. When the secretary was pressed for time, "Motya Kuzkina" chaired the evenings in the role of his volunteer assistant; "Kuzkina" was a lady of initiative, as everyone knew, and he had recently been nominated for a prize in recognition of his contribution to organising Russian literature. You don't happen to know what it was exactly he contributed to our Russian literature, do you?

Click, click – and he reached a site calling itself: "All Russian writers of modernity." The omnipresent "Motya Kuzkina" was listing the members of his little parallel reality. A few well-known writers were mentioned for the sake of appearances, but it was as though the rest had been accidentally omitted.

"Aha, there it is – the injection of a different reality into the real reality," thought Swidersky. "But who knows, it may find acceptance, and grow into Europe like a shaggy root."

When he had struggled to the end of the page, he was overawed by his own prophetic powers. In small letters at the bottom of the page it said that the author of the site, in response to the wishes of foreign philologists, was intending to create versions of this useful internet resource in other European languages.

19.

On the following Monday, Swidersky spied a white envelope in the letter box. It contained a letter from an acquaintance in Moscow, a well-known poet. "It has come to my attention that you have had a misunderstanding with Mr. Sakovich. That is most regrettable. Two such distinguished figures who have both contributed so much to our literature... How could you fail to find common ground? You are stronger: take the initiative – make peace."

"Mmm," thought Swidersky. "A robber is trying to relieve me of my wallet, he's already reaching into my pocket, but suddenly a constable appears at the end of the alley. The robber pretends he was embracing me and walks off at a leisurely pace, whistling a jaunty tune. A Respectable Gentleman approaches and addresses them both: "How regrettable it is that you have had a misunderstanding! Rise above the circumstances, shake hands with one another. How could you fail to find common ground?"

Writers are dangerous people, you know. Every now and then their thoughts land on paper. And so now Swidersky's thoughts landed on a sheet of ruled writing paper, more or less as they had visited him. From there they landed in an envelope which made its way from Germany to Moscow without any unnecessary postal rush, and arrived three weeks later. The Well-Known Poet took offence and kept quiet.

20.

The worst thing about nightmares is not their proximity to reality but their persistence. It is like sailing in the fog: shore is nowhere to be found. "Blessed are those who know how to forget," thought Swidersky. "They should teach that in school, really."

The next week Swidersky received a phone call from the editor-in-chief of a thick journal which had agreed to print his new novel.

'I'm afraid I can't print it,' croaked a senile voice.

'But the issue is already at the printers,' said the writer in surprise.

'Well, they haven't started printing it yet. I've been forced to recall the novel.'

'Been *forced*? Who forced you?'

                                    

'You remember you have a negative hero in your novel? Well, it's bad timing, my dear fellow, bad timing.'

The negative hero in that novel was a KGB official.

"Just like the bad old days," thought the writer as he tossed about on his narrow couch before falling asleep. "I've fallen under the horse. The question is, how come horses are allowed to roam through the rooms in our communal house and squash people? Or are they ghosts of horses, or of bison, from the legends of the Wild Soviet West? But they're very substantial ghosts, if they can squash someone. Yet if you try to tug their tail, there's nothing there, just thick, foul-smelling air or sticky goo. Like that Mandicant. Try catching someone like him by the tail... Our writers' community is like a pond of jellyfish!"

And his grey, diffuse Russian nightmare finally dispersed, replaced by distinctness, in the black and white German kind.

# BRITISH AGENT

## 1.

In the whirlpool of imagination, time ceases to be time and becomes a substance with inconstant parameters; a person ceases to be a person and becomes a shadow that only other people's memories can shape. Let's follow time's backward flow toward the person whose shadow, perhaps, still lives in somebody's memory.

On a cold November evening in 1938 the forty-two year old Irish engineer PJ was sitting alone at a little table in the "Lazy Bar". The Muscovites knew it as the lazy bar because it was on Lazy Street, not far from the Bolshoy Kamenny Bridge. PJ was wearing a woollen sweater with a deer pattern as well as his jacket; he was always cold in Moscow.

Against the wall opposite him there was an aquarium of languid fish with a mirror hanging over it, and PJ could see his far-off self in it. Himself: the Irish boy from the village, the American teenager and the father of two. A framed mirror is as good as any portrait. He tried counting the fish but got a different total each time. When he was drunk there seemed to be millions of them. Magnified by the glass walls of the aquarium, they seemed huge and would turn their greedy, pouting lips towards him, just like the prostitutes on Tverskaya Street. The whole bar was submerged in a dull, yellowy light which transformed it into an oily, watery dimension: man's immersion in his surroundings.

No-one came in. No Irishmen in the bar on a Friday night? Now that was odd. There were five Irishmen in Moscow at the beginning of the thirties. Patrick Joseph Kitt—or PJ—had been the first to arrive, back in the early twenties, and so he was regarded as 'the elder' of this small Irish community. Then there was the engineer and metallurgist, Padraig Beglin from Dublin, and three sales representatives who worked for different British firms and hailed from Sligo, Galway and Wexford. They had adopted the Lazy Bar not because they were too lazy to go elsewhere, but because they could talk in peace there, tucked in behind the aquarium at the stout oak table with four chairs.

The bar didn't serve Irish beer, of course, or whiskey, either, so they drank Russian vodka. The Irishmen diluted their vodka fifty-fifty with water and the Russian clientele would stare at the strange foreigners. Russians don't dilute anything with water, not even pure spirit. And so what? They don't even burn their gullets. It's probably due to the quality of Russian spirit – or the quality of Russian gullets.

'Do you know what I like about this bar? Soviet civil servants don't drink here,' someone whispered right in PJ's ear.

'You don't need to whisper, Séamus,' said PJ. 'Soviet civil servants don't speak English.'

'You can never be too careful... They always look so innocent.'

Séamus McCarthy from Wexford was one of the sales representatives. The others had gone elsewhere, but he'd stayed in Moscow and busied himself with nationwide statistics. He had the dark hair of the Celts, now streaked with grey, and his blue eyes gazed out from the depths of his eye sockets lending him a sad yet mysterious air. He had an intellectual's high brow and the set facial expression of a person seemingly devoid of any emotion. He was always very busy and showed up at the bar less and less often, but he didn't like to miss a Friday night. He needed to unburden his heart after a week's work, as he put it. He certainly wasn't a Communist; he would pour scorn on them behind their backs, and on Sundays he went to mass in the Polish church on Malaya Gruzinskaya Street. It's not that he preferred Poles to Russians, it's just that it was the only Catholic church in Moscow. He stayed in Russia because here he had the chance to use his mathematical skills, which were undervalued in his native land. Russia was made up of numbers, and if you don't believe it, check for yourself – just take a look at the map crammed with unfathomable figures, or at a Russian's head, stuffed with newspaper statistics of dubious usefulness and even more dubious trustworthiness, and which have nothing whatsoever in common with real statistics. Catching up with America, overtaking America, increasing production by thirty percent – thirty percent of what, for Christ's sake?! And where is the money for it all, dear comrades? Where are they, those hammer-and-sickled notes snatched out of circulation? In whose pockets are they accumulating?

'All civil servants here are Soviet. There simply aren't any others,' PJ remarked darkly. 'Just as everyone in this country is a Communist, or at least a sympathiser. And if they're neither a Communist nor a sympathiser, then they have my sympathies, because they're either in the grave or in the nick.'

'Good Lord, PJ, that's not what we expect to hear from a committed builder of a socialist society.'

'I've got nothing against socialism, as you know. It's tyranny I'm opposed to. What they've built here is some kind of Ottoman Empire. The only difference is that they don't impale people here.'

'Maybe they do, how do you know? What do we know about what goes on in the cellars of the Lubyanka?'

'Well, it's a cheery talk you're having, gentlemen,' came a young voice from behind PJ's back.

PJ gave a start and protested softly:

'What possessed you both to come sneaking up from behind, as though you'd made a pact?'

'Yes, we Molly Maguire Irish conspirators are dangerous folk!' Padraig Beglin laughed. He was a young man with a round face and straw-coloured hair. And he came to the bar as often as he could.

He was a fine fellow, Padraig, from Clontarf, in the glorious city of Dublin, right on the sea side. A cheery chap with a twinkle in his seawater green eyes, and never short of a joke. And he sang really well, too, especially once he'd been lubricated with a glass of vodka. He had a wide repertoire which wasn't limited to *Danny Boy* and *Carrickfergus* but included songs from the olden days, too. His family hailed from County Donegal and he spoke—and sang—equally well in English and Irish. The bar always went quiet when he stroke up a song. PJ had noticed that Russians appreciate art even when they are blind drunk.

'It's no laughing matter, Padraig,' McCarthy said, lowering his voice. 'Did you know an Irishman was shot in the cellars of the Lubyanka this week?'

'What?!' his friends cried out in unison.

'Hey, keep your voices down! Don't attract attention. I was told about it in secret, no-one's meant to know.'

'Who was it?' asked PJ. He was quite shocked. 'I thought we were the only Irish here these days.'

'I'd never met him, I've only heard his name. He was called Brian Gould, from County Donegal.'

    

'I think there were Goulds living in Buncrana,' Padraig said in a subdued voice. 'How did he fetch up here in Moscow, and why did he keep himself to himself?'

'They say he was a secret agent. The English thought he was working for them, but in fact he was working for the Russians. But they evidently didn't trust him too much because they abducted him from Spain, brought him to Moscow and held him in the Lubyanka cellars right up until this week.'

'Mmm. I hope they won't think there's an Irish conspiracy,' said PJ pensively.

'Or an English one,' said McCarthy in the same tone.

'Oh, be quiet! Don't remind me about my English passport. Just as well Hitler is still the Russians' enemy number one, so we all see the Soviets as potential allies.'

'Come off it, no-one's anyone's ally. It's every man for himself in this day and age, and that applies to countries, too.'

'Well, we'll soon see who's allied to whom if war breaks out,' remarked PJ.

'Let's prepare for our past,' said Padraig. 'For the battle of Somme, say, or no, the Battle of Borodino. We'll position culverins and howitzers, erect redoubts, and break in the uniforms. Then we'll have to find Napoleon. We can look for him where the Germans looked for Hitler: in the madhouse. And then we'll fight. Many of us shall fall, but they won't even notice it – they'll be ready for their past. The generals will be ready for the past, too, but not their own. And that's all there is to it – not the most difficult thing in the world. It's what they call passing the exam on knowing the future.'

'Mmm. And a gloomy future it'll be if things turn out that way,' muttered PJ. 'It's hard enough to live in this country as it is, I hate to think what it'll be like in wartime!'

'I'd gladly get out of here and go anywhere, but there's no chance of that now,' said McCarthy. 'They might think I was somehow in cahoots with that Brian and arrest me at the border. They'd arrest me, sure as the Pope's a Catholic. I'll have to sit it out. Wait, then skedaddle at the first opportunity.'

'It's easy for you to talk of skedaddling, you're only here temporarily,' put in Padraig. 'You can just pack your bags and go.'

He had left a family behind in Dublin, a wife and two children. And in Moscow he was living with a Russian woman who was already expecting his child. But despite everything, Padraig was still an incorrigible optimist. Well, you had to be an optimist—or a Communist—to live in Moscow in the thirties, and Padraig was both. Born into a Catholic family, he had spurned the faith and joined the Communist Party of Ireland. He had moved to Russia because of his political convictions and was working conscientiously. He was a romantic, pragmatic man and to put it simply, he was happy to help the world along just so long as the world helped him along, too. He didn't know that in Russia it never quite works out.

'We're all of us on this earth temporarily,' McCarthy said dismally.

'Don't fall into the sin of whinging, Séamus,' said Padraig. 'You're a religious man, it's against your principles. And none of us should complain, anyway. There's no point. Let's have a drink instead. It's on me. What'll it be?'

'Jesus, what else is there here but vodka?' muttered McCarthy.

They walked home, filling Moscow's chill suburban alleys with the sound of Irish song. Dogs howled along lazily. The stars slipped out of the Great Bear into the Small Bear, then grouped themselves into the wondrous wild beasts of the newly-established proletarian zoo.

PJ was tipsier than usual. They dropped him off first, handing him over to his wife like a postal parcel. They got her out of bed and, dishevelled, she gave them a dirty look. She didn't have time for Padraig; he was too loud, drank a lot and liked to get her Iosif drunk, too. She drew a line between "drinking companion" and "friend", and Padraig fell into the first category. She only put up with him because for a long time he had been the only other Irishman in town and she realised her husband needed the company of at least one fellow Irishman. She thought McCarthy was a serious man, though, and didn't like to see him drunk. She herself never let anything stronger than weak wine pass her lips, and would dilute even that with boiled water. She would get the holy shivers at the mere mention of vodka, as though that high-spirited substance was the personification of all the ills of the world.

However, she kept a carafe of vodka in her cupboard to use for cold compresses when the children had earache. PJ knew his wife well, so he never suspected any spirits could be kept in the house, even for medicinal purposes; he never found out about the carafe in the cupboard.

2.

A commissar was a sex symbol. Every woman wanted a commissar but there weren't enough to go round, so the women had to make do with someone else instead. Men who looked even vaguely like commissars went like hot cakes. In the 1920's, PJ was almost like a commissar: a handsome figure, a foreigner in military boots, with curly brown hair and gingery whiskers.

Work in a printing-house came along at last. He could already make himself understood in Russian but he would make funny mistakes and the female workers liked to tease and correct him. They liked to talk with him: he looked like a commissar.

And then, years later, an "interesting life" set in.

At night, when the wind was howling and flapping its wings, the black cars were busy reaping a peculiar harvest of their own. There weren't enough prisons of course, and they planned to commandeer space in detention centres. The plan was carried out. More prisons meant more prisoners. People whispered among themselves: X was arrested yesterday. He was a church-goer. Are they going after Orthodox believers now? But the next day the son of a nobleman was arrested, and a secretary of the Party Committee, and then the next day, a foreigner and a Russian engineer. There wasn't any logic to it, but people still looked for some pattern nevertheless.

'Be careful, Iosif,' his wife would say to him in the morning. 'Don't say anything you shouldn't.'

"That would be all well and good if only I knew what I 'shouldn't' say," he thought as he sat on the trolleybus; he did his thinking on the journey as he had no time for it at work. "I hardly ever say anything as it is. The only time I air my soul is on a Friday with the lads. I just mind my own business, and the rest is by the by. A man can get by without contact with his own kind. Animals can, and we're no worse. When did humans become social animals, and what has it brought us? Is Momus tragic or comic? Must Caliban see himself in the mirror of others' words? Caliban... a strange name, that. Sounds Irish: Cailigh Bain..."

Once in his office, PJ looked at the spiky diagram of success and the ubiquitous Lenin in his Irish cap. That wily Pooka* is often credited as the inventor of labour camps – they say, no-one had thought of them until he came along. Mind you, someone had once told PJ that the English had actually been the first to come up with them, during the Boer wars. Not on such a large scale, of course, and not on their own soil. So it seems that Lenin merely adopted the idea and developed it, just as he developed everything and took it to the limits of reality. And he looks just like a sweet, cunning tippler from County Offaly or Tipperary! PJ's secretary had found the portrait and hung it up in the office—an inoculation against arrest—and PJ put up with it because of the cap; it had something Irish about it after all. But he would rather let himself be killed than have that moustached Georgian hanging in his office. He wasn't fond of portraits anyway, no matter whose they were, nor did he like his own face. If he had a god, it was a nameless, faceless god, like the god of the ancient Jews.

His other god was his work. He did his job, and he liked to do it well. His printing house specialised in brochures, the majority of which were party papers, and he had also been commissioned by the Ministry of Defence to print *The Red Warrior* newspaper. PJ read that paper and saw the red warrior not as the hero of future battles but as an insignificant man suffering from hunger and cold, duped by hundreds of contradictory directives. "It's none of my business," he thought. "I'm here to see that the newspaper is printed as it should be, and it is. It spawns future heroes. My Irish scepticism doesn't mean I do a bad job. I wonder how many sceptics there are in this land of compulsory enthusiasm."

3.

Running in spirals, yes, spirals. Here today, tomorrow in the many points which comprise "there". Yesterday it was the back of beyond with the blues, in the morning the symbols of space assemble themselves into some resemblance of a hillock, and you forget that there is a downhill slope on the other side, and the next moment there you are, slithering into something you could write a rather Verlaine-esque verse about, but you only write it in a dream, thank God.

---

*       A creature in Celtic folklore often appearing as a goblin; can sometimes be malevolent.

     

The spiral is the Celtic symbol of life force and inspiration, but where are they, that life force and inspiration? At the other end of the spiral, especially since the Celtic spiral is endless!

In those days Stalin was spinning a spiral with Hitler, and they merged in predatory world-consuming avarice. The world was already splitting in two in their lusting eyes, and each thought the other had the larger half. The caricatures of whiskered fascists disappeared from the papers and were replaced by those of corpulent, tweed-clad British imperialists.

'So what does all that mean for us?' asked Padraig. He'd just got over a cold and was just drinking weak Russian beer that Friday. 'Which side are we on now?'

'On our own side, as ever,' said PJ. 'On Ireland's side.'

'But who will the Russians see us as now?'

'As unwelcome foreigners,' put in McCarthy, blowing out a perfect smoke ring. 'And that's how they've always seen us, by the way.'

'The real question is: who do they take us for, and do they realise that Ireland and England are two quite different countries?' There was a note of despair in PJ's voice; he could feel his English passport burning through his jacket.

'Well, the Germans certainly understand the difference,' remarked McCarthy, sending smoke rings up to the Lazy Bar's stucco ceiling. 'They want us to join forces with them against England. And by the way, Dev* loves the Germans.'

'He's gone short-sighted,' said Padraig. 'A man's applying for a job as director of the National Museum in Dublin. He sends his papers to Dev for a signature – it's an important post, after all, so the head of the government has to approve it. And they tell Dev: everything's in order, but one of the fellow's documents is a bit odd, take a look. Dev says: I don't see anything. Here, look, they tell him. This man's a German, a big cheese in the Nazi party. It's written right here, don't you see? But Dev says: I don't see anything, don't bother showing me. And he signs the nomination.'

'Where do you get hold of Irish jokes?' PJ asked in amazement.

'What do you mean, jokes?! I wish it were a joke.'

---

*      Eamon de Valera (1882-1975), the Republic of Ireland's Prime Minister at the time of these events.

4.

A counter with squares on it. Squares and more squares... But no, wait. They aren't squares but little white cardboard gift boxes. Gifts for everyone. Nobody has anything, yet there is a gift for everyone, a sign that he is remembered, that his work is noted, and that he himself is in full view.

And how happy the people are as they open their little boxes! There is a toy house for one, a toy car for another, a person for somebody else. A toy person, of course. Just as all people are toys.

Someone else gets a box labelled: "Nothing Special". He opens it up and finds another box inside, then another inside that one... And in the very smallest one he finds – who would have thought it? Yes, the very person who created all this. The god-child. With the face of a People's Commissar. And someone up above is wagging a finger at him menacingly, saying: the time has come to give people new toys. More modern ones...

One of the latest toys in the state's household was that gigantic vacuum cleaner of the Lubyanka, a highly economically viable mechanism within the framework of some aberrative—or operative?— state thought. And that mechanism began sucking people in. And in 1940, it began swallowing some Englishmen, too, who were in Moscow on private business and not under the auspices of the embassy or trade missions. Many of them were snatched right off the street.

'Moscow's one big museum of grimaces nowadays,' Padraig said the following Friday. 'Smirking, snarling, faces distorted with malice are peering out everywhere. Some gnash their teeth at the visitors—in other words at us—but others are engrossed in contemplating their own grotesque nature. Before long they'll be announcing a competition for the best grimace, as a national symbol. Have a guess – who do you think stands the best chance of winning?'

'I know who you have in mind, but you can't call Stalin a national symbol,' said McCarthy. 'There's something monstrous about what he's doing.'

'Hitler's not a national symbol, either,' said PJ. 'But that's not the point. Some nations have very strange symbols in these sad times. Have you ever seen those cardboard figures in the fair ground where you can put your face in the hole? That's what Russia is like now, and Germany, too.

     

The whole nation ends up just like whichever ruler sticks his face in the hole.'

'In other words, the hole is the national symbol?' quipped the incorrigible Padraig. 'But why do the Russian people stand for it...?'

'It's not about the Russians. Sometimes the times breed monsters,' explained the methodical McCarthy. 'Now it's the era of the likes of Mussolini, Hitler and another historical figure I could mention. It's a time of tyrants. But who's to say what will happen in fifty years... Maybe democracy's turn will come.'

'In fifty years... But first we have to live that long,' sighed PJ. 'Maybe we'd better stop meeting in this bar?'

'Where else can we meet? Is there an alternative in this city?' Padraig asked. He'd already managed to drink so much that day that eternity finally fitted into the camera obscura of his gaze: the walls of the Lazy Bar glided apart, opening up a never-ending suite of rooms leading into the depths of space.

'Maybe we shouldn't meet up at all? It's becoming dangerous. Who knows, maybe we look like conspirators to them?'

'Ah, so now we can't even meet up any more,' Padraig pronounced with drunken sorrow. 'But why not? Because there's no place for us here. Tell us, o thou who art most wise, where on earth is there a place for the Irish, except the Emerald Isle?'

'You're right, of course, but there's not so much room on the Emerald Isle, either,' said PJ. 'If you gathered up all the Irish Diaspora, all those hordes and hordes of folk, you'd have to find a bigger island for them. Even Australia would be a tight squeeze.'

'True enough, true enough. We are a great nation, it's just that no-one knows it. Such is the huge secret,' sighed Padraig. 'Let's just have drinks and forget about it all. I for one want to enjoy life. I met a girl yesterday, if only you'd seen her... We're going to the cinema together tomorrow evening.'

'Not enough room, you say? They'll find room for us here all right,' McCarthy said, giving his young companion a disapproving look: Padraig's live-in lover would soon give birth and his eyes were already straying. 'And they'll find a fitting article to put us behind bars. As the Russians say: if there's a man, there's an article.'

'Guilty until proven innocent,' Padraig said, trying to make light of it. 'You know what, gentlemen, I think we all look guilty today, as if we'd done something wrong.'

'We did something wrong all right, a long time ago,' McCarthy muttered glumly. 'When we came to Moscow. I for one am trying to get out of here now. I'm going to apply to leave, on family grounds.'

'That's hardly a good idea,' said PJ. 'You said yourself we should sit it out quietly.'

'I can't just sit and wait for them to arrest me.'

PJ knew what he meant. A sort of impatience seized him, too, sometimes: if they wanted to come for him, then for God's sake let them come and be done with it!

That night he dreamt he was having a check-up at the barber's. The inspector was amazed:

'I've seen blonds, brunettes, red-heads... but you've got a tricoloured head!'

'I hope there are a lot of other shades there, too,' said the manifestation of PJ.

'But what do all these lines and contours signify? Why did you draw them?'

'I didn't draw them. They just appeared all by themselves.'

'Your head's very round, too.'

'Yes. And the oceans and continents are all there, blue and green, with patches of yellow, too. Those are the deserts.'

'A real globe, eh?'

'Yeah, that's right, a globe.'

And PJ was ordered to cover his head with a paper hat made from the best patriotic newspapers. And so he sat by a little stream in that stupid hat, sailing little black and white boats on the water and thinking that all streams flow into the blue ocean anyway.

5.

The Soviet skyscraper on Kotelnichesky Quay looked surreal and resembled one of Piranesi's drawings inside an enormous Piranesi drawing commonly known as the Soviet Union. McCarthy lived there but then simply vanished, and no-one answered his phone any more. PJ went over to Kotelnichesky Quay to see if his friend was still there. He roamed the maze of corridors for a long time, bobbing up and down in the lifts. There were five lifts and each one brought him to a different wing of the building where the numbers on the flats began with a different figure. His footsteps raised whispers and he couldn't shake the feeling that someone was following close on his heels, or watching him from the little windows in the lift shafts. And there was that hairdressers' *chic* everywhere: polished, panelled walls and opaque glass with vignettes of grapes.

He came across the door he was looking for by sheer chance: number 505. It was a brown door upholstered in leatherette. There was a large, red seal on the lock, another on the lintel, and a strong rope ran between them. The flat had been sealed off.

PJ knew what that meant. The whole of Moscow knew what it meant: a knock at the door in the dead of night, a "black raven" car waiting in the yard, the Lubyanka cellars, interrogations and beatings, beatings and interrogations, and then, if you were lucky, prison. Or if you were unlucky, the sputter of a bullet in your chest, against the wall of that same cellar.

He walked to Krasnaya Presnya. That was where Padraig lived – he had to warn him, but not over the phone. He didn't take the shortest route but followed the embankment of the Moskva River. The road led him right under the Kremlin walls. For a moment PJ realised he was right between the Kremlin above him and the British Consulate on the opposite bank. There was a certain symbolism in it – a typical position for the Irish, "in between", with an empire to the right and another to the left, and there he was, walking along between them, his "Storm Petrel" boots leaving footprints in the light November snow. But where does our path lead us?

When he had nearly reached an all but identical skyscraper on Presnya, he turned into a side street and came out by a modest two-storey house where Padraig lived with his Russian girlfriend in a large, badly-heated apartment. Half of the house was completely uninhabitable. The apartments in that section had either stood in ruins since the times of the Civil War or had fallen into disrepair more recently, and it never even occurred to anyone to renovate them.

A thought flashed through PJ's mind: what if Padraig's flat is sealed off, too? But no, everything looked OK, and he rang the doorbell.

After a lengthy pause, the door was opened by a young, fair-haired woman of around twenty-five. It had evidently taken her a while to get to the door, and she walked with difficulty now, in her eighth month, PJ realised.

'Padraig's not in. I expect he's still at work,' she said, wrapping the two halves of her dressing gown round her, and PJ thought to himself: why is it that Russian women always slouch around the house in a dressing gown? Don't they have anything decent to wear?

'It's already after seven,' he said.

'I thought he was with you... Jesus, I hope nothing's happened to him!'

'So do I,' PJ said. 'Give me a ring when he gets home.'

But Padraig didn't come home that evening nor the next day. He had been arrested at work, right in his own office.

6.

That night PJ thought about the people who spent their whole life trying to catch up with someone, and about other people, too, who spend their whole life catching up with themselves to the measured step of their wall clocks. The starless blackness seeped in through the window; he was worried about his missing friends. Were they still alive? How could you tell whether a person had already caught up with himself and had nowhere left to go in this world of numbers and clock faces? Maybe he is floating in bottomless, boundless dark waters where there is only ebb and flow, like the plashing pulse in his temples?

But the darkness gave no answer. Instead, it was breeding phantoms of a socialist paradise: gigantic bronze labourers squeezing cobble stones, Pavlov's beheaded dogs genially holding out their paws, a Michurian hybrid of ripeness and conscience. But that paradise is far from cosy: your body merges into a communal body, the shadows dance legless linguistic dances, and the probing rays of the projector search all living beings, inside and out...

PJ began feeling his "marginality". Marginality in the sense of standing on the edge of an abyss, peering down. Well, an abyss is an abyss, nothing more, nothing less, and you can be ensnared by deadly things, but how long can you stay standing on the edge, and will the rim crumble?

He no longer went anywhere apart from to work and back. He'd stopped seeing anyone at all. "Will I manage to "sit it out"? My two Irish friends have been arrested but I, the "Englishman", am still unharmed even though a glance at any newspaper is enough to tell you what the

Soviets think of those "English Imperialists" now. Is there any logic to it? Is there any logic to anything anymore in this day and age? Odd that someone might take me for an Englishman! If it weren't for that little scrap of paper called a passport, who would be able to say where I hailed from or who I was? But here I am, an "Englishman" in a hostile land, exposed to hostile winds as though I were standing on the edge of a half-finished house's roof. And my short-winded, decaying youth is climbing up the spiral staircase, pausing at every window, catching its breath, pretending to admire the sunshine of forgotten landscapes and asking how many storeys I envisage."

## 7.

Days were playing hide and seek with the following days; they ran away followed closely by newly arrived days, making Christmas approach quicker. But no-one celebrated Christmas in Communist Russia, or if they did, they did so on the quiet, and in January. So the printing-house was marking a different celebration: its fifteenth anniversary. PJ was not fond of anniversaries, but this one was special – this was 'his' printing-house!

The celebratory banquet was held in Manezh Square, in the restaurant of the prestigious Hotel Moskva. The building was completely square, and everything else about it was square, too: the facade, the windows, the tables. The faces of those present didn't want for squareness, either. The only thing which was not square was the jokes, and that was because they fell flat.

"Well, what can you expect, gentlemen, from members of the Party's Regional Committee?" PJ thought to himself. "They were born somewhere out in the sticks, didn't have any education worth speaking of, and would have just spent their whole lives vegetating in some local factory but then bang, along comes the Revolution, and Communists are in great demand, especially working class ones. Studying's boring, and why bother when you can already embellish yourself with a nice Party position straight away?" There were representatives of the intelligentsia in the Party, too, of course, but no-one trusted them. It was enough for the Leader to mention the "rotten intelligentsia" and everyone realised what sort of label you could hang on any educated person. Just let the Leader try and say: "the rotten working class"! He'd really be in trouble then! But you could say it about the intelligentsia. The intelligentsia will put up with anything – if you spit on them, they'll wipe their faces; if you walk all over them, they'll get up and dust themselves off, and they might even apologise.

The clamour of the celebratory speeches had subsided, and the celebrating Party workers were now getting blatantly drunk. PJ spotted a bottle of fine Crimean rosé port at the end of the table and they passed it to him readily: Russians drink vodka. If they don't drink vodka then doubt is cast over their Russian-ness.

'We hope that your printing-house won't be publishing *The Red Warrior* on its twentieth anniversary but will have upgraded to *Pravda* or *Izvestia**, one of the honoured guests sitting opposite PJ said with drunken benevolence. He was the head of the propaganda department at the Party's Municipal Committee.

"What a fool!" PJ thought to himself, but aloud he said:

'Yes, that would be wonderful, of course. But we can't print national papers. We're just a small printing-house.'

'*The Red Warrior* is a very important paper, too,' PJ's deputy, Grushin, launched himself into the conversation. He was looking for an excuse to hobnob with the big cheeses.

PJ had taken Grushin on as his assistant some years back. He was a young engineer from Siberia, but a Party member, too, and that's what gave him his upward mobility. He was transferred to Moscow, and the Party Regional Committee recommended him highly to PJ.

PJ had said to his wife:

'Well, let him deal with the Party Committee and that kind of thing. Someone has to do it, and it's not my forte.'

And so Grushin had become the deputy director, and within a year he had already managed to hire another engineer, saying that he himself was too busy with Party business. He had no interest in the printing process, and that suited PJ just fine.

PJ had invited Grushin round to dinner once. He had been on his best behaviour, smiling at PJ's daughters, and his thin little nose had trembled at the slightest movement of his fleshy, pink cheeks. PJ had thought he smiled rather too much – did he do absolutely

---

*        Two major Russian newspapers. 'Pravda' means 'truth'; 'Izvestia' means 'news'.

                                        

everything with a smile? That smile is like a mask... Does he even take it to the loo with him? Grushin was saying about himself: "I am a good person, therefore I smile." But if someone advertised himself as a good person, PJ was inclined to send a private detective after him to find out just exactly how 'good' he really was and what he got up to in those moments when he was not entirely 'good'. All it takes is a gust of wind and that so-called goodness falls away like petals from a daisy. And it's the ones who blow their own trumpets who lose that 'goodness' first. And so—like Stanislavsky—I am not fooled! I don't believe!

When Grushin left, PJ's younger daughter said:

'Daddy, can't you stop Grunty coming again?'

And so the nickname stuck, and Grushin became Grunty. When PJ brought a staff photograph home from some official do at the office, his elder daughter made the most of a moment when her parents' attention was elsewhere and quickly scrawled Grushin's nickname above his head, so that no-one would forget.

But this evening Grushin was particularly animated, as though he saw some as yet unchartered Party horizons opening up before him.

'We do our very best to ensure our paper comes out on time,' he was eager to assure the man from the Party's Municipal Committee, looking straight into the pupils of his rather dull eyes.

'Yes, of course,' the Municipal Committee man was glad of the chance to rectify his earlier slip.

'It's just that your printing-house doesn't like our Party papers!' blurted out the deputy Secretary of the Regional Committee, Kovbasyuk.

His tone was jolly unfriendly although he masked it as a joke.

Kovbasyuk was well known as an anti-Semite of Ukrainian coinage who considered all Jews to be enemies and all foreigners to be Jews. He'd somehow heard that PJ's wife was Jewish and that was reason enough for him to nurture a hatred for PJ.

'What do you mean, we don't like *Pravda* and *Izvestia*? They're both posted up on the walls so the workers can read them during their breaks,' Grushin reported.

'And I really like *The Red Warrior*,' said PJ. 'The military servicemen and women who read it can find material there about their own lives.'

'I'm pleased you like *The Red Warrior*, but does that mean you are less fond of *Pravda* and *Izvestia*?' Kovbasyuk kept on at him.

'Not at all. Each paper has its strengths,' PJ replied diplomatically.

'Come now, Comrade Director,' the head of the Regional Committee began in a friendly tone. 'Go ahead and speak your mind about our Communist papers. After all, we're all friends here, we've known each other for years. And anyhow, Marxism isn't true Marxism without criticism. Lenin said so himself. What would you say are the failings of our two main newspapers?'

PJ ran his eyes over those drunken faces, searching in vain for the slightest hint of intelligence, and he thought: so much for intellect! Genies, you're looking for something where nothing has been hidden. And it turned his stomach, and his head spun, and midnight didn't herald a new day and it was not the sun which rose to its zenith but Kovbasyuk's huge fleshy, round muzzle, and he, PJ, suddenly didn't want to hide his thoughts from anyone anymore.

'So you want to know what I think of *Pravda* and *Izvestia*?' PJ said simply in a cheery tone. 'There's not enough news in *Pravda*, and not enough truth in *Izvestia*.'

Grushin and the head of the Regional Committee were about to roar with laughter but suddenly stopped themselves in fright. An eerie hush descended; people had been locked up for less recently.

The end of the evening sank into silence and small talk.

The joke spread through Moscow like wildfire the next day, whispered into the ears of tried and trusted people. Your wife, husband or brother were not necessarily trusted people; your confidant could be someone else entirely, because we test people's trustworthiness with our own weaknesses and their desire—or lack of it—to take advantage of those weaknesses.

PJ scolded himself on the way home: a fine one, I am. Couldn't keep my Irish humour in check. "We're all friends here"... I wonder which of those "friends" will be the first to ring the NKVD? Friends are always friends – here and there and everywhere, and heaven only knows who else they might be friends with.

8.

However the stream of days was flowing smoothly and PJ was left in peace for the time being. One day passed, then two, then three.

     

"Surely I won't get away with it?" he thought. He didn't mention it to his wife – no need to worry her.

On the morning of the fourth day there was a knock at the door of his office. Two men in uniform and green cap-bands stood there; such men had become an all too familiar sight recently. They said they had a warrant to search his office and suggested he stayed while they searched.

PJ just shrugged, thinking: if you want to arrest me, go ahead, but why bother to search my office? What can you find here?

To his amazement, they seemed to know exactly what they were looking for. They opened the desk drawers and pulled out a book. The golden title gleamed against the red cover: L. Trotsky.

PJ rubbed his eyes. It certainly wasn't his, and he had no idea where it could have come from.

It was a crime to keep books by the disgraced People's Commissar, let alone read them. No doubt Stalin's books would have met the same fate if Trotsky had succeeded Lenin, as Lenin himself had intended. It was ironic, really – these Communists came down more heavily on each other than they did on their class enemies. Maybe it's because they have to share one habitat, so they fight over it like predators?

'Is this your book?' a metallic voice jerked PJ out of his reverie.

"I wonder if they're specially trained to sound like that?" thought PJ. Aloud he said:

'No. And I have no idea what it's doing in my office, either.'

'Well, this printing-house has a fine director, if he doesn't even know what's going on in his own office! Put your coat on. You're coming with us.'

"Who could have planted that book on me?" PJ wondered as they led him along the unusually deserted corridor, now as long as non-existence. There were only two possibilities: the secretary, and Grushin. Then of course there was the classic question of who stood to profit from it. Bearing in mind the recent episode in Hotel Moskva, and his secretary's proven loyalty, it could only be Grushin. He must have decided it was time to take the initiative and avail himself of the director's chair. Deal me the final blow, so to speak. After that scene in the hotel he obviously thought he could get away with it, that it wasn't dangerous. Ah, Grunty, Grunty, you "good person!" No wonder children don't like you! That's always a good indicator.

He finished his train of thought in some dank cellar, locked alone with the dampness, a washtub smelling of urine, and a wooden plank bed with a stinking straw mattress. He was oddly calm, as though it were all happening to someone else. At least there was one good thing: he didn't need to be afraid anymore. He could just stay there, loving his memories and letting his memories love him, attaining reciprocity at last. After all, humans crave reciprocity, even when they have finally reached that final stony, sepulchral reciprocity with the state.

9.

'Have you been here long?' Padraig asked PJ when they were both taken out for exercise.

'They took me three days after you.'

It was hard to recognise Padraig in that doddery ragamuffin dressed in a striped prison robe. PJ wouldn't have recognised him at all if Padraig hadn't called out to him. "I wonder if I look like a station beggar, too," PJ thought. "They don't let us have a mirror, it's against the regulations. They take our own image away from us in the mirrors, as if they were carrying it off on a plate. They claim it for their own as though they hoped the mirrors would go on reflecting what they had reflected previously and not their own protocol faces... Not to see yourself – isn't that both punishment and redemption?"

They were doing laps round the prison's huge stone yard, leaving impatient slushy footprints in the light, fresh New Year snow.

'So, how is it? Do they beat you?' Padraig began cautiously.

'They don't know how to do anything else.' PJ replied gloomily.

'Have you confessed to anything?'

'What is there for me to confess to?'

'Did you know they've shot Séamus? Séamus McCarthy.'

'Good God!'

'He wouldn't confess to anything. That was where he went wrong. You have to confess to something smallish, something they don't shoot you for. I've thought of something: "industrial espionage in the interests of Great Britain." Sounds good, doesn't it?'

'But you're no spy, Padraig, especially not an English one... You're Irish! Surely you can't hope they'll believe you?'

　　　　　　　　ANATOLY KUDRYAVITSKY

'They don't have to believe me. The chap in my cell is a construction engineer from Ukraine and he told them that he planned to bore a tunnel from Moscow to Paris, and that counted as a confession. He got five years. They just have to tick boxes to keep the bosses happy: confessed. If you don't confess they'll beat you to death or shoot you, like they did Séamus. Think about it.'

'In other words, we're guilty from the outset. Something smallish, you say? Five years in prison? OK, I'll see what I can come up with. Best to steer clear of anything to do with ideology, they'd shoot you for that. I suppose "industrial espionage" isn't so bad, after all...'

'Now you're talking,' Padraig nodded.

They plotted and schemed, came up with ideas and rejected them, and weighed their words, but how could they know there could be only one outcome for the likes of them: ten years in the Gulag. And another five years could easily be added once they were already there, in the camp. Or they might be worked to death, effectively making it a death sentence anyway. No-one had been sentenced to immortality yet – that was the capital measure! But they never thought of that, no, they never thought of it.

10.

"Don't go into the shadow of the granite!" warned the Siberian wind as it whistled by. But he did go into the shadows of the granite block of flats. Blue transparent bodies lay on the Moscow pavements. The passers-by obviously didn't see them, and walked on calmly. They avoided the shadow of the granite, they avoided the wind, and that is why they were still alive. When he left the shadow of the granite, the sun shone on the sunny streets just as before. It must be his fate to see millions of transparent shadows, hear the Siberian wind howling even in the very heart of the Soviet Empire, and talk with the dead, for the living don't listen. The living are very corporeal, not at all transparent. They are not hunted by the shadow of granite.

But he sometimes felt the whistle of icy breath on his back. At times like that he would hide in his own house, drawing the curtains and covering his head with the blankets. And people would come and talk to him – dead, bluish people. He cannot forget their words. Perhaps he should write them down. But he was no writer and was not able to sculpt words. And so the shadows remained shadows – unwanted, unseen, unbearable granite shadows.

11.

A cannibal met a huge, shaggy beast in the forest.

"Good day to you, beast," the cannibal growled politely.

"I'm gonna eat you up," blurted the beast out of the blue. "Yes, you. I eat the likes of you, humanoids."

They stared at each other for a long time, then one ate the other. But to this very day, no-one knows who ate who.

There you have it: a terrifying Siberian fairytale. While PJ was in the labour camp, the process of eating up and digesting came to an end, and peace once more reigned over the world of humanoids. And it was more or less clear who had eaten who. But that didn't make things easier for the forest-dwellers.

PJ settled outside the capital when he came back from Siberia; he was still an exile and could have been arrested for breaking the terms of his parole had he shown up in Moscow. His wife and daughters moved out to join him in the suburban village of Malakhovka where he was living in a ramshackle wooden house. A former railway engineer lived in the other half, and had been quietly drinking away his pension for several years.

He had survived; a "British agent" from the times of Stalin's vigilance had come through it. He had returned from the camp having lost his toes to frostbite, i.e. minus a part of himself. Who had he given that part away to? To the cold? To Siberia? To the times? No-one had apologised to him, no-one said: I'm sorry, there was a mistake, please forgive us. Why had they subtracted thirteen years from his life? What had he been guilty of?

As for Padraig, he went straight from the camp to the other world – if, of course, you can say that the camp was part of this world, which is doubtful. A heart attack had finished Padraig off – at thirty-five! Ah, Padraig, how can I live in this huge, cold city without you?

                                        

## 12.

One day, when he had still been living under the terms of parole, he had risked a trip to Moscow. His wife had found out the opening times of the British embassy's consular department and, having smartened himself up, he took a suburban train into Moscow.

The guard at the embassy gates gave him a long, hard stare. Who was that odd man in a tatty black coat, with pensive spectacles and a shaven head? But the embassy guards were trained not to be surprised at anything and if something did surprise them, then they were at least trained not to show it, and to keep their surprise to themselves, modestly and quietly.

Once inside the embassy building, the man in the black coat waited his turn, then showed the secretary a tatty British passport, one of the old kind, and said he wanted to speak to the consul.

He was asked to wait.

Five minutes later, after having spoken to someone on the phone, the girl said:

'The consul's sub-secretary, Mr. Sackville-Large, will see you.'

After another fifteen minutes, a polished man of around forty with fat, rosy cheeks came up to him. He was dressed in a grey suit with an almost imperceptible pattern of pink checks.

'Mr. Er... Kitt, if I'm not mistaken... How are things with you?'

'Not so bad, thank you,' the man in the black coat answered automatically; he had lost the habit of exchanging empty politenesses.

'Take a seat... Tell me, what do you hope to achieve by visiting us? It seems you were a citizen of the United Kingdom...'

'Do you mean I am no longer one of its citizens?'

'We shall, of course, mmm, consider your case. May I take a look at your passport?'

The passport migrated into his hands. He had shiny pink nails.

'Ah, you were born in 1895, in County Mayo. As you know, that is part of another country now. The Republic of Ireland. Ireland doesn't have an embassy in Russia, so we represent the interests of Irish citizens here. But you are, of course, a British subject, if you wish to be one... or if you prefer, to remain one... Would you like tea or coffee?'

'Tea... Thank you...'

Mr. Sackville-Large pressed a bell on his desk.

'They'll bring some tea in a minute... It's quite warm in here, you can take your coat off... Tell me, have you lived in Russia long?'

'Since 1921.'

'Oh! Thirty-two years! I suppose you must like it a lot here.'

'I like some things, I dislike others,' PJ replied warily, finally taking off his coat. 'I would like to go back home.'

'And where is "home"?'

'Ireland.'

'Did you live in Ireland up until 1921?'

'My parents emigrated to America in 1912, when I was seventeen. I lived in the small town of Clinton, Massachusetts.'

'Aha, I thought I detected a slight American twang in your accent... So you came to Russia from America?'

'I served in the American army during the first world war. I fought in Europe.'

'So you are a war veteran... Were you ever a citizen of the United States?'

'No.'

'And you didn't take part in the last war?'

'No. You are no doubt aware of what happened to English-speaking foreigners in Russia in 1940?'

'Well, nothing happened to those working in our embassy. Though of course, many people who were in the Soviet Union on their own private business suffered. You are, no doubt, one of them?'

'Yes. I spent thirteen years in a Siberian labour camp. I was released this year, and still haven't been granted the right to live in Moscow.'

'What were you charged with?'

'The verdict cited state espionage for Great Britain,' PJ said with a grimace of distaste, and thought: Hmm. That's not a pleasant thing for an Irishman; I can't even get my tongue round the words.

'Hmmm. It's a pity the thousands of people who ended up in the camps didn't really work for us,' said the Englishman with a sneer. 'Many of those who survived the camps have now been returned home.'

It was strange to see how the face under the shaven forehead was distorted by some sort of convulsion. Was it hope? He must have gone through so much in the camps...

   

'What do I have to do to return to Ireland?' the visitor asked, looking straight into the diplomat's watery green eyes.

'First of all we have to establish your rights as a citizen. But that is a mere formality... Tell me, were you a member of the Communist Party?'

'I have never been a member of any party.'

'Neither in America nor in Russia?'

'No.'

"I don't believe you!" said the pink smile on the Englishman's well-fed face. "Everyone who spent years in Russia was a Communist, if not by name then by nature!"

'What work did you do?'

'I was the director of a printing-house.'

'Aha, so you were employed by the department of propaganda!' smiled the Englishman. 'The Russian Communists counted you as one of their own, no doubt, if they made you director?'

'I studied in Austria. When the war ended in 1919, the Americans couldn't recall all their GI's from Europe immediately and so they gave quite a tidy sum to those of us who stayed. I decided to study. The following year I passed my exams and qualified as a printing engineer. I set up the printing-house I used to work for myself, many years ago.'

'Don't you work there anymore?'

'No. I'm officially exiled.'

'I see. Tell me, do you have anywhere to live in Ireland?'

'I don't know. So many years have passed...'

'You will have to show us papers proving that your family still lives in the Irish Republic and is prepared to take you in.'

'Is it absolutely necessary?' PJ said with a note of despair.

'Yes. Those are our instructions from the Foreign Office... We cannot just send a person out into nowhere. Don't you have anyone left in Ireland?'

'My parents moved away to Massachusetts with me. I'm afraid they are probably dead by now. My brother lived in America, too, though he later retured to Ireland... It was over thirty years ago. I haven't had any news of them since then. You must have heard that we were not allowed to write to our relatives in the West. It was deemed tantamount to fraternising with the enemy, and you could be locked up for it.'

'Well, write to your folks in Ireland none the less. As soon as you receive confirmation, come to see us again and we will help you. You are in good health I hope?'

'What sort of health can you be in after the camps... Though it could be worse, of course.'

'I advise you to take up running. I go for a run along the bank of the Moskva River every morning, you know. The air is wonderful, and there is a lovely view of the Kremlin on the opposite bank. An hour's run really lifts your spirits!'

And on that note they parted.

No chance, thought Sackville-Large as he finished his tea alone. I feel sorry for the old man, of course. What a life he's had! Seen so many countries! Ireland, America, Austria, Germany, Poland, Russia... Plus fighting as a conscript soldier and thirteen years in the camps! He survived it all and wants to go home! Those Irish must have tanned leather instead of skin. But it's all hopeless. He may write a letter to Ireland, but it won't get any further than the NKVD office. Even if he presented the necessary papers, it would still be hopeless. We only send home the ones we know. And certainly not Irishmen or Communists.

13.

Where is it we are all yearning for? Out of the enchanted circle straight into nowhere, into emptiness. Thoughts, like electrons, trace a circular orbit round an invisible nucleus, and the fads and prejudices of the age act as the centripetal matter. If they scatter – farewell, centrifugality! For the whole world may have once been the Roman Empire, then the British Empire, and then God knows whose empire, but that is not the end; uniformity is still lying in wait for us...

One year later, PJ was given permission to live in Moscow. He went back to his printing-house. They had a new director now. A completely new one, not even PJ's former deputy who had finally got his hands on the directorship after PJ's arrest. He'd since been transferred and given a responsible role in the ministry. PJ didn't know the new director who offered him—the former director—a job as engineer. Still, it was better than starving. Everyone said he'd been very lucky; it was unheard of for a man from the camps to be taken on as an engineer, especially in a printing-house where they made party newspapers! If it weren't for the shortage of specialists, he would never have been offered the job... And who's to blame for the shortage of specialists? PJ thought to himself. And what have you done with them all?

It was as though his past had been a completely different life. He stopped going to the Lazy Bar altogether; it reminded him of his dead friends.

He would sit in the kitchen for hours, a mug of tea on the table in front of him. It was a coarse mug, large and roomy, with a tasteless picture of a tree on a cliff and "Crimea" inscribed below the picture. But for him it was another place entirely, another landscape – an Irish landscape, from his forgotten childhood.

You start believing in God when you go to Ireland, or even cast your mind back to it, and you rebel against your own faith. God is written in the land – the slanting forehead of Ben Bulben, the Teutonic nose of the Wicklow Hills, and the thin hair of the sparse Irish woods. You put this bald Irish god together like a mosaic, taking little pieces from each county. And this rainy, weeping, singing, silver-streamed deity is unmistakeably pagan, and both the implacable Protestants and the convinced Catholics would agree on that, and then they could shake hands, like the wolf and the seven little lambs in the fairy tale, and create something communally. A pagan ritual or a Muslim namaz prayer. Anything would be better than firing at your own reflection in the mirror. And the pagan god gives his demon Crom Cruach a nod, and they lustfully lose themselves in the joint Celtic spiral. And all the streams sing out, all the rivers flow, and at times they carry the people off to some far-off shore...

His brother Thomas had been right, apparently: he should have fought for his country. Ireland was independent now, and it was the only place on earth where he wanted to live. But he was tragically late for his own life, over thirty years late. Does that mean someone else was living his life? Or was it still possible to put things right, to jump into the river which had long since flowed into the ocean?

And how much of the Irishman was left in him now anyway? The accent? The sense of humour? Probably something was still there, buried beneath the surface. They say that a tiger's skin is striped as well as its fur. You can take a look under the fur and check, providing, of course, the tiger lets you.

"All the cells of my body must have been renewed over those thirteen years," he thought, "and I'm not used to my new self yet. Are PJ, Patrick Joseph Kitt, born in December 1895 in the small town of Ballylions in County Mayo, West Ireland, and the Soviet white-collar worker Iosif Kitov, honorary printer of the Russian Soviet Federal Socialist Republic, the same person? If they are, where do the two halves meet? Where do they merge and grow into one whole – if, of course, they can still embody some sort of whole?"

14.

That man with his shaven head and cautious glasses would gaze at the picture for a long time. If you stare at a picture for long enough, you tumble into it, and you might even take root there, for every look has its root, just as every plant has its eye. Would it work now? Would he be able to take root in another reality, in the life which had been aborted years ago? Who knows what that life might have been like...? He had never stayed still, he had always be running ahead. *Homo fugax* – running man. First one country, then another and now – the end of the road: a crooked two-storey house on Taganka, in the low-lying ground not far from the embankment. A house with a crack in the kitchen ceiling and constant damp in the corners. That Moscow damp gets everywhere, from the cellar to the attic, and completely takes over the top floor. A human is one third water, but how about that house on Taganka? Well, just try and check!

But it was all the same to him. He didn't care about his health – it was too late for that. He only did the unavoidable: eating, cleaning his teeth, sleeping, walking. His actions were all automatic. He would take a bath in the morning, and the bath would take him, too, so they would find each other as a keyhole finds a key or lovers find each other. Nirvana in the bath. But it is slippery there, and life slips out of your hands, like soap, and dissolves in the murky water. How can you find it again? Life for life's sake. When it's given, grab it and hold on to it. But now even that tenacity atrophies. Where are the suckers and talons of bygone days? Time had stopped for him. It had doubled back on itself. He was a boy again, and this boyish-ness was growing in him. He wanted to make a universal splash, he wanted to make mischief on a national scale, on an international scale, but they probably wouldn't let him...

In the other corner, the one that isn't damp, a spider is industriously weaving its web. His thoughts follow it: the Spider is no longer in the country. It's croaked, but its web is still hanging here with people glued in it. And I'm on the very edge of it. And you can't rip free...

He had left his wife – or was it the house that had squeezed him out? For houses squeeze out their inhabitants and countries squeeze out their citizens; people are not ideal creatures, after all, and what is good is at odds with what is better. But afterwards the houses suffer from nostalgia and the countries suffer from badly digested history, the history of their own cruel idealism.

He grew weary of the house on Taganka; Taganka is a watery part of town, just as the Kremlin area is full of hot air, but not because cars are belching out exhaust fumes for two kilometres all around it. He grew weary of waiting for a reply from Ireland because it was already clear there would never be one. What else was he weary of? Of the people on the streets, of the planes in the sky. He was weary of getting dressed in the morning and of washing because the shower shot streams in all directions making it impossible to use.

Life came easier when he was asleep. Because for a European, to dream is to dive into the past reality of a world which grew imperceptible into adulthood. And in waking reality, too, each European lives in an illusory world, suspended somewhere between past reality and present reality. Some call that world Ireland, others call it Iceland or Italy. The colours of the flag change—the props of the dreams—but the illusory world never becomes reality. And it is most real in the dream. When you wake up, you begin to notice certain discrepancies. Of course, the wisest course of action is to simply ignore these and carry on living in your illusory Italy, Iceland or Ireland, even if you actually exist in quite a different land, which may also be unreal...

15.

"A mosaic disintegrates over time, littering its tiles everywhere, but what do I have to lose as time passes?" thought PJ, as consciousness gradually returned to him after a stroke.

After his illness, they retired him. His pension was just pennies, for all his pains.

He lay on the creaky metal bed in the badly-heated room. His conscience began its usual loop of metamorphosing objects.

Today he was a heavy old album. An empty one, because all the photos had been taken out; someone's consciousness—a wary dancer—was in danger of connecting with reality. They opened him up and closed him again at once. It felt warm to touch the woollen tablecloth, brown on black. Or was it a blanket, not a tablecloth? Beyond the window a narrow-mouthed Chinese rickshaw ricocheted along the little streets of Taganka. This rickshaw was unobtrusively teaching him the Chinese art of oblivion, and shuffled his thoughts along the map of forgotten faces and objects.

There is probably a country where what we have lost is returned to us, a pink country with two fish in the wheel of its coat of arms. Maybe you can even buy a ticket there, but perhaps there's no point in buying a return...

He had a dream. An *aisling Aonghusa,* Aengus's dream... Was it Irish? Or Russian? In his dream he saw himself in a forest of human trees, both cryptogamous and phanerogamous, and each branch outlined a face. Under the reminiscences-of-rain-coloured sky, he once again let himself be watered and fertilised. Voices wafted over from the kitchen on the smell of onion gravy, the TV was reporting fires and the deforestation of Mars to the emptiness. He inhaled the lakeside wind and looked at the withered trees which had failed the difficult test of others' concern for them, and envied each leaf which had managed to break free – with or without an inscription.

16.

The icicles hanging from the window were vaguely transparent. It was cold inside the house; it was the height of the notorious Russian winter, and it was better to steer clear of the walls. The emptiness in the room was bluish, like crystal, and at night it would ring and ring...

And that ringing turned the walls vaguely transparent, too, and he could see the outline of someone standing there on the other side of the wall...

'Who are you?'

     

But a wall lets no words pass. Instead, it began to let more light through and the image gradually grew clearer.

There was a girl in a while dress in the room. She was playing the harp. So that's where those sounds are coming from! But there isn't anything on the other side of the wall, he remembered. It's an outside wall!

'No, your house is bigger than that, much bigger,' a voice was telling him. It was his own voice.

And suddenly he could see himself on the other side of the wall. He didn't look like himself, but he knew it was him. The girl recognised him, too. Or at least, she wasn't surprised to see him...

The phone rang in the middle of the night. Here, on this side of the wall. Someone was saying something in a slurred voice. They'd got the wrong number. But before they hung up, the voice said:

'I'll be waiting for you at five o'clock, at Hotel Purgatorio.'

The voice was cross now, animated and not at all drunk.

The image on the other side of the wall faded as though the television had been switched off. The wall was opaque once again, though he still thought he could hear the sound of the harp.

He lay there for a long time. Sleep didn't come. But then he must have dozed off, for he could see that other room again, very clearly this time. The harp was playing silently now but he noticed that it was strung with grey hair, not strings. He could see himself. He had aged, a lot. But the girl at the harp was still young.

Then she stopped playing and walked over to the window. He looked out of the window, too. He could vaguely make out a house which was both unfamiliar yet oddly familiar. Then it dawned on him: it was the house where he had been born, except it was the mirror image of that house. There was a sign on the house, and he read the clandestine, mirrored lettering: "Purgatorio."

The girl turned around and walked right up to the transparent wall. She looked at him for a long time. He knew her; he had always known that unknown face. It was Mary Lavelle, wasn't it, his childhood friend? Or maybe it was Caer, the girl whom Aengus the Wanderer had loved, the girl he had first seen in a dream?

Then the girl and he—that other "he"—walked out of the room and appeared in the house opposite. The clock struck five: Freed! Freed! Freed! Freed! Freed!

He was waking up...

17.

...and dozing off again. He dreamt he was driving a car round a race track. The track was warping, and there was another car coming towards him. His family was inside – his wife and two daughters, and there was another him behind the wheel. The cars didn't collide but passed right through each other. They seemed to be writing something with their trajectories, just as someone is writing a book with us. The cars were drawing a figure of eight. No, it was the symbol of eternity, the negation of death. The formula of immortality.

Death was drawn on the race track billboards. She was smiling.

# A Brown Man in Russia -
# Perambulations Through A Siberian Winter
## by Vijay Menon

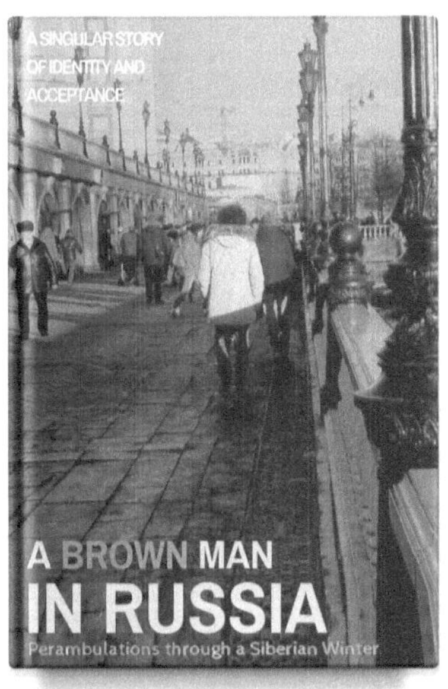



A Brown Man in Russia describes the fantastical travels of a young, colored American traveler as he backpacks across Russia in the middle of winter via the Trans-Siberian. The book is a hybrid between the curmudgeonly travelogues of Paul Theroux and the philosophical works of Robert Pirsig. Styled in the vein of Hofstadter, the author lays out a series of absurd, but true stories followed by a deeper rumination on what they mean and why they matter. Each chapter presents a vivid anecdote from the perspective of the fumbling traveler and concludes with a deeper lesson to be gleaned. For those who recognize the discordant nature of our world in a time ripe for demagoguery and for those who want to make it better, the book is an all too welcome antidote. It explores the current global climate of despair over differences and outputs a very different message – one of hope and shared understanding. At times surreal, at times inappropriate, at times hilarious, and at times deeply human, A Brown Man in Russia is a reminder to those who feel marginalized, hopeless, or endlessly divided that harmony is achievable even in the most unlikely of places.

Buy it > www.glagoslav.com

# Death of the Snake Catcher

## by Ak Welsapar

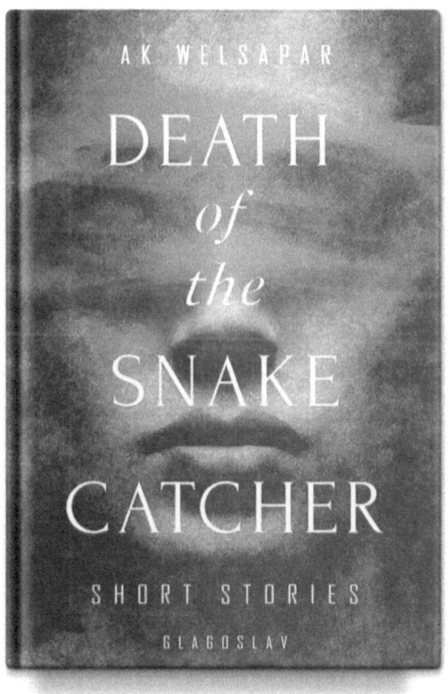

This book features people from one of the most closed countries of today's world, where the passage of time resembles the passage of a caravan through the waterless desert. This world has been recreated by a true-born son of that mysterious country, a Turkmen who, at the will of fate, has now been living for a quarter of a century in snowy Scandinavia. Is that not why two different worlds come together in *Ryazan horseradish and Tula gingerbread*, to come apart in *Love in Lilac*, in which a student from the non-free world falls in love with a girl from the West?

In the story *Death of the Snake Catcher*, an old snake catcher meets one on one with a giant cobra in the heart of the desert. In the dialogue between them the author unveils the age-old interdependence of Man and untamed nature, where the fear and mistrust of the strong and the hopes and apprehensions of the weak change places but co-exist as ever. *Egyptian night of fear*, in which a boy goes to an Eastern bazaar and falls into the clutches of depraved forces, is created in the writer's characteristic style of magical realism, while the novella Altynai celebrates first love, radiant and sad, pure as virgin snow.

Buy it > www.glagoslav.com

# Leo Tolstoy – Flight from Paradise
## by Pavel Basinsky

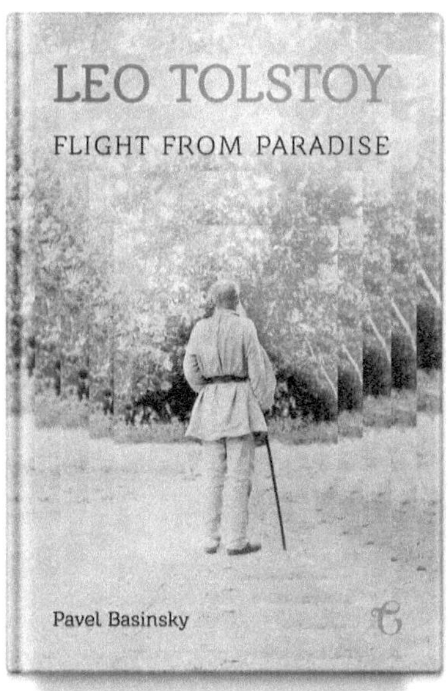


Over a hundred years ago, something truly outrageous occurred at Yasnaya Polyana. Count Leo Tolstoy, a famous author aged eighty-two at the time, took off, destination unknown. Since then, the circumstances surrounding the writer's whereabouts during his final days and his eventual death have given rise to many myths and legends. In this book, popular Russian writer and reporter Pavel Basinsky delves into the archives and presents his interpretation of the situation prior to Leo Tolstoy's mysterious disappearance. Basinsky follows Leo Tolstoy throughout his life, right up to his final moments. Reconstructing the story from historical documents, he creates a visionary account of the events that led to the Tolstoys' family drama.

*Flight from Paradise* will be of particular interest to international researchers studying Leo Tolstoy's life and works, and is highly recommended to a broader audience worldwide.

Buy it > www.glagoslav.com

*Glagoslav Publications Catalogue*

- *The Time of Women by Elena Chizhova*
- *Andrei Tarkovsky: The Collector of Dreams by Layla Alexander-Garrett*
- *Andrei Tarkovsky - A Life on the Cross by Lyudmila Boyadzhieva*
- *Sin by Zakhar Prilepin*
- *Hardly Ever Otherwise by Maria Matios*
- *Khatyn by Ales Adamovich*
- *The Lost Button by Irene Rozdobudko*
- *Christened with Crosses by Eduard Kochergin*
- *The Vital Needs of the Dead by Igor Sakhnovsky*
- *The Sarabande of Sara's Band by Larysa Denysenko*
- *A Poet and Bin Laden by Hamid Ismailov*
- *Watching The Russians (Dutch Edition) by Maria Konyukova*
- *Kobzar by Taras Shevchenko*
- *The Stone Bridge by Alexander Terekhov*
- *Moryak by Lee Mandel*
- *King Stakh's Wild Hunt by Uladzimir Karatkevich*
- *The Hawks of Peace by Dmitry Rogozin*
- *Harlequin's Costume by Leonid Yuzefovich*
- *Depeche Mode by Serhii Zhadan*
- *The Grand Slam and other stories (Dutch Edition) by Leonid Andreev*
- *METRO 2033 (Dutch Edition) by Dmitry Glukhovsky*
- *METRO 2034 (Dutch Edition) by Dmitry Glukhovsky*
- *A Russian Story by Eugenia Kononenko*
- *Herstories, An Anthology of New Ukrainian Women Prose Writers*
- *The Battle of the Sexes Russian Style by Nadezhda Ptushkina*
- *A Book Without Photographs by Sergey Shargunov*
- *Down Among The Fishes by Natalka Babina*
- *disUNITY by Anatoly Kudryavitsky*
- *Sankya by Zakhar Prilepin*
- *Wolf Messing by Tatiana Lungin*
- *Good Stalin by Victor Erofeyev*

- *Solar Plexus by Rustam Ibragimbekov*
- *Don't Call me a Victim! by Dina Yafasova*
- *Poetin (Dutch Edition) by Chris Hutchins and Alexander Korobko*
- *A History of Belarus by Lubov Bazan*
- *Children's Fashion of the Russian Empire by Alexander Vasiliev*
- *Empire of Corruption - The Russian National Pastime by Vladimir Soloviev*
- *Heroes of the 90s - People and Money. The Modern History of Russian Capitalism*
- *Fifty Highlights from the Russian Literature (Dutch Edition) by Maarten Tengbergen*
- *Bajesvolk (Dutch Edition) by Mikhail Khodorkovsky*
- *Tsarina Alexandra's Diary (Dutch Edition)*
- *Myths about Russia by Vladimir Medinskiy*
- *Boris Yeltsin - The Decade that Shook the World by Boris Minaev*
- *A Man Of Change - A study of the political life of Boris Yeltsin*
- *Sberbank - The Rebirth of Russia's Financial Giant by Evgeny Karasyuk*
- *To Get Ukraine by Oleksandr Shyshko*
- *Asystole by Oleg Pavlov*
- *Gnedich by Maria Rybakova*
- *Marina Tsvetaeva - The Essential Poetry*
- *Multiple Personalities by Tatyana Shcherbina*
- *The Investigator by Margarita Khemlin*
- *The Exile by Zinaida Tuluh*
- *Leo Tolstoy – Flight from paradise by Pavel Basinsky*
- *Moscow in the 1930 by Natalia Gromova*
- *Laurus (Dutch edition) by Evgenij Vodolazkin*
- *Prisoner by Anna Nemzer*
- *The Crime of Chernobyl - The Nuclear Goulag by Wladimir Tchertkoff*
- *Alpine Ballad by Vasil Bykau*
- *The Complete Correspondence of Hryhory Skovoroda*
- *The Tale of Aypi* by Ak Welsapar
- *Selected Poems* by Lydia Grigorieva

- *The Fantastic Worlds of Yuri Vynnychuk*
- *The Garden of Divine Songs and Collected Poetry of Hryhory Skovoroda*
- *Adventures in the Slavic Kitchen: A Book of Essays with Recipes*
- *Seven Signs of the Lion by Michael M. Naydan*
- *Forefathers' Eve by Adam Mickiewicz*
- *One-Two by Igor Eliseev*
- *Girls, be Good by Bojan Babić*
- *Time of the Octopus by Anatoly Kucherena*
- *Soghomon Tehlirian Memories - The Assassination of Talaat*
- *The Grand Harmony by Bohdan Ihor Antonych*
- *The Selected Lyric Poetry Of Maksym Rylsky*
- *The Shining Light by Galymkair Mutanov*
- *The Frontier: 28 Contemporary Ukrainian Poets - An Anthology*
- *Acropolis - The Wawel Plays by Stanisław Wyspiański*
- *Contours of the City by Attyla Mohylny*
- *Conversations Before Silence: The Selected Poetry of Oles Ilchenko*
- *Nikolai Gumilev's Africa*
- *Zinnober's Poppets by Elena Chizhova*
- *The Hemingway Game by Evgeni Grishkovets*
- *The Secret History of my Sojourn in Russia* by Jaroslav Hašek
- *Mirror Sand - An Anthology of Russian Short Poems in English Translation* (A Bilingual Edition)
- *Maybe We're Leaving* by Jan Balaban
- *Death of the Snake Catcher* by Ak WelsaparRichard Govett
- *Hard Times* by Ostap Vyshnia
- *Duel* by Borys Antonenko-Davydovych
- *Vladimir Lenin - How to Become a Leader* by Vladlen Loginov

*More coming soon...*